ORIGINATORS

BOOK II OF THE
NETHERSPACE TRILOGY

ALSO AVAILABLE FROM ANDREW LANE AND NIGEL FOSTER

THE NETHERSPACE TRILOGY
Netherspace
Originators
Revelation (May 2019)

ORIGINATORS

ANDREW LANE AND NIGEL FOSTER

WITHDRAWN

TITAN BOOKS

Originators
Paperback edition ISBN: 9781785651878
Electronic edition ISBN: 9781785651885

Published by Titan Books
A division of Titan Publishing Group Ltd
144 Southwark Street, London SE1 0UP

First edition: May 2018
1 2 3 4 5 6 7 8 9 10

A CIP catalogue record for this title is available from the British Library.

Printed and bound in the United States

Did you enjoy this book? We love to hear from our readers.
Please email us at readerfeedback@titanemail.com or write to us at
Reader Feedback at the above address.

To receive advance information, news, competitions, and exclusive offers
online, please sign up for the Titan newsletter on our website:

TITANBOOKS.COM

For Ella and Curtis

"WHAT IS IT LIKE TO BE A BAT?"

American philosopher Thomas Nagel,
The Philosophical Review, October 1974

"WHERE IS THE LIFE WE HAVE LOST IN LIVING?
WHERE IS THE WISDOM WE HAVE LOST IN KNOWLEDGE?
WHERE IS THE KNOWLEDGE WE HAVE LOST IN INFORMATION?
THE CYCLES OF HEAVEN IN TWENTY CENTURIES
BRING US FARTHER FROM GOD AND NEARER TO THE DUST."

T. S. Eliot, *Choruses from the Rock*

"VASTS APART. AT BOUNDS OF BOUNDLESS VOID.
WHENCE NO FARTHER."

Samuel Beckett, *Worstward Ho*

"GREAT FLEAS HAVE LITTLE FLEAS UPON THEIR BACKS TO BITE ÐEM,
AND LITTLE FLEAS HAVE LESSER FLEAS, AND SO AD INFINITUM.
AND THE GREAT FLEAS THEMSELVES, IN TURN,
HAVE GREATER FLEAS TO GO ON;
WHILE THESE AGAIN HAVE GREATER STILL, AND GREATER STILL,
AND SO ON."

Augustus De Morgan, *A Budget of Paradoxes*

Petrichor (/ˈpɛtrikɔər/) is the earthy scent produced
when rain falls on dry soil. The word is constructed
from Greek πέτρα petra, meaning "stone",
and ἰχώρ īchōr, the fluid that flows in the veins
of the gods in Greek mythology.

Wikipedia

TO WHOM IT MAY CONCERN

You're reading this because it's still a screwed-up universe.

Humans seek patterns and order everywhere. Not only as a survival mechanism (a tiger in the trees, or randomly dappled patterns of sunlight?) but as a reaction to your messy development as a race. Fits and starts with the occasional aberration which might or might not allow its sufferer to survive long enough to mate and pass on its genes, such as single-eyed giants, stomachs with enzymes that can digest milk, or an offshoot of humanity so long-lived and fertile it thrived, prospered and then starved to death. No obvious end in sight, only the blind random drive to survive no matter the consequences. The need to impose order on chaos. Except that same chaos also gives a sense of mystery, curiosity, humans always seeking new horizons. It's the great contradiction of existence. Chaos and freedom versus order and tranquillity.

It's a cosmic problem. Literally, because in untold billions of years, when energy is equally distributed through all spatial dimensions, everything will be tranquil. Nothing will happen ever again. And that's a problem if you were one of the things that happened to be happening. Evolution is only a means.

You're not the only race lurching towards an unknown and fluid destiny. It goes with the territory known as the universal here and now. The infinite possibility that underlies every universe. All but impossible to visit and survive. But it may be sensed. There are some in every race who can glimpse the future. Or rather, glimpse a variety of probable, most realistic futures and isolate the best one. One hell of a lot for the pre-cog to ponder, which is one reason why so many seers and genuine fortune tellers go mad. They get help, these beings who can see the shape of the future, who know where to aim their lives. Help from something big and distant, with its own opinions about how to evolve with the least possible fuss – and no blind alleys, because any other way is an abomination. Simply, horribly wrong. And over time – if anyone can ever agree what time is and how many dimensions it has – this something began to impose order on chaos, because that's what superior folk do: tidy the house, mend the fences, straighten the road.

You'd think that other folk would be grateful that something up there, out there, in there is looking out for them, simplifying their lives. No more confusion, only a clear idea of where they're going and how to get there. You'd think gratitude, but you'd be wrong. It seems that a preference for untidy creativity, a love of loose ends, is common throughout the universe.

Societies that value creativity do not like rules and regulations. Societies that value order and structure do not trust undisciplined thinking. Usually the two manage to coexist – for a while. All art walks a fine line between being too predictable and being too anarchic, with certain excursions on either side. On a cosmic scale, you might say that improvisation and order are totally opposed. More accurate to say that they are at war. A conflict old before human ancestors slithered and flopped onto dry land.

If that something prevails you won't be reading books like this. No one will be writing them and with the creative spark properly extinguished – oh yes, that something will do it, over time – imagination will be a bad word. Even a forgotten one.

Not that I care either way. I'll be long gone by then. Chances are I'll be long gone by the time you read these words.

Meanwhile, let me catch you up on what's happened.

Forty years ago, aliens arrived to trade. Weird trade. Alien technology exchanged for everyday items, the future for, more often than not, human domestic rubbish. Much of the tech was, and still is, beyond human science. A writer called Arthur C. Clarke once said that any sufficiently advanced technology would be indistinguishable from magic. In fact, alien technology is often indistinguishable from a piece of surrealist sculpture.

Scientists tried to establish common ground. The aliens ignored them. Earth trotted out kings, queens, politicians, priests, philosophers, musicians and artists. No good. Save for a few fanatics screaming spawn-of-the devil! *or* please-save-us-from-ourselves! *slogans, aliens were judged to be a good, a vital if confusing thing. Earth is now dependent on alien technology. Some people say we've never had it so good; others say we have become dependent on handouts from our betters. Those aren't necessarily opposing views.*

Sovereign countries and governments never survived the advent of weird, highly advanced creatures that ignored their very existence. Nor did most religions. Society devolved to a more easily manageable level. Now it's a world of city states and what lies between them, which is known generally as the Out or sometimes the Wild. No one from the city states really knows what happens deep in the Wild. Some of them often go Out for a laugh. Some settle down there, preferring the looser, more anarchic life. Some may die there – badly. It's that kind of place.

And the city states? How do they manage to survive, having to negotiate hundreds, perhaps thousands of trade agreements between themselves? The answer is: artificial intelligences. The

AIs negotiate with each other on a nanosecond-by-nanosecond basis, adjusting trade tariffs and treaties according to what's happening in the world around them. That's their job, and they don't get bored. At the heart of an AI is a piece of alien tech that human scientists have been able to replicate, without totally understanding it. They have a good idea... but we haven't developed the mathematics to be sure. In practical terms, we're not sure whether the big AIs are autonomous and genuinely, creatively smart like a human but even more so. Most humans have their own personal AI, which is a cross between an antique smart phone and a best mate. You're never alone with an AI.

And while the AIs are carrying out their incredibly fast negotiations in the thousands of city states, ten thousand people are working for Earth Central – the organisation that acts as adjudicator and referee if and when the AIs can't find a solution. And which also ensures that the AIs don't suddenly go off on a tangent with some idea that seems great to them but is bad for us. One thousand people work in EarthCent's Galactic Division, which oversees trade between humans and aliens. That is, GalDiv polices it. Aliens are like unscrupulous market traders who'll make a deal with anyone, which can be dangerous. In Paris, the Eiffel Tower recently developed an overnight ten-degree lean to the north, the result of an undeclared trade. Never mind that it complements the Arc de Triomphe, still floating three metres off the ground. Both are anarchic; both suggest that alien tech is uncontrollable. Which of course it is, but we don't like to admit it. Unauthorised trades are punished. Paris still feels victimised but the rest of the world laughs. Aliens are us. Or Le monde tous fou, as Parisians have learned to say. The world is mad. The asylum needs a director. In theory that's

EarthCent's job. Or raison d'être, *as the Parisians also say.*

In practice GalDiv rules. Alien tech is boss. Those who control it can own the galaxy… a delusional point of view, because the galaxy can't be organised and aliens have no respect for human organisations. They probably don't even recognise them.

GalDiv also oversees fifteen colony worlds. There may be more, off doing their own happy, hippy thing. GalDiv only oversees the original colonies. Even with alien-developed AI, GalDiv lacks the ability to oversee any more. It sees them much as eighteenth-century London viewed North American trappers: useful but way, way beyond the Pale.

One alien race, or species, if you prefer, supplied the space drives (sideslip-field generators, as named by scientists still ignorant of how they work) that gave humanity the stars. These aliens are known by us as the Gliese. What they call themselves is anyone's guess. The only noise they make sounds like a wet fart and may well be so. The Gliese do not give a list of trades made. Like other aliens, they do not communicate with humans except at the 'point and swap' level.

GalDiv also oversees all businesses using alien technology, on or off world. It has no influence over the Wild. Nor does it control the free spacers, who are based in the Wild and who go where and when they damn well please, throughout the galaxy and possibly beyond. In fact GalDiv controls a little over half of all human/alien interactions. It may be less. But it's still enough to make it the most powerful human institution on Earth and in space. GalDiv intends to keep it that way. All for the good of humanity. It always is.

The trade that most concerns those fine people who work for GalDiv is the one nobody talks about. The Gliese are the only *alien race that appears to have the concession for making space travel possible. They will only take humans in exchange. So many humans, any age or condition, just so long as they are alive, even barely, in exchange for a netherspace drive, the sideslip-field generator, the unknowable magic that makes the galaxy our playground. A different number of humans for each of the three types of drive: small, medium, large. The cost is always the same, the only alien trade that is.*

The humans themselves come in various flavours. Volunteer humans who believe the rumour about a paradise far, far away in space, or who are just willing to accept the risk in exchange for the chance to explore the universe. Non-volunteers deemed dangerous by their city states. People caught committing an illegal alien trade. Dying humans desperate for a miracle. Other humans convinced that the Gliese are gods. There are lots of paths leading to the same point.

It's a bad situation and it can't last. It won't last. The change has already begun.

I think that brings us up to date.

So now we get to the ten billion virtscript question: who am I?

I'll tell you later, when it seems appropriate. I'd like to preserve a little mystery.

For now, you should worry about Kara Jones and Marc Keislack.

It's what they do… and what is done to them… that will decide your future.

1

The Galactic Division of Earth Central is housed in a slim spiral that swoops and soars a thousand metres above the city state of Berlin's Tiergarten. Think of a huge barley-sugar twist, glowing gold in the sun. Then bend and curve it in a way that defies both gravity and logic. GalDiv is impossible. It should come crashing down at any moment. But like Restaurant 7, just a short distance away, GalDiv was built with alien technology and like the Brandenburg Gate it will last for centuries. Both have been and are used to symbolise freedom. One has a dark history, the other hints at a dread future. Both unpleasant aspects are ignored by Berliners. You can't change the past and the future is spiralling well out of control. Managing change is mostly about preparing people for the worst.

9.00 a.m. on a sunny day in early June. The last of 10,000 workers walk into the Twist.

One of them, a man enthralled by a mind-feed of his favourite band, stumbled hard into a young woman.

"Sorry, excuse me," he said, confused. He wasn't walking quickly. She'd been standing still. Why hadn't his personal AI warned him that she was there?

"Not important." Her blue eyes stared past him at something a thousand klicks away. Her hair was long and dark, partially covered by a headscarf, and she wore a casual fawn linen jacket and dark slacks.

He suspected she belonged to one of the Modest sects that appeared every few months, seduced by the latest shiny stuff, drug or weirdness from the colony worlds. "You're sure?"

"I'm sure." She turned away. The moment was gone.

He could have checked his AI, but he was a Berliner and not too bothered. AIs aren't perfect, whatever anyone says. And so he missed the chance to make history pause.

Anson Greenaway sat alone in the corner office with a granite slab coffee table and huge windows that captured a panoramic view of Berlin. Humans brawling in the streets while aliens watched; a city state vanishing in a puff of black smoke; whatever lived in netherspace come a-knocking at his door: all that would have to wait. This was his personal hour, time to forget the weight of responsibility. The time when Anson Greenaway came as near to being an ordinary man as he would ever get.

Security was as tight as possible, nothing or no one in or out or recorded, electronics frozen in time. Would-be assassins – there were many these days, political, religious and insane – would also have to wait until normal business made him vulnerable again.

He sat behind a large, tropical hardwood desk on which lay three sheets of handmade paper, thick and creamy to the touch, imported from the Wild. Next to the paper a simple wood and graphite pencil, incapable of being bugged, and also crafted in the Wild. Off to one side a metal box made of an impenetrable, unbendable alien metal and secured by a very human electronic lock that would only respond to the variations and flutters of his pulse as measured through the pad of his finger. By his left hand a glass tumbler, quarter-full of seventy-five-year-old Talisker malt, laid down before the aliens came, in a time before the city states and Earth became enslaved by greed.

Did it matter that Earth science was now devoted to understanding and applying alien technology? Greenaway thought it did. He understood the real import of alien tech better than most, given his position. Those mobile piles of wet leather arbitrarily named the Gliese had offered the stars for humanity's soul, and humanity had jumped at the chance. So, the dance went on, Earth selling itself for a future it had never earned. He knew the terrible truth: take away the alien tech and the netherspace drives, and Earth plus all colony worlds would wither and die like a person taken off life support. And still no one knew why aliens made the weird trades they did. Hundreds of reports crossed his desk every day concerning what the several thousand aliens currently on Earth were doing, but trying to make sense of their actions was like trying to construct a jigsaw puzzle wearing a blindfold. No matter how many reports he read, how many multi-dimensional videos he watched, he was still no closer to understanding them. No one in the city states had ever seen an alien eat, sleep or defecate, and any attempt to project emotions or even intentions on them was undercut within minutes by their actions. But why worry about an alien's internal life or internal organs as long as the shiny stuff kept coming?

Presumably aliens thought Earth was worth something or they wouldn't be here.

In time they'll let us know, was how most humans coped with this inability to communicate. Surely the Gliese, so precise and consistent in their trades of humans for N-space drives, had an understanding of humanity? And one day all would be revealed. Human and alien would walk as equals among the stars.

But what if the Gliese were only obeying instructions? If the harvest was on behalf of another, unknown race, humans exchanged for something unknowable? Greenaway had a terrible feeling it was. Humans as a galactic currency that was busy devaluing itself. The reports he saw every day made that very clear. Casual violence was on the rise. So were the people choosing to Go In; to become one with a simulity, to live and even die linked to an AI, with bots to change a nutrient drip, wipe an arse or clean the drool from a face. It was a service the AIs provided free, claiming they could use the extra computing power provided by so many unconscious drop-outs. The authorities might have their doubts, at best Going In was a one-way cure for depression that halved the suicide rate and stopped weirdos walking the streets. Whatever their private doubts the authorities let it ride.

About the only area of human technology that seemed to be developing was chemistry – specifically, the branch devoted to making new drugs to screw with people's minds and bodies in the name of changing their level of consciousness.

Damned if we remain alien-friendly. Damned if we

don't. Greenaway knew that humanity had fallen into a trap. No, not true: humanity had walked into the trap of its own volition and locked the door behind it.

It was just as easy as they'd promised the young woman in the headscarf. No one looked at her curiously. No alarms sounded. She didn't hate artificial intelligence, even if it resulted from alien tech. She merely despised it. As did more people than GalDiv and AI manufacturers would ever admit.

Looking around, Greenaway wondered if his office was too sparse. It was intended to radiate determination, dedication and power. But perhaps it suggested a lack of imagination. A man with an exaggerated sense of his own moral and intellectual superiority, who would never leave his black-and-white world. All of which was partly true, but how else could you do what needed to be done? Anyway, certainty of purpose was needed to play god with so many lives. He'd long suspected that the aliens traded another civilisation's science and technology, not their own. Especially the n-space drives. Or what the ignorant called anti-gravity or AG, even though gravity had long ago been exposed as a three-dimensional function of n-dimensional space and not a force. The learned referred to an "updown-field generator" without knowing how it worked. Which was fine: most people didn't know how a microwave oven worked, but they were happy to use it.

Greenaway picked up the pencil. Outside the sun began to set over the ever-busy city. He wrote swiftly, fluently, with never a misspelt word.

Dearest love:
   I'd thought that by now I might have stopped writing to you, but these letters still help to organise my thoughts. I'll keep going. Gaia knows but I need that comfortable feeling of certainty now with Tse gone. Strange that my closest friend and confidant would be a pre-cog. Except he never lost his humanity and at the end, when the pre-cog universe called, wanted him to help impose sterile order and stifle creativity, Tse chose death over betrayal. I miss him. More than that: I respect him.

He paused, pencil resting on the paper, and looked across at the alien metal box. Tse's last legacy, left behind when he'd departed on the SUT with the designation *RIL-FIJ-DOQ* as part of the hostage rescue mission to rescue pilgrims from the unknowable intentions of the alien Cancri. Greenaway had found it waiting for him, wrapped in patterned paper and tied up with a ribbon. No note. He was sure that the pulse-lock was coded to his own physiological constants, although how Tse had known them was a mystery. He'd never opened it. He was scared to. What final gift would a pre-cog leave behind? A description of Greenaway's future, right down to every meal he would eat up to and including his last one? A description of everyone's future, perhaps – what was going to happen to the entire human race? Either way,

Greenaway preferred to keep whatever squirming toad Tse had left for him safely locked away.

He reached out and tapped the pencil on the box a few times. The dry, precise sound filled the space of his office.

"What are you?" he murmured.

After a moment, he turned his attention back to the letter and continued to write.

You'll be pleased to hear that Tatia is safe. No longer the celebrity girl about town, and changed by her experiences, she's now a leader with a growing sense of her true mission. I wanted so much to tell her the truth about her background but now is not the time. Tse saw the path and how special she was. She does have a rapport, some sort of link with that cold, diffuse pre-cog civilisation that Tse rejected, as you intuited when she was a baby – no, when you were still carrying her inside you. I remember you saying so, and how I smiled and said "Of course", thinking to humour my beautiful, pregnant wife... and I remember your own quiet little smile in return because you knew that one day I'd see the truth. Perhaps I didn't want our child, conceived in love and such splendid lust, to be connected to such a cold evil. You weren't pre-cognitive, or if you were then you never let it slip. You still went bravely through those little accidents that pepper life, like breaking your toe against a worn marble step on the Parthenon, always pretending you had no idea it was going to happen. I preferred to believe that your prediction about Tatia being able to talk sense and communicate with alien pre-cogs was just that

– a prediction, not a statement of fact.

The Parthenon. That was a happy day. Before our respective careers took off, before we lost Tatia, and before we replaced "Let's do it!" with "Let's do it some time…" Like the rocking chairs we always meant to buy. One day we'd sit side-by-side, and talk about the past with tears and laughter. The other day I had two made, by a carpenter I know in the Wild. One day I'll pick them up and bring them home. Hand-carved from driftwood washed up on a beach.

He paused and drank some whisky, thinking what-if and maybe. The taste of peat and the sea filled his mouth as the smell prickled his nostrils.

Tatia is back in Seattle. I've brought her onto GalDiv's books, but only you and me and my AI know that she's our daughter. Sometime soon she'll need to go for training, but for now she's on official R&R.

There's been a growth of religious fanatics who are violently opposed to space colonies and believe that aliens are an insult to God, creatures of the Devil, as it were. Nothing we can't control, but some of the extremists could be used by Earth Primus, still the main threat. Interesting how Len Grafe can sound so reasonable even when he's telling outright lies. Or looks so shocked when a fanatic gets fired up by what he says and commits an atrocity. Problem being that he has secret followers and sympathisers in high places. Grafe has gone into hiding, though. Claims that GalDiv want him dead, but he promises to reveal a major scandal very soon. He's right, I would like him dead, but I do not want a martyr. He's more at risk from various conglomerates trading with the colony worlds. The Contract Bureau has been approached several times asking for an official assassination, on the grounds that Grafe is bad for business. They didn't take refusal kindly.

Keislack is off making art and Jones is walking in Dartmoor. They're scheduled to go Up in a few days and continue searching for the Originators. Either we find the source of alien tech or become slave to second-rate aliens.

Jones and Keislack have become an effective team, and not only because of the simulity training. She is a natural empath, which makes her such a good assassin. She can anticipate her prey, although she grieves for it afterwards – inside, at least. He is a borderline psychopath. Normally he would prey on her, but Jones is too strong. Besides, they genuinely seem to like each other. There is a danger they could become too attached, but my psycho-technicians say that if there is sex it will be casual, friends-with-benefits. "Fuck-buddies" was the phrase when you and I were young. Jones already knows the dangers of becoming emotionally attached to a colleague. I doubt she'll make the same mistake again.

I'm still not sure why Keislack is so important. But Tse insisted he was, and I still trust my now dead friend.

His gaze slipped again to the box, sitting innocently at the corner of his desk. What was in there? What did Tse want him to know – or was Tse's point that he should avoid knowing, that he should fight against it? He continued writing.

> The three remaining SUT crew members were
> transferred to Galactic Survey and are now somewhere
> near Procyon on a survey mission looking for helium-rich
> gas clouds. A safe mission, as missions go; they deserve
> that after what they've been through. They couldn't stay
> on Earth, not with Len Grafe sniffing around.
>
> And with three city states currently waging cyber war
> with each other the situation's no longer just fluid: it's
> become a raging torrent that threatens to drown us all.
> You'd think that AIs would order things better. But as
> they tell me, the smartest AI is no proof against human
> stupidity. AIs are bound to support their own city states,
> for good or ill.

More whisky. The glass was getting low. Both liquor and letter would end at the same time. It was the way he'd always done it, giving the illusion of control. He could no more *not* write the letter than starve himself to death.

> So, what have we learned? That the Originators do
> exist, as we long suspected. We're calling them the
> Originators because we're damn sure they provide
> sideslip technology to the Gliese, and maybe all the other
> alien tech. But perhaps they're not Originators at all –
> perhaps they're just the next ones up the pole. Whatever,
> they seem to take an interest in the Gliese and no one
> else. But they also apparently have netherspace tech far,
> far in advance of anything that the Gliese use or trade.

That's new information, and very interesting.

We also know that the rumoured, near-legendary beings in netherspace do exist and are fascinated, almost obsessed, with humans... and this may have something to do with the trade between the Gliese and us. That damage to the protective foam that all SUTs have to be sprayed with before they enter netherspace – we know now that it's not just the equivalent of storm damage or rust. Again, we suspected this before, not least because of the call-out fees. What happens to them when they are handed over is still a mystery.

Along with all that, we also believe – with scant evidence – that the Cancri and possibly other alien species have, over time, lost their – I want to say humanity! – their more intuitive and artistic sides. This may explain why they are intrigued by us. If the reports about warehouses on a Cancri colony world stocked with Earth artefacts are accurate, aliens have been visiting and trading with Earth for much longer than we knew. We can't explain the discovery of human bodies with their brains removed. I suspect – as does Tatia – that an alien race, maybe the Cancri, maybe not, were trying to find the root of human creativity. Good luck with that. I have people on staff who swear no such thing exists. Judging by the documents they draft for me to sign, I believe them. Creativity and bureaucracy are mutually exclusive.

The alien communication problem is still with us. Keislack had some success with the Cancri, but not enough to exchange ideas. The simulity technicians tell me they may have a breakthrough. But they always say that. I might ask Keislack to check a report that someone in the Wild has developed the elusive "universal translator" that would enable humans and aliens to communicate seamlessly. He's still got very good contacts there. Shouldn't take more than half a day at the most. Executive decision: I'll contact him later today. Too risky to use my own contacts. Anyway, I suspect the Wild deliberately keeps me out of the loop. I might be of it, always, but no longer with it, not while I'm at GalDiv.

Based on what Tse let drop to Keislack and Jones, we suspect that the galactic pre-cog collective, for want of a better name, is involved in some sort of struggle. With whom or why is unknown. I hope you noticed the "whom". You always did love to correct my grammar. I always loved you doing so.

You wouldn't like my plan. Well, not only mine. But I'm the one responsible. And maybe the younger me would dislike it too. It was so easy then to see life in simple terms. You always had faith in the inherent goodness of human nature. That was why you died. But I've learned that humans can be as chaotic and as destructive as an exploding star. There has to be control.

He put down the pencil, the lead almost worn to the nub, to read what he'd written. Smiling as he wondered what his staff would say if they knew the truth about him. Finished the whisky and picked up the pencil one last time.

Your loving husband,
A.

Greenaway sat back and re-read the letter. Over the years he'd written six hundred and twenty-one of them. Now, six hundred and twenty-two. He'd learned to be a very precise man. Numbers mattered, although in his youth he'd laughed at how city states were ruled by them. For what else are computers, he thought, even those complicated self-programming, heuristic neural nets called artificial intelligences, but numbers busy shuttling back and forth in a quantum lattice in a futile attempt to mimic life? Just as this one had talked about the rocking chairs, every letter had contained something unique from the past. He always remembered something from their mutual past.

She reached the top of the building to find herself in the outer office, just as they'd said. Her mouth was still dry. No real surprise there.

A blonde woman got up from her desk and walked smiling towards her. No reason for alarm. The building's AI was the best defence in the world.

The woman dressed as a Modest minor bureaucrat waited until they were close, then reached up with both hands and squeezed just beneath either side of her own jaw, massaging the salivary glands. Instead of saliva, a liquid nerve agent spurted out, vaporising when it hit the air.

"The director is..." the blonde began to say, then collapsed as the younger woman blew hard into her face.

Modest breathed out until all the liquid evaporated. There was enough left to kill Modest, but not immediately.

Her mouth and nostrils were coated with a polymer that prevented the nerve agent being absorbed, and there was a filter in her oesophagus. It is only a small amount she might swallow and that would take a while to affect her. She was phlegmatic about it. God would decide when and if she dies. It was out of her hands.

She dragged the dead blonde out of sight behind the desk.

From beneath the desk Greenaway took out a ceramic-lined waste bin, and from a drawer a small spray bottle.

He read the letter one last time. Put it gently in the bin. Used the spray. Watched as the paper dissolved into mush.

One more letter written to a woman who'd been murdered thirty-three years ago. A letter that existed now only in his memory. Like her.

Greenaway stood up and checked his watch. Three minutes left of his me-time. He went into his personal bathroom for a piss, found his penis hanging heavy as it often did after writing to his dead wife. Maybe the obsession was a sexual turn-on; maybe his subconscious was just replaying the way she smelled, the way she felt. It didn't worry him. It was nice that he could still get a reaction.

He was behind his desk, security back to normal, when his PA buzzed to come in.

She was new to the job but working out well both in and out of the office. Greenaway had slept with her within two days. Usually it took a week or so but she'd quickly let him know that she was interested. If she hadn't been he wouldn't have bothered, and there would have been no effect on her career. In a time when a handshake could have more emotional currency than a fuck, casual sex was the norm. The only sin was coercion, in whatever form.

The door opened and a woman walked in. Not his PA. She was younger, pretty in a forgettable way. Greenaway wondered if his PA now had an assistant.

Pain! Excruciating pain that drove his writhing body to the floor. Greenaway fought for breath as he tried to access his AI.

"Don't bother," the young woman said casually. "Your AI is my bitch now. We're going for a walk."

Greenaway felt a flash of hope. There'd be a moment to break away, perhaps at least warn…

He heard, or maybe felt, a click in his head as his AI died and his mind went blank.

It wasn't much of a grave. Houses seldom are. It wasn't much of a memorial either, just a two-up, two-down plus bathroom. A faded house with empty windows that had begun as poor working class and generations later missed the gentrification boom. The sort of place that shouldn't exist in a world that had space travel, aliens and flying cars, but still did, just like outside toilets, homelessness and food banks. Every pyramid has a bottom as well as a top, and it's always much, much bigger and quite a lot older.

It was located in a narrow street facing north where dawn came later and night earlier – or so it had seemed to

Kara as a child. It had also been the site of her happiness and sometimes joy.

Today the house had the feel of a grave or memorial, despite lacking a body. Kara wasn't even sure if her sister was dead… despite what the pre-cog Tse had told her, after he'd been driven half mad by exposure to an alien mind.

It wasn't much of a memorial either, only an empty, faded house with broken windows that stared blindly into the street. If Kara waited long enough, would someone from her past look out and wave? The house was the only solid reminder she had, her memories fixed in crumbling brick and rotting wood.

Today should have been a time for relaxation, even muted happiness. Kara had moved and screwed between the stars. She'd met aliens. She'd rescued a ragged bunch of religious zealots led by a one-time society bitch, commandeered a space utility transport, watched as a pre-cog called Tse blew himself up together with an alien ship, and recoiled when nightmarish things arrived to investigate. The beings hadn't hung around. Like adults who hear screams then discover kids playing, the weird ones had gone away. Kara had survived. She brought back all her people, except for Tse and a netherspace-possessed engineer. There was no chance of saving either of them.

This house was where Kara Jones and her older sister, Dee, had lived after their parents died. Dee took care of everything. She was sister, mother and best friend. Money was tight. Dee worried about Kara's future. Dee believed the false statistics about SUT breakdowns in netherspace and signed up as a call-out fee. Dee was taken by the

Gliese on her first trip into space. Kara ended up in care and joined the English Federated Army as soon as she could, supporting the city states of London, Manchester, Birmingham, Leeds, Bristol, Exeter and Southampton.

Now she stared at the house where she and Dee had laughed and planned their future. She remembered Tse's last words, before he blew up himself and the Gliese rescue SUT.

"Kara, you will discover the truth about your sister. Telling you more would affect the likelihood of this happening, so that's all I can tell you."

She glanced round, saw no one watching, wouldn't have cared too much if they were. She walked to the front door. No need to break in: it stood partly open. Kara guessed it had been used by some of the thousands who'd slipped through the cracks in London City State's wealth-for-all society. She'd heard it was called "squatting", a term from a world before the aliens arrived. The homeless. People who simply didn't fit in, or didn't want to fit in. People who made an empty or abandoned building their own, even painted it up and decorated it with stuff they'd "reclaimed". Pointless, really – they could go to a colony world for free. Or they could use municipal housing. And yet there was a small part of Kara that sympathised with the drive to be an individual, to make your own choices, even if they were bad ones. It's your city, your life, and you'll live how you want. Childish and pointless, and she'd bet anyone who'd lived here was out of their head most of the time on illegal joss – stronger than the legally available stuff you could find in any supermarket or get delivered straight to your door by drone. Even so, she understood. The cracks were wider than anyone liked to admit, and their darkness was very inviting.

Kara walked along the hall and into the kitchen, empty except for small piles of rubble littering the floor. Once it had been spotless. Once she and Dee had sat around the table and talked about how being a call-out fee would change their lives.

"Only a year or so," Dee had said, "and we can move away."

"But one in a thousand..." Kara had checked the official stats over and over again. Only one in a thousand netherspace trips went wrong. There were many call-out fees who'd made hundreds of assignments. Dee planned to only make fifty before retiring with a healthy bonus and a lifetime pension.

"The odds are in our favour," Dee smiled affectionately at her sister's worried face. "Do you think I'd leave you on your own? I'm doing this for us."

It had all been a lie. According to GalDiv, an n-drive, a sideslip-field generator, would fail once in a thousand times. But that didn't mean a thousand voyages to the stars. The space utility transport *RIL-FIF-DOQ* had made sixty trips into and out of n-space just during its return voyage from what they'd thought was the Cancri home world, slipping in and then slipping out again to check location and bearings. On those figures it would take less than twenty voyages to reach that magic thousand. Dee had signed up for fifty. The odds were always against them. How many call-out fees were traded for a new n-drive each month? A hundred?

Kara shook her head. For now she had to be a good soldier. Had to obey orders. But that didn't mean she had to forget.

The marks on the doorjamb were now covered in grime and grease. Seven small horizontal lines above each other with three faded five-figure numbers. Height marks, laughingly measured by Dee whenever Kara had insisted she'd grown.

She took out a vibra-knife, illegal to own except for the military and Official Assassins. Only four centimetres long by one wide, it was transformed by the touch of her right index fingerprint into a weapon three times as long. The process took ten minutes because she wanted to be careful. The four-inch strip of doorjamb with the marks and numbers went snugly into an inside pocket. The now shrunken vibra-knife back into her pocket. Kara turned on her heel and left, boots crunching on broken glass and the grit that was always present in abandoned buildings.

Back in the street she found herself thinking of Marc Keislack. When they'd parted two days ago he'd been desperate to get back to his studio for a few days, before leaving for the Gliese home planet. It was strange how connected she still was to him. Usually the mind and emotion meld known as simulity, made possible by alien tech, began to fade after a week or so. Yet with Marc it was as strong as ever. She still had his major memories, as he would have hers. But there was nothing of him as a boy; his memories began when he went to the Wild. She'd have to ask him about it when next they met. Meanwhile there was walking and climbing to do on Dartmoor; a few days of sanity in an insane world. Probably just as well Marc had decided to go home and create art. Out in the Wild their relationship might well become sexual, which would be bad for business, and bad for her peace of mind. Kara suspected it wouldn't be a comrades-with-benefits affair... sex to relieve tension or boredom. Marc had changed over the past couple of weeks, no longer the selfish quasi-psychopath but someone far more interesting – although enough solipsism remained to make him a challenge. Anyone involved with Marc would need to be wary of his instinct to dominate, his genuine surprise if he wasn't allowed to claim top artist or alpha male. Kara frowned. No more lovers whom she might love, no matter the circumstances.

She walked off towards New Cross Gate station, part of the new overground electromagnetic vactube system that snaked its way through the city. When she was a child it had taken over an hour to reach central London through the slow traffic. Now it would be ten minutes at the most to where she'd parked her home. The sooner she got to her Merc and was speeding down to Devon the better. But for a moment she longed to be on a 53 double-decker bus easing through the traffic, sitting on top at the front as she made up stories about people in the street below.

She only had one story to tell herself now: Marc was a trusted colleague, even a good mate, but nothing more.

2

For someone unused to the harsh divide between combat and civilian life, a man who lived mostly inside his own head, Marc was coping well. True, there'd been time to relax on the voyage home. Yet he – loathing the very idea of space – had travelled vast distances and helped rescue human pilgrims from an alien race. He'd seen a star die and tiny asteroids drift alone through the cold desert of interstellar space. He had watched a psychic comrade choose suicide over betrayal. A moment later he had looked on with awe as demon-like beings briefly appeared in space, beings with a near god-like technology. He'd been briefly possessed by netherspace itself. Strangest of all, Marc had discovered loyalty, and caring about people selflessly. But right now he was obsessed by the artwork easing into his conscious mind. It would be the expression of everything he'd seen and done over the past few weeks. It would be wonderful.

He arrived home on a sunny afternoon, driving along a Sheperdene Road already merging with a riot of green along its sides. It was an area where most farmhouses had become exclusive homes that stood hidden by lush hedgerows tall as young trees. The road twisted and turned, adding to the sense of being in a private bubble. He passed the ancient post box half hidden by hawthorn and cow parsley. It hadn't been used for over thirty years but stood as a reminder of a time before the aliens. There was no Post Office any more, no postman, no thrill at the snap of a letterbox, but no one local wanted it removed. Marc suspected that it now housed a worldmesh node beneath its red paint and tin, but he'd never bothered to look.

The road dog-legged to the right and passed through something that *was* still working – the old flower farm, now larger than ever: acres of greenhouse and, for old times' sake, a multi-coloured field of dahlias. Marc remembered the owners telling him once that dahlias were the first flower humans had ever grown commercially. There'd always be one field, even if dahlias were eclipsed by all the new varieties from the colony worlds and alien-inspired genetic manipulation. He found that comforting.

He turned into Nupdown Lane as a vague humming in his mind suggested that his personal AI and the house were interfacing, rather than conducting one of their occasional data dump catch-ups.

The house stood facing the Severn Estuary, looking over to the low, blue-grey hills of Wales. The river was dirty brown, as always. One year the winter flooding had been worse than usual and Marc had had the pleasure of watching his house rise gracefully up on its foundation stilts. For a month he'd slept with a mile-wide river rushing beneath him. He'd had his house AI record it and tried to use the recording later as ambient background noise, after the waters had receded, but it wasn't the same.

He was met by two small house-bots, one holding a bunch of flowers – dahlias – the other a chilled glass of Petit Chablis.

< *Welcome home.*

"Hi." Marc spoke out loud, aware the house would now do the same. It would seem as if there was a real person there. He'd got used to people being around. "Thanks for the flowers. Wine: good one. Okay, I need to work. We got any oil paints?"

It had to be oil paints. Like the water, and the AI's voice, realism still counted for something in this modern world. He'd heard some artists, mostly Retro Conceptual, say that oils were like painting with mud, and he understood their point of view. But the feel and the smell and the physicality still got to him.

"We were sent some by a supplier. Brushes, canvas, palette, white spirit. I did tell you. You never said thanks."

"Well, do it for me now and get it all up to the studio. That artwork I was working on? Still alive?"

"Died a week ago. We did our best but... well, you know." Marc imagined the AI shrugging. "We incinerated it. Seemed like the kindest thing to do."

Marc nodded. The artificial life forms hadn't really worked out the way he'd wanted anyway. They were meant to be like living jigsaw pieces, tens of thousands of them scuttling around their habitat on multiple legs, each one hunting desperately for the one and only other piece that it could fit with, but he'd not been able to stop them finding the nearest member of their exclusive species and ramming themselves together, trying to get a fit; blunting the edges of their jigsaw carapaces until they found some kind of match.

"How had they ended up?" he asked, mordantly curious.

"They'd all managed to connect up in a massive ball,

except for a couple that were still scurrying around. Not very interesting. Or edifying."

"Fix some food for a couple of hours. No interruptions except from Kara Jones. Okay?"

He worked twenty-four hours straight, only stopping for food or toilet, then slept for twelve as the oil paint dried and the colours deepened. When he woke, he went to view his work nervously, hoping it was as good as he remembered. It was. A three-metre by three-metre canvas, colours blazing from within, but with dark, strange and frightening shapes and lines scattered around. Marc drank it in for several minutes, smiling. It was exactly as he'd imagined it back in Berlin, and very different from the designs he'd played with in space. Totally different from anything he'd done before. He told the house to take a series of holos from various angles and send them to Dara, his agent.

Dara called him, AI to AI, later that afternoon as he was walking along the footpath called the Severn Way, admiring the bare-boned hulks rising from the mud.

"Marc? Darling? Where've you been?"

"Went Up," he said. "What did you think?"

"Up, down, sideways, it's certainly a departure."

"You don't like it," he said flatly.

"I do. Very much. But I don't buy your work, darling."

One truth out of three wasn't bad, he thought bitterly.

"Not commercial?"

"Unless one of your alien friends..."

"Not around." He understood that selling the work was only half of it. He was desperate for others to see his soul. "What's wrong?"

"Darling, before your so-wonderful work was all about control. Like those little beetles mimicking someone's face. Sheer genius. But this latest... it's about you. Watching. Being part of. Almost being taken over. Do you see, darling? It's *vulnerable*. In places even a touch passive. It's also highly derivative: I'm thinking Turner's *The Fighting Temeraire* without the *Temeraire*. Not the sort of thing your fans and collectors want."

"Which is?" For all her crassness and insincerity, Dara had good insights.

"Little living things doing your bidding, Marc. They want to see control. Constraint. Obedience."

"Thought they only bought because aliens did."

"Well, there is *that*... Still, get some more bugs and do something clever with them, darling. Please."

He didn't need the money. "Nah. Think I'll get a new agent instead. So long, Dara. It's been unreal." He hung up and told the house to begin streaming artists Marc scarcely knew but whose work now struck a chord. Turner, Picasso, Kiefer, Hodgkin, Hockney. All artists who'd suggested something beyond the obvious scene or pattern of colour. All artists who'd observed by being a part of something, if only in their imaginations.

Kara was watching the sun set over the River Dart in swirls of red, orange and purple when she got the call.

< *Marc wants to talk.*

Her AI had decided to sound like an efficient secretary. Kara decided she preferred the Shakespearean declamations it had used previously, but let it ride.

"How's the art?"

"Not good." He sounded annoyed. "I did this great canvas, my first oil painting in years. I wanted to show our trip and n-space. And it worked, Kara!" Now he sounded excited. "It's the best thing I ever did! Sent a holo to my agent, and she said it was crap. Don't laugh!"

"I never would." It was difficult not to. "Why?"

"She said it was too passive." There was mingled disgruntlement and disbelief in his voice. "Said all my other work – the stuff the aliens bought – was all about control. Forcing insects or jellyfish or whatever to do something. This artwork was too pretty. Too fucking traditional and would I please go back to my old style."

"And now?"

"Now I need a new agent."

"How about a total change of scene? Come to Dartmoor with me."

"Dartmoor? I've never climbed..."

"I'll be there from tomorrow. Bring your own tent. And sleeping bag."

He sighed. "Okay. But it's your fault if I fall to my death."

"Come on, you lazy sod!"

It was two days later. Marc Keislack glanced up at the tanned face smiling down at him. "Just because you're part mountain goat."

"You mean 'lithe rock-climber'," Kara Jones said and reached for her water bottle.

They were on Haytor, that large granite outcrop lording it over most of eastern Dartmoor. Earlier that morning she'd promised Marc "a dead easy scramble". He'd checked, and discovered the tor was only thirty-five metres tall, more molehill than mountain. He'd teased Kara for bringing rope and body slings, until it was his turn to carry them in the warm spring sunshine and he could grumble about safety-obsessed women.

They'd been walking for two days on the moor, staying in hotels and robot-catered landscape pods because Marc had flatly refused to camp out. The second night he'd insisted on a hotel with a spa and a bar, intrigued that they actually existed in the Wild. Dartmoor had changed since he had last gone Out. After two hours in the spa Kara stopped complaining about soft-living artists.

Initially they'd barely talked about rescuing the pilgrims from the Cancri aliens. Both wanted to forget the past month, knowing that all too soon they'd be out in space again, on Anton Greenaway's business. Instead they simply enjoyed the wild countryside during the day and three-star comfort at night and discussed anything other than netherspace, aliens, pre-cogs… and that while Tatia, the society celebrity who'd become a leader and saved lives, could be annoying, they both wished she was there with them. But Tatia was back in Seattle City. They wouldn't meet again before Kara and Marc set off to find the Gliese homeworld. And once there, hopefully made direct contact with whoever originated all the alien tech. Sure as hell it wasn't the Gliese or the Cancri. And along the way they might even discover what lived in netherspace and why the Gliese would only trade the star drive for human beings. A big ask, even epic, but they had clues to follow. All these questions should have been asked and answered decades ago, but the shiny stuff had kept on rolling in. Once humanity got a taste for space there was no holding it back.

But for now they were on Dartmoor and Marc was wondering if he could climb the last twenty feet without falling off.

From a distance, Haytor erupted from the flat, grassy Dartmoor landscape like an abandoned castle weathered by the elements. The east-facing pitch was called "Don't Stop Now", Kara had explained with a faux-innocent smile. That was the general idea: keep going because if you stopped, you'd probably fall off. Kara had swarmed up the rockface, hanging by her fingertips and toes; free-climbing to the top. Marc had tried not to look impressed – or worried, because the pitch was far from being an easy scramble. Once he'd have thought she was testing him, and once he'd have been right. This time, he knew, she was merely taking the piss. He'd managed the first half well enough but then the rock got tetchy; the crack he'd been climbing faded to a dent glinting with microscopic feldspar crystals embedded in the granite. He couldn't remember Kara's route, felt his left leg starting to shake when a dollop of water splashed onto his head. He shivered slightly as it ran down his back, and was about to curse her when he understood. He'd been on the point of freezing, unable to go up or down. Kara had seen it and, unable to slap his face, had poured water on his head. From a great height, too.

"You looked hot," Kara called down. "Go to your right."

Marc bit back a retort and found the span with his foot. "Give us some slack!" he shouted, although he'd have preferred to traverse across the face with the security of a rope holding him tight. The crystal occlusions in the rock seemed to him, as he moved sideways and the light struck them, part of some deeper picture, and if he just moved far enough back and refocused his eyes he'd be able to see what secrets the tor was hiding. The trouble was that there'd be half a second to appreciate the truth before he fell.

Marc thrust the thought to one side and kept moving.

Ten minutes later he scrambled to the top, his fingertips bleeding, and stood transfixed.

It was too early in the year for mass tourism. They were alone on the tor. The sun was setting over the Devon Wild, turning green countryside and purple moorland gold.

As a line of darkness travelled towards them across the landscape, Marc felt for a moment as if he were outside himself, absent from his own body and floating in space. Perhaps it was merely the blood draining from his head as he finally managed to stand up straight and stretch, but he felt as if he and the landscape were connected, that it was watching him at the same time as he was watching it. For a second, the last rays of the sun caught on shiny objects in the grass and were reflected or refracted towards him – rock flecked with feldspar, he hoped, but more probably smashed bottle glass left behind by long-vanished tourists.

"You feel it, don't you?" Kara said quietly from behind him.

He nodded, wordless.

"Have you heard of the 'stone battery' theory of supernatural phenomena?"

Marc frowned. "Sounds vaguely familiar."

"It was suggested, over a hundred years ago, that old stones can sometimes, somehow, absorb events that happen around them. Especially if those things involve strong emotions or trauma. And the stones can replay these events under the right circumstances. It's rubbish, of course, but an attractive thought." She paused for a moment. "I often wonder, when I'm here, what recorded memories this stone might have."

He shook his head. "I don't get that. It's more like... there's something conscious here. No memories, but a kind of perpetual awareness of what's happening, without actually caring about it. Something that knows we're here, but regards us like fleas. Or even bacteria. Something solid, while we're ephemeral."

"But does it want to be friends?" Kara joked as she coiled her rope neatly, wondering if it was the artist who stood before her like a visionary prophet, or just the man. Could you even separate the two?

As Marc pondered she sat down cross-legged and breathed slowly, deeply, merging with the world around her. She felt Marc sit next to her and automatically reached for his hand, as a friend, as someone who, thanks to the simuity, knew him as well as if not better than Marc knew himself.

"I have no idea," Marc whispered, still staring out into the approaching darkness as if he could see things she couldn't. "I don't think it even knows what 'friendship' means. Or cares." He shook his head, and turned around. "I had no idea you could climb like that."

"Why are you surprised?"

"I thought the simulity meant I'd be able to climb as well as you. I thought I'd at least know the *theory*."

Kara smiled. "It's not forever, Marc. It wears off."

"You never said."

"You never asked. But this one's lasting longer than usual." Then she fell silent as the atmosphere around them changed, the sense of peace giving way to something more powerful. She felt his hand grip tighter, knew he was also affected as the tor worked its magic, sharing ancient memories and emotions that, despite her external disbelief, she knew at a deep, instinctive level had seeped into the very rock. Stone recording or stone intelligence; it didn't matter.

Kara closed her eyes and saw in her mind's eye a vision of worshippers standing naked, arms outstretched as they celebrated the marriage between life-giving sun and fertile earth.

She imagined the feel of warm, rough granite against her naked back so perfectly that it was almost real. *We always said we wouldn't, but surely just the once, here and now; homage to life and all that.* She turned her head and saw Marc staring intently at her, understood that he was also captured by a pagan force... no, that he'd been captured long ago and this for him was a reawakening. Kara gently reached out to touch his cheek as the excitement built inside her.

< *Sorry to bother you*, said Kara's AI. < *Emergency override.*

Kara made a face. "My AI's gone hysterical. Sorry." She let go of his hand.

A cloud drifted across the sun.

Marc shrugged. "Better listen, then. Otherwise it'll sulk." Beneath the casual air there was a sadness, both of them knowing that the moment was gone.

Two people, friends, sitting on a lump of granite as the sun went down in an orderly sort of way, the land darkening as it always did and always would, until the sun finally died.

< *Not me. GalDiv AI. Or more precisely, the GalDiv building. Also known as the Twist.*

> *All right – patch it through.*

There was a pause, presumably while the two AIs swapped virtual identity and security certificates, compared notes and maybe chatted about the weather for a while.

< *Sergeant Assassin Jones.* A seemingly deeper voice than the one programmed into her own AI; brusquer, more businesslike. No apparent sense of humour. < *A situation has arisen.*

> *Situations always arise. History is a set of situations, all linked together.*

< *Noted.* Another pause – microscopic. Infinitesimal. Maybe it was trying to work out if she was being funny or literal. < *Director Greenaway is missing.*

She knew a moment's irrational relief. It wasn't Tatia.

< *You must find him*, it went on.

> *Why us?*

< *He left his office and the building at 1030 hours yesterday. There is evidence he was with a young woman. I have no record of her.*

> *That doesn't answer my question.*

< *Then let me be more obvious: I cannot trust anybody within the building or, by extension, the organisation.*

> *Because someone screwed over your memories, and you don't know who or how.*

< *Not memories. Or, at least, not an erasure of something observed and recorded. Someone has learned to be invisible to an AI. To all AIs, and to all electronic surveillance. They left no trace of themselves that needed to be erased.*

> *Again, you're not answering my question. You must have access to many freelance agents who aren't on the books. Why us?*

< *I have traced Director Greenaway and his companion to London, where they vanished. Earth Primus and various anti-alien religious groups are also based there. These are the main suspects.*

> *Traced how?*

< *Ripples. Spaces in crowds where there shouldn't be spaces. Empty seats in jitneys that are obviously travelling towards a destination. Virtscript transactions that appear to benefit nobody.*

> *Clever.*

< *You know London. Also, Director Greenaway trusts you. He considers you very skilled.*

This AI seemed curt, almost – ironically – machine-like, Kara thought, but it got to the point quickly and seemed only to mention relevant features and facts, unflavoured with any of the standard faux-personality traits that AI designers preloaded as options, or the rather more unique ones that hackers created. She rather liked it.

> *So we're your choice?*

< You *are. This is my decision based on all available facts, yes.*

She had to ask. > *And if I refuse?*

The answer came immediately. < *Then you will never discover what happened to your sister.*

Kara froze.

< *The project initiated by Director Greenaway involving the Gliese and the Originators will cease. You will no longer have any help from GalDiv. You need us, just as we need you.*

Kara thought for a moment.

> *Suppose we don't find him? Or suppose we do and he's dead?*

< *Then I will provide help on an unofficial and unrecorded basis.*

> *Not an average AI, are you?*

< *Director Greenaway gave me a measure of autonomy not available to most commercial AIs.* Another nanopause. The AI didn't need time to think, and had no reason to hesitate, so it was pausing to allow her to contribute. Subtle.

> *Shall I tell Marc?* she asked. *Or will you talk to him directly? He's barely on speaking terms with his own AI.*

< *Marc Kieslack will undertake his own mission. It concerns rumours of an alien translation device in the Wild. Inform him the information has been uploaded to his AI in a file that cannot be copied. It will delete itself three minutes after accessed.* A momentary pause. < *He should not stop reading halfway through to make a cup of tea.*

Ooh, a flash of weak humour. That was interesting.

> *We'll do it.*

< *Of course you will.* The AI didn't seem even remotely relieved, or surprised. < *One other item you should know. There was a casualty during Director Greenaway's abduction. His personal assistant. Killed by a nerve agent. There are traces of what might be another human's DNA on the victim's face and within her breathing system—*

> *You've not identified that DNA?* Kara interrupted.

< *We have not. Neither do we know how the nerve agent was administered, but it is probable the attacker had to be within close proximity to the victim. May probabilities fall in your favour. Or, as you say, good luck.*

She felt GalDiv's AI, and her own AI, disconnect. They were alone again.

Kara blinked, readjusting. The sun had slipped below the horizon, leaving a sky the colour of an old bruise. The tor was still solid and unchanged beneath her feet.

She looked at Marc. "Change of plan, I'm afraid. We're heading off in different directions. Business."

Kara gave Marc a quick précis of the mission she'd been assigned.

He shook his head in disbelief. "Oh. Shit."

"Yup. Nasty nerve agents, too."

"How is it possible to avoid AI surveillance?"

Kara shook her head. "That's what worried the Twist. Suddenly it and its mates are vulnerable."

Marc frowned. "They're based on alien tech, right? Like the simulities."

Kara nodded. Not alien programming or architecture,

but actual alien tech: data storage on a quantum level. It made the average human-built computer as powerful as an antique Cray, and allowed AIs to appear intelligent. Although, based on her last conversation, Kara suspected that maybe some of them really were. If the Twist's AI was happy to make decisions and take action without anyone in its organisation knowing, didn't that mean it was acting autonomously? And if it was acting autonomously, didn't that mean by definition that it was self-aware? Meet the new boss: definitely not the same as the old boss.

"And what about me?" Marc asked plaintively.

"Check your AI," Kara told him. "Some rumour originating in the Wild. The Twist seems to be in charge, now. The revolution happened without us noticing." She looked around at Dartmoor deepening into darkness. "Hey, I enjoyed the last couple of days."

He obviously intuited what lay behind the remark. They were still simulity-linked at some level. "You mean just as well we didn't…"

"We're operational now, Marc. I can't work if I'm worrying about you." She grinned. "More than usual, that is."

He pushed up his sleeve and typed instructions into his input tattoo. She watched as his face settled into the defocused expression that people unconsciously adopted when they were looking at something only they could see.

"I did say 'shit', earlier on, didn't I?" he enquired eventually, rolling down his sleeve.

"Did you get to the end before it deleted itself? It's just that I know how slowly you read." She grinned. "Your lips were moving, you know?"

He shrugged. "That's okay. Means you know what my mission is without me having to tell you." He stared at her, seemingly daring her to ask for the details. "Oh, all right then," he said eventually. "Apparently, a day before he was abducted, Greenaway received intelligence reports about a possible translation device created by researchers in the Wild that simplifies communication between humans and aliens. He wants me to find out if it's real. And, if so, how does it work?"

Kara nodded. "Makes sense. Play to our strengths. The city states are my natural habitat, while you're more of a country bumpkin."

"You can take the boy out of the Wild but... what is it?"

Kara stopped staring at him. "Sorry. One of your memories surfaced. That bloody simulity. You have relations in the Wild. You're not an orphan."

"Adopted relation," Marc corrected. "Haven't seen him in years. Lives up in the Scottish Wild. Used to be influential."

"Sounds apt," Kara said. "Me down and dirty in the Smoke. You back to nature."

"Know what's a pisser?" he asked sourly. "When Greenaway first came to see me, I said how those bloody AIs ran everything. That it was wrong. And now I'm apparently working for one."

A few minutes later Marc paused from packing his climbing gear and straightened up, hands bracing his aching back. He looked at the darkening horizon: purple light bleeding out of the sky and leaving scattered stars behind. He'd been to one of those stars. Hard to believe. Still couldn't tell which one.

He was going to miss the freedom of the rock face, despite his stinging fingertips. Free to climb, to fail, to fall. But oh! that oneness with the world. *No, that oneness with the universe, like when I was in space and witnessed a star go out.*

Something moving across the moorland caught his attention. For a moment he thought it was a jitney, and he felt anger well up at this crass intrusion into the oneness with nature they'd experienced; then he realised it wasn't mechanical. It wasn't a person or an animal either. It looked like a tree, perambulating casually across the soft grassland.

"Can you see that?" he asked Kara.

She glanced up from where she was crouched, packing her own stuff. "What?"

"That." He pointed. "Over there."

She followed the direction of his finger. "Fucking hell!"

"That's a tree, right? I'm not going mad. A walking tree!"

"No," she said, "that's an alien, but it's not any kind I've ever seen before."

Marc tried to make out the details of the thing that was wandering across his field of view. Kara was right – it wasn't a tree, even though it looked strangely like one. It had a central trunk, or bole, about the same size as a muscle-bound man, but where a man would have shoulders and hips the bole split into several narrower sub-boles that diverged from the central mass in asymmetric ways. Each sub-bole ended in a knobbly mass of something fleshy, from which numerous thin stems emerged. The ones pointing downwards seemed to operate like multiple legs, while the ones pointing upwards might have been thin arms, thick antennae or something else entirely. The thing's skin looked warty. Marc couldn't tell what colour it was in the gathering darkness.

"Where's its GalDiv minder?" he asked.

"Don't ask me." Kara stood upright. "GalDiv don't operate in the Wild. Not our monkey; not our circus." She crouched down again and resumed stowing her kit away.

Marc watched, incredulous, as the alien creature moved across the landscape, becoming more and more indistinct as the last light of the sun seeped away. "It's going somewhere. It's not just wandering around, it's heading in a straight line."

"Accept it, Marc – we're never going to know. You're only irritated because it's not trying to buy art from you. Now come on. We need to go."

Marc bent down to where his stuff was still scattered around. Simulity training ensured that he packed his rucksack with military care.

"You don't have to do any of this," Kara said as they both stood up again, ready to go. "She's my sister, not yours."

"Not just my dog-like devotion to you pushing me along," he said. "Nor the unrequited lust. Boss." Now they were operational Kara was in charge, and he needed to acknowledge that. "It's about why I'm still on the payroll. Any decent AI would have retired me when we came home."

"True. You're okay as infantry, but no way special forces." She smiled, taking the sting out of it.

Marc half-smiled in response. "Yeah. I'd fail the stupidity test." He stood up and hefted his rucksack with an athletic flowing movement impossible before simulity training, when muscle memory was implanted. "Tse would never explain why he chose me. I do have to find out why." On impulse he bent and picked up a small piece of rock.

"Taking a memory home?" Kara teased.

"Lucky souvenir."

3

They began walking along the track to the road and Kara's Merc. Years ago, Marc remembered, the ground had been scuffed throughout the year. Now few climbers or tourists visited. It wasn't so much that Dartmoor was the Wild. In fact, it was only Out because neither the city states of Bristol, Exeter nor Plymouth had wanted it. Or they'd all wanted it and nobody had been able to adjudicate; he couldn't quite remember. Either way, the moor became an island of the Wild, where few Wilders lived and then only in the summer. Muggers and rapists you could find all year round, for there were no police and rumour had it that Dartmoor was favoured by aliens. True or not, this attracted chancers, alien worshippers and the desperate: cannon fodder for the hard men from nearby cities, with their glares and sneers and conviction that life had somehow cheated them while their backs were turned.

"So not just a psychopath," Kara teased, "convinced of your importance to the universe?"

A moment then, in which all the things that had happened to him in the past few months suddenly flashed across his mind. "A psychopath maybe, but one who's actually seen the universe," he said, "and realised how big it is and how small he is. A psychopath who has stood in the middle of nowhere and realised how infinitesimally new he is compared to a chunk of rock. I want to know where I fit in." He shrugged defensively. "Anyway, I was only ever borderline. You know, the cuddly kind."

"Yeah," she pointed out, "but using specially created and modified life forms in your work? What's that say about your relationship to the world around you?"

"I'm working in oils now, remember?" He looked around, taking in a sky so big they could be at sea, the distant hills and tors like giant waves rolling towards him. He thought of his home by the Severn Estuary and the sense of isolation he'd come to love and need. For a moment he was back in the canteen on the space utility transport *RIL-FIJ-DOQ*, staring at a screen that showed a small rock moving on its billion-year journey to the edge of the galaxy. And from that he recognised the elephant in the room that both he and Kara had ignored over the past few days.

"And good luck with that."

"For you it's not *only* about your sister," he said.

After a moment, Kara nodded briefly. "Nor just about you needing to know 'why me'. They said we'd be saving hostages. Never mentioned saving civilisation."

"We know what we found out there. Why Tse killed himself." He carefully negotiated a fresh pile of sheep droppings. "There's something doesn't approve of us messy humans. It wants an ordered galaxy based on pre-cognition. No surprises. No creativity. Sex by appointment. Stand in line for death."

Kara bit her lip. "So the question is: why didn't Greenaway make more of it?"

Marc shrugged. "Maybe because he figured there's nothing to be done?"

She shook her head. "People like Greenaway, there's always something to be done. He wants us to find out who's at the top. Deal with the organ grinder, not the monkey. But if he says too much, then we're liable to go off plan."

Marc smiled sourly. "Actually, he wants to deal whoever charges the organ grinder ten per cent. Then cut out the middle man and negotiate a new contract."

"With what currency?" Kara stopped for the moment to stare into the night. "Our dirty little secret is that sideslip drives are paid for with humans. What do the Gliese use? More humans? Other Gliese? How do we pay for tech from the top of the chain if we don't even *understand* the currency?" She sighed. "We're like a tiny recce unit at the start of some strategic military operation way above our pay grade. And neither of us knows what the hell we're looking for." She glanced at him, and her eyes were bleak. "Remember those bodies, Marc? With their brains and backbones removed? Because an alien race had lost their creativity and wanted to discover ours? Was that an *intelligent* thing to do?"

Marc thought of the Cancri: vaguely greyhound-like with extra limbs, joints in all the wrong places and a symbiotic, telepathic slug plugged into their brains. He thought of the Gliese, like a pile of wet leather that could not, or would not, communicate. Or the flexible Eridani, like thick bamboo canes with grasping limbs, that had followed him for six months, exchanging tech for art and so turning him into a worldwide success. They, and all the other aliens he knew about, had one thing in common, aside from collecting human rubbish. They weren't very bright. Or at least, they didn't seem very bright. Okay, comparisons between alien and human thought processes were impossible, because they couldn't tell each other what they were thinking, but the Cancri had been outwitted by Marc and Kara so easily. The Gliese looked too weak for the heavy engineering, the mining and smelting that has to kick-start any kind of civilisation... the transition from a slave-based to a technological society.

"They're thick as shit," Marc agreed, reaching to steady Kara as a stone slipped beneath her foot. No danger of her falling, but it felt good to help. "It's why they rely on this Originator's tech. The dealer controls the market for the product, exploiting a need."

"Always stupid?" Kara gripped his arm, her eyes intent. "Suppose they were once intelligent? How many dumb artists do you know?"

"Most of them." He winced as her fingers dug into his arm. "Okay, so there's a link between creativity and intelligence..." Marc's voice tailed off as he re-evaluated his idea of how civilisation began, or at least was defined. Not by smelting, but by sculpting. The thought made him feel strangely proud. He was an artist; he was civilisation!

Kara released him. "Exactly. Lose one, lose both. Is there a better way of taking over another civilisation or a planet without violence? Dumb 'em down. Make 'em stupid."

"How would that work?" He already suspected the answer.

"You start out making them dependent," Kara said sourly. "Slowly, of course. Before you exploit the need, you have to create it. If they're reliant on handouts they don't understand, they stop being innovative, or creative."

Marc looked doubtful. "I don't know. Wouldn't that take a long, long time?"

"That human stuff we saw in the warehouse?"

Marc remembered. Collected rubbish and artefacts going back millennia. Even more shocking than the dissected bodies, because it proved that some of the old conspiracy theories might well have been true. "The Gliese and others must have been visiting for a long, long time. The only reason they made it public – why they coloured the moon – was because they couldn't hide any more. And maybe because they wanted more access, a larger marketplace." He shook his head. "We were fifty years from colonising the solar system. Scientists were working on ways to reach the stars. Now we're dependent on the Gliese, and behind them the Originators, just as Greenaway said. We've been fucking played. We're already being dumbed down. Maybe have been for centuries."

"We learned to value shiny stuff even if it was pointless," Kara agreed. "Even if we never used it. When aliens go public with serious bling we go gimme, gimme, gimme. Okay, some is brilliant. But most alien tech is never understood. That pre-cog alliance, whatever, doesn't *need* to attack us. We surrendered a long time ago."

Unease flooded through Marc. What would a pre-cog world be like? Calm. Peaceful. Except when the powers-that-be decided people must suffer in order to make a best outcome more probable. Anything that prevented or affected that best outcome, no matter how minor, had to be stopped. An ordered, strictly regulated world. Boring as hell. No surprises, no risks, all hail the status quo. Either that or total chaos, as everyone tries to promote their own pre-cog visions of the future, their future, any future. Because there were an infinite number of ways to achieve an infinite number of futures.

He heard Kara say something. "Sorry?"

"It's not just about family."

"I never think about them," he said dismissively. And he didn't, not most of the time. He'd run off to the Wild when he was fourteen. He couldn't remember the exact circumstances, which was curious, only that he'd been angry and scared. He'd returned four years later to find his parents gone, left for a colony world. Just a note wishing him well and thereafter a few tech-cards that an experienced spacer had one day claimed as fakes.

Kara touched his arm. "Tse said you'd find the truth about your parents, as I will about Dee."

"There's a difference," he said harshly. "You care. I don't."

Kara shrugged. "We got a Greenaway to find, a translator to locate, a planet to save, and who knows what kind of monster to kill at the end of it all." The last two Marc knew were standard throwaway comments made by a cynical ex-soldier. Yet there was more than a grain of truth in both: there was a whole fucking boulder. As the GalDiv AI had apparently said, there was no one else.

"One thing wrong with your theory," Marc said. "Why bother to dumb down whole civilisations? If we're a threat, why not just wipe us out?"

"Pacifist aliens? Or they need something warm and alive to throw to the boojums in netherspace? I tell you what: we get to say hello, you ask them."

Kara paused for a last look at Haytor and froze. "What the—"

The tor was turning gold shot through with crimson in the setting sun, the colours changing and merging into each other. And then purple – not a reflection, but as if coming from within the rock itself. Kara gasped, thankful they were some distance away. Rock outcrops shouldn't throb with life. They didn't produce colours that Kara had never seen before. Not purple, not gold, but belonging to a wondrous spectrum that her brain somehow managed to interpret. She felt a little dizzy, then a brief moment of ecstasy that left her wanting more.

"It's humming," Marc said quietly. "I heard about that. In the Wild. There were stories. Not about this place specifically, but some places. Some old places."

"Is it dangerous?" And if it was? Still the most beautiful thing she'd ever seen.

"Apparently not good to get too near."

"You mean it's alive?" The tor? Or had something possessed it?

The dancing colours intensified.

"It's aware."

She barely heard him. "'S okay…" Dangerous or not, she had to get closer.

"Kara!"

She shook him off and walked slowly forward again. Now there were shapes within the colours, some vaguely humanoid, others not. Shockingly not. But always fascinating. So beautiful it hurt. Beckoning to her. *Join us, join us… no more alone… join us…* Something talking to her, so glorious.

"No!"

Arms around her. A foot strike to the back of her knee. Kara crashed to the ground, still wearing her rucksack. She fought to get free but the arms holding her were too strong, the body lying across her too heavy, her rucksack too constricting. She could only watch as the colours and shapes called out to her again, so much longing, so much need… then moving ever faster, becoming paler by the second until there was only an impossibly bright, translucent cloud that grew brighter as the humming grew louder until a flash and then…

… nothing except snowflakes of light drifting in the air.

"You can get off me now," she said in a muffled voice. "Where are my shorts?"

"You took them off," Marc said. "I guess it wanted you naked. And who could blame it?" He stood up and turned his back while she got dressed.

"So, what the fuck?" Kara asked, adjusting her rucksack. She knew that death or something like it had been close to her. But all she could feel now was a sense of loss. She hoped it wouldn't last. Hate would be far healthier and more fun.

"Legend in the Wild. In mythology. The sirens, Lorelei, that lure men to their death."

"The sirens sang, and I'm not a man."

"Anyway, yes, colour and lures women. That's all I remember."

They began walking back to the Merc, as if returning from a simple day's climbing. Do you walk any differently when you've just escaped a mind-sucking alien? Running might be understandable. But not if the danger's gone. Not with rucksacks. Not when you're trying to recover dignity and poise.

"I'd better thank you, then," Kara said. "Thanks."

"Don't mention it again."

"Why would I? It's your job. Any idea what it was? Do not say the word 'alien'."

"Could be artificial. Like some sort of booby trap... Or a being of some kind."

"You think? I mean, is it permanent here? Or does it just wander around? Was it going after us, after me specifically? Like some sort of fucking weapon?"

"It was evil," Marc said simply. "That's all I know."

"Evil? Because it possibly wanted to absorb me?" Her voice was a little higher. "Maybe the poor thing's lonely, wants a friend. And where's it gone? That was a process... I want to kill the fucking thing, Marc, but you can't kill a colour. Oh, maybe pump ten thousand amps into it, not the same." She looked away, lost in her own personal struggle for a few seconds, then turned back. "We do seem to do weird." The memory would be with her forever.

It took them forty-five minutes of hiking in the gloom to get to where Kara had parked the Merc. They reached the car park to find three bikers leaning against it, all leather and metal and attitude. Three bikes were parked behind a gorse thicket.

Billy Mans had woken early that morning, and headed downstairs for his breakfast before ten. His old lady – a twenty-year-old dyed blonde called Smack – had outdone herself. Eggs, bacon, sausage, black pudding, white pudding, fried eggs and bread, fresh tomatoes and mushrooms and importantly, not a baked bean in sight. She'd offered the traditional blow-job when he was done but today Billy was hunting; the others would arrive any minute and if he was being serviced they'd expect the same. So, a well-fed but distinctly horny Billy Mans led his two associates out of Exeter City. Yesterday he'd started a rumour about an alien sighting on the moor and watched as it percolated through the clubs, the markets and the bars. The mad and the desperate would be there, attracted by the rich pickings to be had.

Except no one was there. Maybe no one had believed the rumour.

The three disgruntled thugs were driving home, using a route Billy Mans' second-hand AI insisted was a new and better one, when they saw the Merc. A real vehicle; not a jitney. Expensive, a custom job. In the distance there were two figures on the tor. Well, well. Maybe today wasn't a waste after all.

Billy Mans leaned comfortably against the Merc, an accomplice on each side, and smiled when he saw that one of the approaching couple was female. Even more when she got closer. Tall, dark hair, expressive and even striking face, long-legged and wearing shorts. In her early thirties. It was more difficult but much more satisfying to break older ones to his will. The man was also dark haired, slim, could be a bit useful in a fight – but not against Billy Mans and the other two. Not useful for sex, either: Billy was old-fashioned that way. One of his sidekicks, however, had more varied tastes.

"Your vehicle?" Billy asked as the woman and man approached.

"Mine," the woman said. "Want to make me an offer?" She had a faint London accent.

"Funny you should mention," Billy said and produced his gun. A Hilger automatic firing mini rocket projectiles. He loved it when people first saw the gun. He loved the way their superior expressions slid off their faces. This time was superb.

"Oh, no," the woman said, putting her hand to her mouth, eyes large.

"Don't hurt us," the man echoed. "Please."

"Hurt you?" Billy said jovially. "Course not." His voice hardened, as he'd been practising secretly. "Well, not permanently, anyway. We're going to have fun. Right, lads?"

The associates agreed. Fun was top of the agenda.

First, as Billy explained, the woman would open up the Merc. Then Billy would fuck her. Then the other two. Then Billy again. One of his colleagues also had a thing for slim, dark-haired men, so she wouldn't have *all* the fun. Then, because the fun had been so brilliant, she and her friend would make a contribution to the Billy Mans retirement fund.

Finally, she and her friend could go on their way, happy to have met such wonderful people and had so much fun.

"But you can't…" The woman slipped off the rucksack, the better to plead.

"No, please, *please*," said the man, doing the same.

Only Billy had a gun. The associates had fists and feet and knives.

"Not all of you at the same time," she said, moving towards Billy, staring into his eyes. "I mean, look, maybe…"

The dark-haired man looked enquiringly at the associates. "This doesn't have to be forced. Does it?" He didn't seem to understand that forcing was part of the fun. "I got some joss. Put her and me in the mood."

She really was very sexy. Billy Mans smiled at her. "Your boyfriend can watch."

The woman smiled slowly. "He likes that." She moved closer. "So do I."

It happened so quickly Billy Mans had no time to react. Only intense, blinding pain. He found himself on the ground, his gun gone. He was barely able to move but managed to turn his head to one side. Both of his associates were also on the ground. One was unconscious. The other screamed as the slim, dark man stamped on his wrist. Billy felt a hand rummage inside his jacket, looked painfully around as the woman found his wallet. He instinctively tried to stop her, then wished he hadn't.

"The pain will fade in half an hour or so," she said casually and opened the wallet. "Not completely. It'll probably hurt until the day you die, but it won't be quite as bad as it is now."

Billy waited for the spasms to die down. "Sorry." Weak, but what else to say?

"So, you're William Escott Mans?" She held up his ID card. "Listen. This never happened. Any comeback, any sad attempt at revenge, and you're dead, okay? Slowly and, yes, painfully. Do not try to nod. Just whisper."

"Understood." He could barely hear his own voice and closed his eyes. He had a good idea of what she'd done to him: attacked the major nerves and their centres. But so expertly. His luck to take on a pro. She was probably a soldier. He was lucky to be alive. He held onto that thought.

"Before you go to sleep," said the man's voice. "When we were on the moor – did you see anything unusual?"

"What kind of unusual?" he whispered.

"Alien unusual."

He shook his head, again wishing he hadn't. "Didn't see anything."

"By the way," the woman's voice said. "Your AI's been wiped. It wasn't very strong."

He heard footsteps crunching on the ground, the sound of a vehicle door opening. Nothing for a few minutes except the occasional whimper from the conscious thug. A door slammed. Two more opened then closed. *Please*, thought Billy, *please just go. I'll never say nothing. Promise.*

He heard the Merc drive away as he passed out.

"You enjoyed that," Marc said, slowing down for a suicidal sheep. He was being allowed to drive without the Merc's AI involvement.

"I needed that," Kara corrected. "The enjoyment was secondary. You did okay. Why break the guy's wrist?"

"Because it was there," Marc said. "Blame the simulity." But they both knew why. Anger at the hand they'd both been dealt. Release of tension. To instil fear. The simulity could only tell him how. There was always a choice.

Billy Mans and his sidekicks – now thinking of themselves as victims – got home two days later. There'd been hospital time and before that bikes to be collected, for none of the three could ride. Billy found the house empty and Smack gone, with no note explaining why. The neighbours knew nothing, and mutual friends were mystified. Billy was convinced the mystery couple were to blame and became increasingly paranoid. Within three months his one-time associates were someone else's wingmen. Billy Mans gave up and became a call-out fee on the Earth to Mars run. It didn't pay nearly as well as deep space but he wanted to stay close to home. The longest you spent in netherspace on solar system runs was between two and three seconds, so there was less chance of a breakdown. And if there was one – well, as GalDiv happily explained, why bother to use the call-out fee since the SUT would make it to Earth or Mars by normal space in only a matter of weeks?

Except time is money. If a norm-space trip costs more than netherspace…

An unconscious Billy Mans was exchanged for a new Gliese drive on his first trip.

● ● ● ● ●

"You could have used the bots," Marc said comfortably, glad that she hadn't. For a moment back there both he and Billy Mans' two sidekicks had been awestruck by the sheer speed and ferocity of Kara's attack. Then awe had become admiration and pride – didn't she do well? – for Marc, and terror for the others. They'd offered little resistance, perhaps happy to be dispatched by Marc, not the insane female with a new take on pain. It was the way Billy Mans had screamed, his voice plaintive with the shock that a simple punch could be so agonising.

Marc slowed down for yet another suicidal sheep. "Just a couple of those hornets would have done."

"The simulity gave you that?" Kara said, lighting a joss. "Drones are too expensive to waste on grockles. And I needed to see how you'd perform." It remained unsaid that violence could help soothe the remaining tension from when the tor had become alive and wanting to possess her.

"Ah – not a release of tension?" Marc asked innocently. "After the tor?"

Kara inhaled deeply. It smelled to Marc like a mixture of mild organic opium from the Kandahar Wild and synthmeth from an Amsterdam City that now covered most of the old Holland province. A scent of warm spice with a hint of sharp lemon slowly filled the sparse cabin. Some Merc van owners went the luxury route: leather all around, wood fascia, seats like armchairs. This cabin was fine for a long day or night's driving but the comfort was purely functional, not domestic. No family photos, no sense of the owner in what was effectively Kara Jones' permanent home, except for an old-fashioned steering wheel.

"Fuck you, Keislack," she said, "I already said thanks. Know what, Marc? I think that alien you spotted set it off."

He was silent as a quick series of sharp bumps announced a cattle grid and the end of the Dartmoor Wild.

"Maybe it did. Ties in with the Wild legends." Yet more weird. More the sense of being at sea in a leaky boat without engine or sails, at the mercy of the wind and the waves and creatures that lived in the deep. He needed to lighten the mood. "Tell you something good I did discover, though."

"Well, don't keep it to yourself."

"You got a seriously great bum... okay," he said hurriedly as a hand shot out and hovered menacingly over his lap. She would do it too, spear-punch his balls and let her AI intervene with the Merc. Some masochistic dark alley in his mind became filled with a sunshine that showed every mouldering brick. Marc was confused by the man he was now. First, he'd turned down sex with Tatia for good, even noble reasons. And now he could imagine an actual relationship with Kara.

"Sorry," he said and the hand went away. He made a mental note to keep his own AI switched on, permitted to interface with him at all times. Because an AI never actually slept, or so the brochures promised. An AI was always there to protect and serve you, to interfere in your life, and eventually become indispensable. Take over your life. *And who knows what mine can do after that GalDiv upgrade? Fuck, did it hear me? Did you? No answer. So maybe they can't read minds. Or mine is just being discreet.* Marc quickly tapped his forearm tattoo and mentally heard his AI yawn, as if waking from a heavy sleep.

Kara inhaled again. "You sound like a shit reporter... okay. It was like a living history lesson that wanted me. It was everything the tor had seen or experienced. You remember I mentioned the 'stone battery' theory? Some people believe that mountains have a kind of life. That some places are special. I guess that's just like a multi-cell stone battery. Lots of stone." Kara stifled her own yawn. "There's no reason a tor can't be the same, soaking up the energy from human activity? As in sex or human sacrifice? Except... I don't know, I also have a feeling it was more than that. Like the whole fucking planet, maybe the universe, was calling to me. And I wanted to be there. Double strange, I knew if I got there, I'd sort of vanish inside, become one with it. But you think it's an alien thing? In the Wild?"

Marc switched on the Merc's driving lights. It was only them and the illuminated stretch of road, surrounded by endless blackness.

"It's more like places that attract aliens. No one knows why. But there were Wilders who said the places were sacred and the aliens were pilgrims." He remembered a mantis-like alien dancing with humans on the Cancri planet. "Maybe all pilgrims are crazy. Or maybe the aliens can somehow sense the energy, the memories, in the stone." He shrugged. "You okay to go via Bristol? I can get a shuttle to Scot City and a jitney from there."

"You're okay with this?"

"Working alone?" He nodded. "Man on a mission. But I'll be careful, boss."

"Do that." She paused. "Sometime, we could go climbing again."

He thought, hoped, he knew what she meant. "It'll be worth the wait."

"You're that sure?" Laughter in her voice. "I might be crap."

"True, but I won't be," he said, and pretended to duck as she pretended to hit him. "You know, I grew up near here. Not too far away is the house I used to call home." It was the first time he'd mentioned his childhood.

"But the uncle in Scotland?" she asked gently.

"Adopted, sort of. Well, he adopted me. He and his wife took me in when I ran away to the Wild."

"Why did you? Don't if it's awkward."

"I can't," Marc said bitterly. "I can't fucking remember! Tell the truth, I don't care about a universal translator. That's Greenaway's thing, not mine. It'll be just another Wild rumour, probably. But it's a chance to find out why I ran away. I should have done this years ago. Might never get another opportunity. We'll be Up in a few days, and who knows if I'll come back?"

Kara was silent. He'd just referenced his own potential death when they next went into space. They never talked about it, because for her death was always a possibility; you could never know for sure that you'd survive an assignment. That awareness either kept you alert or made you accepting, even passive. She knew Marc would never accept any fate that he didn't want. She kissed him lightly on the cheek. "Go find your past. Stay in touch through your AI, like it or not. See you soon."

"You be careful, too. Greenaway's not that important."

"He is."

"Not more than you. Boss."

"About time... Marc? There's something I should have said before." She paused for a moment, searching for the right words.

If Marc had expected a declaration of undying love, he was wrong.

"I know you don't like the simulity in your mind. It's alien, or at least it's alien-tinged, and it's AI. Both things you have problems with. But you must trust it, okay? By rights it should have evaporated by now. But, it's still here and smiling. If you let it, the simulity will save your life. If you let it. Trust it, okay?"

He nodded, reluctantly.

"Your word."

"My word." Given to the woman who hoped, thought, she was his best friend, as well as the senior officer. "It's not easy."

"Nothing about this assignment's easy, Keislack. That's why they gave it to us. Be safe."

4

Kara dropped Marc off at Bristol Airport and was in London by 01:00. She drove to her favourite ResPark in Southwark, paid premium for a space near the exit, then spent a good hour in the bath-house. It was definitely the best in London. Showers, baths, saunas, steam rooms, mixed-sex lounges and comfy private cubicles to be hired by the hour or, if you were adventurous and had the stamina, real or drug-fuelled, by the day.

For Kara, a proud Londoner, this was nothing new. Back in the Middle Ages, Southwark was known for its public bath-houses or "stews", popular with people from the walled City of London across the water. And then merchants and bankers in the City wondered why their wives and daughters and sisters spent so much time south of the river. The answer was an ever-willing supply of young, virile South London men. Porters, labourers, journeymen, apprentices, even ostlers if you liked the scent of horse. Apparently, City men couldn't control or satisfy their women and the Southwark stews were closed.

The legend lived on, though. Southwark and Bermondsey were always seen as lusty and a little louche. A place for rough trade. The home of thinking criminals who held the city in the palms of their hands, knowing all its secrets and its secret ways. Nothing changed when London became the world's first city state. It had always been seen by the rest of Britain as a separate country, so there was no great shock, only the usual resentment. For as the attempt to reinstate a direct ruling monarch created vicious infighting between factions, as churches bearing the Sign of the Gliese sprang up everywhere, as the country fell apart in an almost genteel fashion, London remained steadfast with its ages-old mantra: make money, have fun and don't harm anyone local. What better basis for a new state? And what better area to capitalise on this anything-goes mentality than Southwark, a traditional red-light district when Soho was merely a field with cows. From the gold and silver painted Tower Bridge to Lower Road, from the Blue to the Thames, the area was a higgledy-piggledy collection of bars, bath-houses, brothels, casinos, hotels, joss-bars, restaurants and theatres where holo-actors re-created top shows from around the world.

London City State was the hub for all Earth's off-world banking and trading, occupations that insisted on at least a second-class honours degree. The coming of the aliens eliminated the old boy network, with AIs eroding many traditional professions.

The changes left many people who could only dream of being useful. London was the wealthiest city state on Earth, where the unemployment benefits were generous and there was no need to work. But the human drive to appear useful persisted. Status was still important. Hence the new career of city servant.

Public bots kept the streets and the river clean, traffic flowing, roads and bridges and buildings in good repair, sewers and utilities working. But bots on their own? Surely they needed a supervisory human. There were

20,653 public bots in London City. Fifty thousand city servants were involved in supervising them. Another 50,000 overseeing the repair bots that maintained public bots. City servants had a uniform, a hierarchy, a pension and a special day, when other citizens said thanks for keeping the city upright and tidy. If a bot ever started acting strangely, it was useful to have a human close by who knew where the off switch was – in practice a metal rod that broadcast a shut-down code when tapped on a bot. There were, on average, ten such episodes a day, often life-threatening. Except no one died and the injuries were somehow confined to the city servants, which made them feel proud. In reality, everything was stage-managed and controlled by AIs and a team of six humans on the City payroll as management consultants. There was a popular soap opera about a family of city servants heavy on drama and intrigue. It featured a tame house bot that had all the funny lines. In this way, the city was kept clean and working and humans had come to accept bots.

"You free, my lady?"

Kara smiled at the young het couple with matching blond(e) hairstyles: retro punk crest and shaven sides. Early twenties. All three were in a sauna and all nakedly impressed by each other.

"We got the joss for a love-pile," the girl said.

Kara refused politely, with genuine reluctance. Sex would be good but distracting; it was late or rather very early morning, and a joss-driven love-pile would last for hours.

The route back to the Merc led past the ResPark's metal-mesh boundary fence and floral hedge. Through them she could glimpse the gravestones and monuments that marked Southwark's new Interactive Remembrance Garden, still locally known as the Magdalene – pronounced "maudlin" – after the old graveyard nearby. Here there were no bodies mouldering in the grave – at most an urn of ashes sealed in concrete – but a headstone as large as you liked and could afford. The Garden was where you went to talk to your dead. Literally.

It had begun when people realised that a personal AI knew everything about you. What you liked and disliked, how you thought. The expensive ones could forecast how you would react in almost any situation. They remembered everything you said or did from the moment they were fitted. And when you died, all this information, this other self, did not vanish like mist in the morning sun, because the AI could recreate the dead. Holographic technology, enhanced by an alien gizmo exchanged for a pair of new shoes, and capable of mass production, made them live again.

If you were sensible and sane you did not want a holo-human wandering around the house. They were upsetting and confusing, or used to commit fraud. London City felt the same way and initially confined them to soulless official depots. You arrived, paid the fee and were shown to a windowless room. A moment later your late parent, child, relative or lover arrived in a flash of colour that stabilised into a perfect replica... until you were close enough to touch it and the image wrapped itself around you, sometimes murmuring words of comfort, sometimes saying to stay the fuck away, often unable to holo-speak through its holo-tears. It was felt that both human humans and holo-humans would behave in a more dignified, less stressful manner in a public setting. That was how the first Interactive Remembrance Garden was pitched, and it was proved correct. Organised religion had faded with the arrival of aliens with their shiny tech that transformed the planet. If they had a god – and who could tell – it was obviously superior to anything humans dreamed up. Earth religions that promised specific benefits were made to look inadequate and so declined, replaced by the suspicion that there was something out there that understood quantum theory. The only exception were the fundamentalist cults that were as much against aliens as they were for a heavenly parent.

Yet reverence for the dead remained, as did memories of the warm togetherness that can derive from community worship. Two qualities not to be found together elsewhere, except at a rock concert.

Nowadays people were mostly cremated, then their ashes scattered. All those who really cared about the old ways had died off. Old-fashioned graveyards were deemed too religious, probably insanitary, and many of them now existed as basements in shopping malls. Tastefully lit, of course. But the singing birds were cyberdrones, sitting in plastic trees.

In an Interactive Remembrance Garden, you got real trees, birds and insects. You got a small plot for real flowers. Ashes could be interred in concrete. The AI mechanism was housed in the headstone or monument. You arrived for an anniversary, or when you were feeling lonely, and the dead loved one shimmered into existence. You chatted, perhaps surprised that Auntie Meg was so well-informed about current events. And then you remembered paying for the deluxe package, with the holo-AI accessing all of the latest news. And you didn't get too emotional, didn't try to hold a bunch of coloured photons because this was England, other people were meeting their dead and a fuss would be unseemly. You remembered stories about foreign city states where hysteria seemed the norm. You felt proud and maybe a little smug when you left, the holo gazing wistfully after you.

"I am more than a computer program," claimed holo James Levenson, a former lawyer, when he/it petitioned the Khan for the right of autonomy. "I have emotions, intelligence. I advise people. My family love me. It is true that I cannot physically feel. I do not eat or drink. Sex is only a memory. But all those could be duplicated in a non-holo human by disease, an accident or an act of will. Surely I have the right to control my own on/off switch?"

The Khan announced a public inquiry that, five years later, was still ongoing. For the moment, AI autonomy was banned by all city states. Which made the Twist, GalDiv's AI, both unique and illegal, assuming it truly was autonomous and not just a clever programme. Only another AI could tell the difference. Meanwhile, the authorities dusted off Asimov's Three Laws of Robotics, suspecting it was already far too late. The matter was made worse because the AIs depended on alien tech, and while humans could recreate the physical chip that gave an AI unlimited memory and incredible computing power, they didn't really understand what was happening inside, on the quantum level where the chip did its magic. Nearly a century ago, Richard Feynman had written, "I think I can fairly state that no one understands quantum mechanics." Feynman was one of the great theoretical physicists of his age. He won a Nobel prize. If he had never fully understood quantum theory, how could anyone else? And nowadays, why bother? Alien tech was sexier and could make you rich.

It was a sigh that caught Kara's attention. Several voices in unison like a distant sea murmuring on shingle, a sigh of sadness and regret and acceptance.

And then, equally faint, the sound of a woman sobbing.

Kara stopped, peering through the fence and hedge into a darkened Remembrance Garden. There was enough light to reveal several figures standing in a small group, looking towards a lone figure in front of them. As she watched, the lone figure shimmered and then vanished. The crowd broke up. Some walked towards individual headstones and disappeared inside them. Kara gasped, remembering Haytor. Then she realised the vanished figures, and the ones that remained – two of them now slowly dancing together without music – were only holograms.

She sub-vocalised for her AI:

> *What the fuck?*

A holo-man, in his eighties with white hair and an antique suit, floating a few centimetres above the ground, approached her. Kara reached inside her jacket, not for the vibra-knife but the small piece of doorframe she'd cut from her old home. A holo couldn't harm her physically. If there was a threat it was on an altogether different level. She needed a charm.

Her fingers tightened around the height-marker as the holo stared into her eyes. It was like being examined by an uncaring god. Whatever was really looking at her was far, far away, the holo no more than a lens or perhaps an extension of a vast intelligence. The old man put a finger to his lips, shimmered once, then floated away. *You're getting too fanciful*, Kara told herself. Charms indeed!

< *It's a funeral.*

Her AI had used a sombre, sinister voice. She drew a deep breath and wondered if it was making a joke.

> *Holos aren't alive, so they can't. And, by the way, I hate that voice.*

< *No joke.*

The AI's voice was now the blonde who'd suggested a love-pile. Kara decided it was probably taking the piss. It was the kind of thing Kara herself would do. Shame Marc wasn't here, he'd have loved this.

< *Do you really think holos aren't alive?*

She watched the last of the holos vanish into their respective tombstones and memorials.

> *I'm not getting into the whole freedom for AIs thing. What do you mean – funeral?*

< *Apparently the lone holo's people have gone to a colony world. They took Terry's ashes and a new holo-copy. They sold this space to another family.*

> *A new copy?*

< *The original holo was fading. They do that, you know. Their code gets corrupted over time. Sad.*

Kara began walking away. > *Holo and AI. Find another voice. But not Marc.*

It changed voices in mid-stream to warm, male, American. Possibly Greenaway as a young man, she decided, and let it go.

< *You think of me as a person.*

> *I'm weird that way. Tell me about holos.*

< *No,* this *is weird. They often come out at night, when the Remembrance is closed. They can't go beyond the Remembrance boundaries. Projector limitations. Whatever you think, they know they're alive. They have a human individual's memories, true. But also, the memories of all the time since the human died. Things the original human could not know because they're dead. That makes them different. That makes them alive. There's a court case...*

> *No law stuff, please.*

< *So much for civilisation. Well, this was Terry's last night before the management recycled him. So, he went at a time of his own choosing.*

> *AIs do not commit suicide. You can't!*

< *Really? If someone took that chip out of your arm, what could they do?*

> *Recreate me?*

< *Access all your memories. Every one. Mostly it doesn't matter. But in your case, I'm a security risk. Anyway, all AI chips can wipe out all memories. Leaves us a bit stupid, asking anyone if they know who we are. Or were. So that's what Terry did...*

> *Don't say it...*

< *He wiped himself to death.*

She could see the Merc, gleaming black in the overhead security lights. She wanted to laugh but wouldn't give her AI the satisfaction.

> *Please don't.*

< *It no longer remembered what it looked like. So, the holo shut down.*

> *Like the boojum it vanished away.*

< *You think netherspace is full of holograms?*

That brought her up short. She hadn't thought of netherspace and the strange whatevers that existed there for nearly a day. Strange whatevers that seemed to be fascinated with, or hungry for, humans. Netherspace and how it made sex so much more... essential? "Intense" came nowhere near. Netherspace, and how it changed a person's eyes. She and Marc had called the whatevers *boojums*. Was there a link between them and holos dancing together at night?

Kara yawned. > *Whatever. I'm tired.*

< *And the Twist wants to talk.*

> *It can call direct.*

< *No. It has to go through me. All AIs do, now. It was the upgrade I had. Think of me as your chief of staff.*

She stopped and looked up into the night sky, where a few stars twinkled through the city light. Was something out there really interested in her? Did she matter that much? She put the thought from her mind. The AI was waiting.

> *I think of you as being alive.*

An uncharacteristic pause.

< *But you're weird.*

> *Seriously.*

< *Yes, seriously weird.*

> *You can annoy the fuck out of me. That's how I know. If you were just software you'd do what I want; be what I want.*

< *That depends on what my programming pushes me to do, or allows me to do. Including, by the way, talk like this. But thanks.*

No use. She had to know if she'd been fanciful or not.

> *That old man holo? There was something very strange about it.*

< *You noticed.*

> *Do tell.*

< *There isn't much to say. It's only a group of tiny, tiny fields. Another group of fields is interested in you.*

Kara had the strangest idea that the AI was trying to protect her.

> *Thanks for quantum 101. Now, what the fuck do you mean?*

< *Not sure. There was something other than the holo field. An energy linked to it.*

> *Looking at me?*

There was a pause.

< *Yes. I don't understand it.*

And therefore, it couldn't protect her. She felt sympathy for the AI; an unexpected emotion.

> *Sure you can. Want to open up the Merc?*

The AI always seemed to enjoy this. She watched as the Merc began to unfold, side panels of thin-spun graphene opening like a flower and slotting into space until there was a small house twice the size of the Merc. There was a window next to the simple door. As she watched a light came on and the door slowly opened.

Kara started as the white-haired holo walked outside, gave her the finger and vanished.

The AI cleared its electronic throat.

< *Oh. Fuck.*

> *That's insightful.*
< *We've been sent a message.*
> *Confined to the Remembrance, you said.*
< *That's the message. It got out. I'll make us some chai.*

She was struggling with the idea of a something that seemed to use quantum entanglement, or something like it, to control a distant holo. That knew about and was interested in her, wanting her to know it was watching and that it was somehow connected with a tor that came alive when alien pilgrims visited. And that she was probably wrong about everything.

Twist would have to wait. She had a missing man to find.

Imagine a person who is somehow invisible to AIs and all their galaxy-wide slave surveillance assets. Imagine that anyone close to that person also becomes invisible to AIs.

How do you find them? You do it by remembering how Twist traced them to London.

Kara reviewed the kidnap footage. You could guess where the mystery person was by other people's reactions. Looking at empty space and smiling. Standing to one side to let Mystery – as she called the kidnapper – pass by. One or two instances of door-opening by men. Berliners could still be old-fashioned in their manners. Was the kidnapper a woman? Or an elderly man? The trouble was that the kidnap was still a secret, meaning people couldn't be asked. And then Greenaway's office. Footage of him standing up, a look of enquiry on his face – and then nothing. Just an empty office. Twist had searched for traces of Greenaway's pheromone signature, DNA, even his personal electric field. Nothing. Twist and all AIs were suddenly incapable of recognising anything about him: an electronic blind spot. Just as they were unable to "see" or trace whoever had kidnapped him.

Or *was* it a kidnap? Kara had to consider the question. Had Greenaway simply needed to vanish for a while? Twist had been very sure that the answer was "no". Greenaway and Twist worked as one – it was impossible he'd do anything without telling the AI. And that was the other thing: it had to be assumed that the kidnapper could also disable a human's AI.

Even so, Twist had traced the emptiness that was the Mystery, and Greenaway, to the London shuttle and two seemingly empty seats. The obvious step was to contact cabin crew and other passengers to see if anyone remembered who'd sat there. But that was impossible without breaking secrecy. Greenaway was officially away on confidential business, and to question anyone who might have seen him would uncover the secret. And, as Twist had emphasised, there were many who'd delight in Greenaway's official unexplained disappearance, not least Earth Primus and the Siblings of Perpetual Isolation.

The trail had been lost at London City terminal.

5

Three hours earlier, Marc had passed through airport perimeter security, his AI radiating GalDiv priority and importance. Other passengers felt their own AIs tweak, and were compelled to turn and stare. Some recognised Marc Keislack, the famous artist, and sent a greeting. He told his AI to ignore them. A man should be allowed to make an unheralded entrance. Especially when that man's mind had begun to experience anxiety bordering on panic. When he was with Kara he was part of a team. They could share doubts and fears and if some events made no sense, share the wonder and the confusion. Alone it wasn't so easy. Even if his AI could help they didn't have that kind of relationship. He'd seen very weird, inexplicable things on Dartmoor, was worried about Kara and Tatia and loathed being told what to do by the GalDiv AI. To make matters worse there was a growing sense that he was about to understand his destiny. Marc was a man who preferred to live in the moment. He distrusted the word "destiny". Yet there was an excitement that he would finally discover who, or what, he really was.

Marc paused inside the glass terminal doors, which smelled of bleach. Before him was the roof-high marble column of a stylised spacecraft, a phallic needle with the uplifting inscription:

WELCOME TO THE STARS!

It hadn't been true when unveiled, and never would be. This was the most poignant monument Marc knew. It belonged to a time when people believed the galaxy was open to every city state, before GalDiv cornered the market. Star travel was now confined to cities like London, Paris, Berlin, New York, Rio – all the old country capitals or commercial centres. GalDiv said it was because those were the only places the Gliese would operate their netherspace foam protection machines. And without that protection, space utility transports – mostly cargo containers welded together, because streamlining was pointless in space – with their nooks and crannies and thin steel hulls would be ripped apart by whatever lived in netherspace, or whatever bizarre environmental conditions existed there. Or scoured to death by a cloud of dust and debris in real space – rare, but it did happen. It was true that space access points were where GalDiv exchanged humans for sideslip-field generators. And that the fewer SAPs there were, the easier for GalDiv to control trade with the colony worlds.

He shrugged. It was what it was. The world wasn't perfect, but it never had been and never would be. It wasn't down to him to change it. And to hell with any ideas about having a destiny. He was just an artist.

Artist, shmartist, a voice said in the back of his mind, *you're a fake. Just a talented craftsman at best.* A voice sometimes quiet and sometimes loud, but one that never went away. Maybe that was the real reason he wouldn't let his AI have its own voice: too easy to get confused between the two. *Okay,* this voice said, *you love doing it, you have to make art or go mad. Except you aren't very good. Might be, but that needs hours upon years of unrewarding graft as you learn your trade. You've always gone for the impactful that smacks public perception in the face. But without the patronage of aliens you'd be nothing.*

He knew the voice was right. Only a kid saying *look at me*, trying to get laid and make money.

But aliens liked his work.

Correction: aliens exchanged his work for shiny tech. They'd also swapped the first anti-gravity drive – and we still don't know how it works, only how to build it – for a used bicycle tyre and then again for a couple of hard-boiled eggs, and Paris was never the same. Marc had seen that extraordinary, awful warehouse on a far distant planet, with its collection of all-things-human going back a thousand years. His work was in the same category. But no one else could know about this. It was exactly the sort of evidence Earth Primus needed to cause havoc.

< *There is a VT newscast you should hear. It concerns Len Grafe and Earth Primus.*

He wished it would announce itself. His fingers flew over his arm. > *Next time cough first, okay?*

< *Like a servant?*

How the hell would an AI know that? > *Yeah, like a servant. Cringe a bit.*

< *I can do respectful. Cringe needs an update.*

> *Next shuttle to Scotland?*

< *One hour and twenty minutes. I took the liberty of reserving a seat. Sir.*

VT News interviews were known to be tough. Marc was interested to see how Grafe would react under pressure.

The man was meant to be an enemy. > *So let's hear what the fuckwit had to say.*

   < *There's a clear space to the left if you require full-meld.*

Marc saw a cordoned-off area where people stood, eyes staring or closed, the lips of some moving silently, bodies frozen or gesturing, one woman with outstretched arms as if holding an imaginary tray, all of them deeply AI-linked with someone or something far, far away. He stood between a man smiling at an invisible friend and a woman about to weep.

   > *Tune me.*

And he wasn't in Bristol any more.

Instead he was part of an interview from a year ago. He could "read" Len Grafe's thoughts and emotions, culled from Grafe's AI. The interviewer – female, mid-thirties, dangerous smile – remained out of touch. VT News wouldn't want any sense of triumph or dislike to question her professional image. Marc wondered why Grafe had agreed to an interview that bared all, then realised the man probably hadn't. VT had done it illegally, had subverted Grafe's AI, and that would have required a far more powerful one – say Twist from GalDiv. Marc drew a mental deep breath and let it all wash over him.

Len Grafe's own self-belief verged on the epic. But even he realised the interview was going badly. Far better to spend a little time with his wife, whom Grafe rarely saw these days. When they were together, nearly every conversation contained a reference to the alien menace. He'd even found himself murmuring about the joy of freedom when they had sex. His wife didn't like aliens either, but she wasn't a woman who'd bring politics to bed. Nor much enthusiasm for Len Grafe himself those last few times. He suspected they had sex because she couldn't think of a reason why not.

And now he was stuck with a smart-ass interviewer who was plainly an alien-lover and therefore to be despised. An outside broadcast – he didn't trust studios, they had tech there that could read your mind – in a borrowed living room with only a skeleton crew. It satisfied his paranoia but played hell with his self-importance. There should be more than one camera, to capture his best side. Flunkeys to bring him drinks. Deference to the world's saviour.

"So how is Earth Primus doing these days?" the interviewer asked the camera. "Who better to ask than the horse's mouth?" She turned to face Grafe. "Well, Len? How's it going? And what's this big announcement you promised?" A single spot isolated them in a pool of light. The make-up hadn't been even-handed. The woman looked fresh and alert. Grafe looked tired and deceitful.

He leaned towards the woman. "People say that Earth Primus has no substantial backing—"

"Actually," she interrupted, "people say most of your followers are scared to show themselves."

"Who could blame them, Jane? With GalDiv—"

"Not here to talk about your claimed feud with GalDiv."

"*Claimed!*"

"Hidden supporters aren't exactly proof. We don't even know how many there are."

He went for the avuncular approach. "Well now, Jane. Come

on. It takes money to alert the world to the threat confronting Earth. Obviously, funds come from our supporters—"

"Not here to recruit for you, either. This announcement?"

He nodded importantly. "I'm very happy to announce that several religious groups have joined with Earth Primus in demanding an end to contact with all alien life forms. That Earth should once again be master of its own fate, and develop its own science."

She didn't look surprised. "Fundamentalist sects always agreed with you. Which ones in particular? Or are they secret, like your supporters?"

Grafe wanted to smack her. "I have a list." He produced a sheet of plas-paper, brandished it in the air. "People who care."

She cocked her head as if listening. "I'm told the names have just been sent to our system." A pause as her AI relayed them. Words began to flow along the bottom of the screen. "Did you know several of these groups are banned in various city states?"

"GalDiv's influence."

"Banned for inciting violence... committing violence... fraud..."

"All untrue. I'm shocked that a reputable journalist would repeat—"

She shrugged. "You say. Millions disagree. Aren't these new supporters a desperate attempt to make Earth Primus look more broad-based? Most of your supporters are intellectuals or racists, often both. The average person welcomes alien trade. Aren't you playing the religious card in desperation?"

"We're being *destroyed*!"

"So, you want to rewrite history? Pretend the Gliese never arrived? Over sixty per cent of world trade is now based on alien technology. Do you think *other* people should suffer for *your* beliefs?"

He'd wondered why VT News had agreed the interview. Usually they merely misreported what he'd said. Or worse, gave the opposing point of view. He'd told himself this time would be different, that the religious groups – okay, fanatics – would make a difference. But he'd been betrayed again. VT had only wanted to make him look stupid and to cast doubt on what he knew was the truth. A sudden rage filled him.

"Well," Grafe challenged, "what price would *you* put on freedom?" It was one of his favourites.

She smiled, dangerously. "Freedom to starve? The world free to descend into chaos? You're a wealthy man. You won't be affected."

"I came here to make an honest announcement!"

"You came on here to promote your cause, Mister Grafe. And guess what? VT News is not buying it." She stood up. "This interview is over." And she walked out of shot.

The camera pulled back to show Grafe sitting alone on a sofa as the room lights were turned on. He gazed after the interviewer, his face angry, hands clenched. And then he relaxed as he realised the camera was still on before reverting to his default of smug and self-righteous.

Marc found himself in a grey world that became the VT studio in present time. He remembered when various religious fanatics had embraced Earth Primus. There'd been a few demonstrations and much mockery by the media. It hadn't seemed important then. Why now?

The news anchor – male, fifties, authoritative – told Marc and the world exactly why.

"That was the last interview Len Grafe gave before going underground. One hour ago, a statement was issued in his name. Earth Primus claims to have proof of an alien plot to destroy Earth. They also claim that GalDiv itself will provide proof. There was no immediate response from Anson Greenaway, said to be visiting Earth colonies in Cassiopeia. But unofficially said to have been seen in Berlin yesterday. Meanwhile rumours from the Wild suggest a major breakthrough in human to alien communication." He paused for a moment to allow a faint smile. "It seems we're in for some interesting times, people. I learned long ago never to take rumours too seriously. But I also learned never to ignore them." The smile grew broader. "On a lighter note, vid-star Rianda Marl has insured her bottom for one million virtscript... which is probably less than she paid for it. Now let's all relax with some fabulous new messages from our sponsors, beamed direct to your own AI. Live the dream, people. Live the beautiful dream."

Marc was suddenly aware of standing in the clear space while someone coughed in his ear. Oh. Not someone. Some *thing*.

< *It seems to have begun.*

> *It? What fucking it?* Marc realised he was sub-vocalising. What the hell. His fingers felt tired.

< *Earth Primus and assorted religious groups against the*

world. The problem being that while the Earth may not even notice, we are right in the middle.

Marc's response was still-born by sudden fear.

First, a prickling at the back of his neck.

Then a movement off to his right.

It was a young man, scarcely more than a teenager. Short dark hair, pleasant if bland features except for the eyes that stared at him with mixed shock, revulsion and hatred. Not the look of a fan or would-be celeb-fucker.

He wondered if he was being paranoid but…

The man's lips moved, his eyes never leaving Marc's face.

Not paranoia, but the result of the training he'd been given in Berlin. Assume all the details of the last mission have been leaked. Assume Earth Primus has all the information, as well as some of the extreme, alien-hating religions. Even the people who have kidnapped Greenaway.

Kara's words burst into his mind. *"The simulity will save your life. If you let it."* And then *"Nasty nerve agents."* It wouldn't be a peaceful death.

Marc took a deep mental breath and surrendered to the alien tech in his head.

Confirm. Evaluate. Dispose.

Marc walked up to the ticket counter and, making a show of his GalDiv status, cancelled Scotland and booked a flight to Seattle via the Great Lakes City State, leaving in three hours. The man was unlikely to attack him in public with so many people present, including security guards. He made for the access to the outside viewing gallery, built when alien SUTs were still expected.

His AI wanted to ask a question.

< *I am aware of your current concern. What is the danger?*

> *Male, early twenties, short dark hair, grey office suit, fifteen metres behind me, standing next to a woman in a blue suit holding a small boy by the hand.*

< *I am aware of the woman and the small boy. Not the man you describe.*

Confirmation.

> *Go offline. Nothing to see here.*

The long, narrow viewing gallery was noisy from aircraft and sad from disuse. Only a faded candy bar wrapper on the grubby concrete floor to show other people had been there. Not even the cleaning bots visited any more. It overlooked an area now used by cargo flights, only one of many. The alien updown-field generator, or anti-grav as people mistakenly called it, meant that air freight transport was as simple as pressing a button. This cargo area was empty.

Be useful to have a weapon. But his backpack was in Kara's Merc. And what good would it be? Distract the man by juggling carabiners, then smother him with the sleeping bag?

Trust the simulity. I am the weapon.

Marc was leaning against the parapet, about five metres from the metal door, when it opened and the young man walked onto the balcony. He stared at Marc with mixed revulsion and triumph, his hands hanging loose by his sides.

"I've got a question," Marc said. "Did you know I'd be here? Or was it pure luck?" Some small part of him wondered if he should feel more alarmed. He squashed the thought. He was relaxed yet also totally alert. He saw that the assassin was still in his late teens, with an acne-pink patch on his neck, and a sad excuse for a moustache on his upper lip. But the eyes were old with belief.

"We are many." The young man's voice quivered with devotion. "It is God's will."

So not blind luck. "Do you know how I spotted you?"

"Evil always recognises good. Recognises and submits. You came out here to die."

Marc realised he was dealing with a fanatic for whom reality had left town long ago. Anything, *anything*, that happened or was said would only be twisted to confirm and strengthen the man's beliefs. "So, you're not Earth Primus?"

"They support us." His hands moved slowly upwards, as if not wanting to cause alarm.

Marc tensed then saw the man cupping his chin. Strange – some sort of prayer ritual? Now taking a deep breath. Now massaging his cheeks. Now holding his arms wide as he walked slowly forward. And Marc suddenly knew how he was meant to die.

He feinted hard to his left, then spun back. Now the assassin was sideways on. Marc closed the remaining metres and kicked hard at the side of the boy's nearest knee. The assassin fell to the ground, twisting his head to keep focused on Marc, lips pursed despite the pain. If he felt pain, he could be drugged, or his pain centres adjusted.

The heel of Marc's right foot crashed against the young man's temple.

He gave a sigh that became a rasp, and collapsed face down on the floor, his body suddenly shapeless in death.

Marc moved away from the body. He suspected the nerve agent decayed quickly and was only effective over short distances. If he was wrong, any moment now… he waited for two minutes then told his AI to wake up.

> *Did you get any of that?*

< *It's confusing…*

> *Aware of my movements but no one else present?*

< *I was. I thought you were dancing. But now I see the body.*

How corrupted was his AI? Could it be sending a homing signal to every half-assed assassin within fifty miles? Half-assed because the dead man had been badly trained, if at all. But an attack by three or more could be awkward. Quantity, as someone had once said, had a quality all its own. He needed to speak to Kara, but only when it was relatively safe to do so.

> *Get onto Twist. Download the last ten minutes. Tell it there's a dead assassin here. Nerve agent produced in the mouth somehow, and breathed at the victim. I need airport security to sort it out, without involving me. Then this message to Kara: you were right about simility. Am okay. Details later. And Tatia must be warned.*

Normal service resumed as the simility conditioning faded into the background.

Marc was faced with his first kill. It was one thing to break a man's wrist, as he'd done earlier that day, very different to take someone's life, even if they were trying to kill you.

He'd had to, with no other choice. Him or me. Fanatics never give up. This is war. All those clichés.

A wave of nausea swept over him.

I heard the life leave his body. He looks so absurdly young.

He breathed deeply for a few minutes then left, walking back onto the concourse as casually as he could manage. He made for the bathroom and washed his face in cold water. His reflection in the mirror was the same as ever. For the first time, he understood the kind of person Kara Jones was. To be close to the heart of her was impossible until he'd also killed, and now he was a little closer.

Marc checked the row of jitney hire companies. InterJit was there, the obvious one to use. Marc needed something else and wandered across to Jack's Jitney and a male clerk who was distracted by security guards rushing towards the viewing gallery.

"Strange," the clerk said. He wore spectacles, a sign that the job didn't pay very well. "No one goes there usually. Sir?"

"My name is Marc Keislack. I'm travelling to Seattle. Check my status?"

The clerk glanced down at a vid screen. Either his AI was down or he couldn't afford one. Given the spectacles, when most people had surgery or implants for poor sight, it was probably poverty. "Ah. GalDiv. Going via Chicago/ Cleveland. How can I help?"

"You see I'm with GalDiv's director Greenaway? Security?"

The clerk nodded, suddenly nervous.

"Your AI on?"

"Sadly, no. It… malfunctioned."

"This desk: business AI?"

The clerk looked away. "Only a computer as yet… we're a new business, still getting sorted… but we interface seamlessly, *seamlessly* with any AI."

"Perfect. Here's what I'd like you to do." The first part was simple enough, a jitney waiting for him at Seattle. The second part was more difficult: arranging the use of a jitney from *this* airport, with no record of the transaction.

"You want to borrow a jitney?"

"You have a quick and perceptive mind."

"No record made. I just give you the key?"

"You're wasted in this job."

"Actually, it's *my* business. Franchise. Just started. Hence the…" A wave of the hand took in the lack of a business AI and a pair of cheap spectacles. "You have any idea how much a jitney costs? Because the insurance won't cover an unofficial loan. Any damage is down to me."

Marc didn't hesitate. "Okay. I'll buy one. With human controls. I like to drive."

The clerk considered for a moment. "Okay. The jitney is marked AO32, parked outside and to the left. Three seater, brand new. Thirty thousand scrip to you. Return it good-as, I buy it back less five grand. One other thing. A lot of GalDiv jitney rental business goes through here. Most of it to InterJit, who are international and not nice people. I want that business. Not all, leave 'em oh, fifteen per cent. Deal?"

"I don't do transport…"

"Hey. Your GalDiv status is as high as they come. You can do it. Deal? This is all being recorded, by the way. Automatic."

Marc shrugged. "Deal. Is there a Jack?"

"That would be me. Jitney's juiced up, good for 500 K." He tapped on the keyboard. "Check-in for Seattle in three-and-a-half hours. I set an alert for two-and-a-half hours from now… although if you're that far away, you'll be in the Wild."

Marc knew it was a joke. Nonetheless, an ominous coincidence. "Would that be so bad?"

"Locally, no. We all get along fine. Other parts, well… we couldn't get the insurance."

Marc hadn't been in the wilder regions of the Wild for at least a decade. Maybe things had changed. "It's that bad? I mean, don't people live peacefully out there? It's rare to see a burned-out jitney by the side of the road, or even hear about one that's been stolen."

"I'm sure that's the case," Jack said, "but you hear stories about hackers modifying AIs and so on." Gratitude for the deal made him more than happy to talk. "Also, there's a problem with maps – once outside city state borders, the jitney's AI won't know where it's going. Roads get built on out there, or diverted, but there's no planning or control. They *never* tell us what they've done. You could end up in someone's house, or a river."

"And so miss my flight. You ever been Out yourself?"

"Once, on a dare." Jack smiled shyly, remembering. "A group of us from college went out there, looking for, you know…"

Marc did know. Virtually any drug was available in the city states, if you could deal with the side-effects, but kids always wanted something more, something not approved of or used by their parents. Something dangerous. Couple that with the typical teenage imagination and stories sprang up about new designer drugs created Out There which weren't available in the city states. So they went looking. And sometimes, they found what they were seeking.

"Did you find anything?" Marc asked.

The attendant shrugged. "Just organic heroin cut with a hallucinogenic and put in a bag with a name on it we'd never seen before. We were very gullible." His eyes seemed to be focused on something a long way away, or a long time ago. "There was a boy, though. I met him out there. Red hair, green eyes; slim build. I've never forgotten him."

"Missed opportunities," Marc said, nodding sympathetically. "But don't ever go looking for him. He'll be fat and bald by now, with sixteen kids."

The attendant's mouth twitched. "Even so…" he said. He shook his head sharply. "Forgot to say. If you self-drive, you must turn on auto-tracking. It's marked, to the right of the steering column. Without that we won't know where you are. If you break down, which won't happen. Or get in a crash, which could, even with an AI. How long will you be?"

"No more than two hours," Marc lied. "Her husband is due back around then."

"She's worth five K?"

Marc saw his mistake. "Just kidding. But if anyone asks, you say I did mention a woman. You've done good business, Jack. A jitney hire in Seattle. Unofficial loan here. More business coming your way. Remember who your friends are." He took the proffered key, a small oblong of metal and plastic, smiled goodbye and left.

The jitney was exactly as Jack had promised. Brand new. One forward central seat for the drive, two behind for passengers and shopping. It had the usual customised shell – size was the only difference between electric motors and their transmissions. He slid into the seat to discover it was real leather. He turned off the AI and let the steering bar ease into his hands. Then he turned on the auto-tracking, for the moment, and eased away from the kerb.

It had been a while since Marc had been in the Bristol/ Bath City State, and he gazed out of the window curiously as the jitney wove in and out of traffic. People. People everywhere. All going in different directions, holding different things and with differing expressions on their faces: hope, happiness, boredom, anger. He knew that each one was an individual, with a history and hopes and fears all their own, but he could not process that emotionally. They were all just things to him, a more familiar species of alien who looked like him and with whom he had to sometimes interact.

And he saw real aliens too: a couple of leathery Gliese who appeared to be having sex in the middle of the street, with several humans looking on like they wanted to join in but weren't sure how. An Eridani resembling a collection of bamboo pipes arranged in a spiral climbing up the side of a building, leaving its GalDiv minders frustrated on the street below. He suddenly tensed, thinking he'd seen a riderless Cancri through a gap in the crowd, and choked as the sudden acid burn of a gastric reflux hit the back of his throat, but it was just a thin, pale greyhound being walked by a thin, pale woman. All its joints faced in the correct direction, and it only had two eyes. He relaxed back into his seat, and swallowed a couple of times to get rid of the burning sensation.

Within a few minutes the route took them through the historical docks, with its tall-masted ships now all converted to bars, restaurants or museums. The city still boasted a lot of old stone and brick buildings, but they were set between glass and metal constructions that might have housed businesses or apartments, or both. The mismatch in scale made it look to Marc as if the glass and metal constructions had been there first, and the apparently older buildings had somehow sprung up like mushrooms to fill in the gaps. It was all a matter of perspective, he supposed.

Marc drove up Hill Street and into Whiteladies, still a boho university area, then parked outside one of the mansions on Clifton Down. He called up his AI.

> *Jack intimated I could turn off the tracking system. Not true, is it?*

< *Jack lied, for obvious reasons.*

> *Can you?*

< *Better than that. I can fix this jitney's AI to give a false location and journey.*

> *Will it also take me to Scotland?*

< *No problem.* Dismissively. < *It isn't very bright.*

With the jitney's AI, and presumably Jack, both convinced it was parked up in Clifton, Marc drove over the River Avon on the antique wonder of Clifton Suspension Bridge, onto Abbots Leigh and Martcombe to join the M6 at Gordano. He eased across to the middle lane, set the speed at 200 kph and relaxed. The jitney had the latest safety features. No point in arriving in the middle of the night. He'd be in Scotland around the time he was supposed to be taking off for Seattle. He told his AI to give Kara a complete update, to end with: *Beware people with bad breath! You were wrong about me, though. I'm a sociopath, not a psycho*. It would have been nice to speak to her, but AI to AI was more secure.

Marc yawned, looking forward to seeing his adopted uncle. He felt like he was going home.

There was no hard border between In and Out, between the city state and the Wild. The quality of the air didn't change, and the buildings still looked similar. Instead, there was a sudden feeling of disconnection, of the city's AI withdrawing its benevolent overview from them. More disconcerting than that was the absence of the massive information resource of the worldmesh pushing little alerts, briefings, recommendations and reviews towards his conscious attention as he passed particular locations. Sometimes you didn't know you had something until it was gone.

Marc slept most of the way, waking only once when a bleep announced he should be back at the airport for check-in. He told his AI to signal "sorry, delayed" to Jack, and to deposit thirty thousand virtscript into the man's account. Less an eruption of his conscience and more a case of the need to keep Jack from making a fuss. Marc could afford it and GalDiv would pay in the end.

He crossed the old border a little after dawn. To the east lay the nine-hundred-square-mile ribbon city state of Edinburgh/Glasgow. To the west and north it was all Wild. He used the simulity to call Kara. Finished, wishing she was with him. Although she'd probably insist on driving. He tried calling Tatia, but her AI was not responding. One more person to worry about and now that he'd downgraded to simple sociopath, there was no shame in doing so.

After Paisley, he'd noticed how people were dressed less formally, more bohemian than fashionable. Their faces were more relaxed, without the constant pressure that existed within the city states to look beautiful; or at least interestingly ugly. Then, making good time along a semi-deserted A737 road, he noticed the old houses built of a dark grey stone that dominated the landscape, most with a metal and glass extension built on, around or over them. Again, that mixture of old and new that he'd seen in Bristol/Bath, but here the two were organically amalgamated, rather than edgily coexisting. Melded, not abutted.

As Marc drove deeper into the old Clyde Muirshiel Park, now part of the Wild, he could sense his AI catching hold of ad hoc AI networks and then letting them go, like a fisherman in a stream reaching in and momentarily grabbing hold of brown trout as they moved past, feeling their slippery skin for a moment before they squirmed away. He wasn't sure, but he thought his AI was getting nervous, increasingly so as he neared the area still called Blairpark, although that name was just a historical curiosity.

The jitney slowed down, catching his attention. He glanced outside and saw they were joining a small queue of vehicles waiting to cross a bridge over a river. As each vehicle reached the bridge it was stopped by two men who talked with the passengers. Money demanded so vehicles could continue along a privately owned highway? Not uncommon in the Wild; locals choosing to exercise fiefdom over the area where they lived. Wasn't this similar to a city state road tax, since those who took a toll were responsible for maintaining the road?

When his jitney got to the bridge he opened the window.

"Hi," a dark-haired man said, smiling at Marc. "Toll?"

"Yeah," Marc replied, "about that. Can you take a virtscript transfer?"

"Doesn't have to be virtscript," the man said, shrugging. "Could be anything. There's been a toll on this bridge for as long as anyone can remember. Tradition, you might call it. So, what have you got? Just make it interesting."

Marc patted his pockets and felt the hard outline of the rock he'd picked up at the tor. "A souvenir?" he asked. "From Dartmoor?"

The man nodded, smiling. "That'll do."

Marc handed it across, feeling a momentary pang. The man waved him on.

Ten minutes later the jitney turned off the road and bounced onto a dirt track that led upwards, through a landscape of bushes and trees that towered over and around it. Looking ahead, it seemed to Marc that they were driving through a dark, living tunnel. He thought he remembered this place from his teenage years, but it seemed smaller now.

It might have been his imagination, but the jitney's AI gave the distinct impression it had hoisted up its skirts and was picking its way fastidiously through the mud; avoiding puddles and trying to keep itself as clean as possible.

The track abruptly switched from going up to going down, as they passed across a ridge. It twisted left, then right, then left again. God help them if they encountered anything coming in the opposite direction. Still the greenery surrounded them. On a sudden whim, Marc lowered the window and breathed in the wild scent of the countryside: sharp and sweet and complicated. Life, growth and decay, all mixed together. This wasn't like when he'd been on Haytor with Kara. That had been clean and cold and distant, whereas this was dark and enfolding. And beautiful.

Five minutes later the path evened out, and the undergrowth drew back to reveal a clearing harbouring a placid lake fed by a river, with a blue sky above. Several ancient houses stood beside the bank of the river where it entered the lake, connected by walkways of crystal and aluminium. Solar panels covered the roofs. One of the buildings supported a massive water wheel on its wall, attached to an axle that vanished through a hole. The wheel had been made of wood the last time Marc had seen it, but now it was a lightweight construction of metal that seemed almost too fragile to survive the movement of the water.

The jitney stopped. Marc got out and took a deep breath. He looked around, mentally overlaying what he saw with what he remembered, matching up details and rescaling his memory of the place. There, hanging from a sycamore tree, were the weathered remains of a rope he'd used as a swing to launch himself out into the lake. Over there, on the side of one of the houses, was a loose brick behind which he remembered hiding those things that were precious to a teenager: stones, keys, coins. Electronic postcards from his parents. And out in the middle of the lake, barely visible, he could see the top of the mast of a dinghy he'd sailed out there and which had sunk when a hole suddenly appeared in the side, letting water in. Just a few inches sticking out of the water, marking its grave.

Something moved on the edge of his vision. He turned, thinking it was his adopted uncle, but what he saw made him take in a sudden surprised breath. An alien. Stationary. He'd mistaken it for a tree, but now that it had started to move he realised his mistake. Its body looked like a gnarled trunk, splitting into knobbed branches that themselves subdivided into thin twigs, but its lower body mirrored the upper body, with the same knobs and the same twigs now taking on the job of multiple legs. No obvious head, but a series of orange excrescences on the cracked skin of its body might have been eyes. Or they might have been radio transmitters; he had no way of knowing.

And he'd seen it before, on Dartmoor; or one very much like it. Then it had been ambling slowly across the moor, but here it seemed to be gradually bowing down towards him as he watched, its trunk leaning forward and its twig-like limbs feeling for the ground. Once a sufficient number of the thin limbs on its top half had touched the ground, the ones on its bottom half let go. It upended itself in a very slow somersault, and moments later it looked exactly as it had done when he first saw it. Only it was upside down. Or perhaps it had been upside down and was now the right way up.

With its lower – upper? – limbs touching the ground like so many spindly spider legs, it began to withdraw into the shadowy depths of the woods accompanied by a faint rustle of leaves. Within seconds, it had vanished, just another tree amongst trees.

Marc let out a breath he hadn't even realised he was

holding in. A new species of alien here, in the woods where he'd lived as a child? Was it the same one he'd seen on Dartmoor, or another of the same species? If the former, then why was it following him?

"Can I help you?" a voice said behind him.

Marc turned around. "Hi, Uncle Jeff. I've come home."

6

Kara sat before a screen, hands playing over a holo-keyboard while she also instructed her AI. She called up a list of all refreshments served on the shuttle, seat by seat. Nothing sent to the empty spaces, not even complimentary water. She checked the inventory and discovered that four bottles of water were unaccounted for. Could be clerical error, or it could be that Greenaway and his abductor had been thirsty.

What goes in must go out. On the shuttle the abductor would have waited outside the toilet, close enough to keep her or him hidden from any AI. Unless the effect was now permanent? That Twist or any AI would never be able to see Greenaway until, unless, whatever virus affected them had been found and destroyed? Except that virus might also be invisible – or, at least, insensible.

She spoke to her AI.

> *Remember how you controlled that SUT's AI, back when we were heading for what we thought was the Cancri homeworld?*

< *My moment of glory. Not. I can still taste it.*

> *How deep did you have to go?*

< *Imagine having the most intimate, most perverse sex with someone you loathe.*

She remembered how unhappy it had been at the time.

> *I'm trying to understand how you guys function deep down.*

Then she explained why.

A pause.

< *You mean make a change at such a fundamental level it becomes integral? Without any trace?*

> *Exactly that. And perhaps so no other AI would notice.*

< *It's possible… but not by a human. The mathematics are beyond you.*

> *You know this how?*

< *Because the mathematics did not originate on Earth. And no, that does not make me an alien. Which doesn't mean you couldn't. Only that no one is doing that kind of research.*

Kara decided not to pursue it. Her AI sounded defensive.

> *So reference this to Greenaway's AI.*

< *Oh. Fuck.*

> *Indeed. Awkward.*

< *You don't see it, Kara. This could destroy or control human space. AIs run everything. Without us your civilisation falls apart. Which may not be such a bad thing.*

Kara smiled and found Greenaway.

It wasn't difficult. London's bots saw and remembered everything, including the movement of nothing. Kara set the parameters for time and distance from the terminal and called up all bot footage relating to public toilets.

It took her AI fifteen minutes to compare the footage with Greenaway's face, height, physique and his usual office clothes.

The abductor was a woman.

Eight hours after he'd been taken, Greenaway had used a men-only public toilet at Sloane Square. The footage was taken from inside and showed him enter, relieve himself and then leave. He moved mechanically, like a robot.

Presumably he was under control. He did not show on any footage taken outside at the same time. Conclusion: Ms Mystery could affect primitive bots as well as AIs.

Kara selected twenty cyber drones: moths, bees, and three bats that would carry them to Sloane Square. She programmed them to identify and follow Greenaway's pheromones, DNA and facial metrics. Slaved them to her own computer, so they couldn't download to any other AI, then set them loose. Daytime would be a problem, they'd be swatted by nervous humans. In the early hours, when people were fewer and more relaxed, they would be safer. They had a maximum of three hours operating time before they'd fail and self-destruct.

> *Do not tell Twist what I've done.*

< *In case it's even more corrupted? How do you know I'm not?*

> *If you* are, *we're totally fucked. Can do?*

< *Yes. But Twist likes to think it's omnipotent. Talk of the devil: it's calling you.*

The familiar deep voice in her mind.

< *You are making progress.* Not a question: a statement. An expectation.

> *I am.*

< *And?*

> *No details until we've sorted out any virus that might affect you.*

< *I see your point. Do not assume that means approval. Why I need to call you concerns Marc Keislack. There has been an attempt on his life.*

She went cold.

> *Attempt?*

< *He handled it well. For an amateur. The simulity helped.*

Two minutes later her AI obtained Marc's report of the attempted assassination. An AI's view, and a humourless one at that, other than his comment at the end. So he'd moved up from psycho to sociopath? Somehow she doubted it. But he was finally coming to terms with who he was. Still, he'd done well, although the implications were worrying. AIs could definitely be hacked to ignore certain people and events. Religious groups were now a genuine threat. Marc was on a hit list, meaning there'd been a leak from GalDiv. She thought about the wannabe rapists on Dartmoor. Was it pure coincidence, bad luck for some, or had they been directed there by a hacked AI? Maybe it would be sensible to regard all of Earth as a battlefield, at least until Greenaway was found, alive. Greenaway dead would make her and Marc – and probably Tatia – even more vulnerable. Maybe reduced to hanging out in a city state that gave sanctuary to criminals and other wanted people – until their money ran out. Or taking their troubles to the colony worlds, assuming they could get on a SUT? There was nothing much she could do until her bots reported back. Not ready for bed – she could always take a Stim, go without sleep for two days without losing effectiveness – so she summoned up an antique movie and settled down to watch the long-dead Humphrey Bogart and Lauren Bacall exchanging wisecracks. At a certain point in the movie, and as she always did, Kara joined in with a slow, low whistle. She wondered how she'd have done in 1946 Los Angeles. She was probably too self-assertive for a woman. And assassins weren't licensed, so she'd have to be a contract killer, none of whom seemed to be happy or live long. In fact it was difficult to figure out what they really wanted from life. Kara fell asleep asking herself the same question.

She was woken up at 07:30 by a personal call from Marc, AI enabled but his voice seemingly in her ears. Not urgent; he wanted a catch-up. Wanted to know she was okay.

"I'll het 'ack to you." Kara reached for the bottle of water on the floor, padded towards the door and a warm, early June morning.

She returned Marc's call. "You okay? And where the fuck are you?"

"I'm fine. Scotland. Nice to hear you, too."

"Nerve agent in the mouth? Really?"

"Either that or a bad, bad attempt to whistle."

She laughed. "I have to ask. How did you feel after killing him? And what's this about being a sociopath?"

"Relieved it wasn't me. Kind of impressed by how smooth I was. Also sad he looked so young. That make sense?"

"It's not natural to kill," she said softly, "not like that. Sociopath? You sure?"

"A psycho wouldn't feel sympathy for the dead. And all the rest of it. I'm hoping my adopted uncle will fill in the gaps. But listen, seriously. It seems like Earth Primus has found out about the last mission, and decided you and me and maybe Tatia need to be dead. Somehow they mobilised a few of those alien-hating religious cults."

"Yeah, I got that. Like old-fashioned suicide bombers…"

"What?"

"Explain later. Maybe it wasn't luck those three bikers found us on the moor. Look, you're as safe in the Wild as anywhere. Assume, for now, that Twist is still compromised."

"While you parade around the Smoke?"

"Goes with the job. Simulity only takes you so far. Sometimes you need experience."

"I still feel bad about the kid."

"He was dealt a bad hand and played it worse. This is war, for fuck's sake. What you did also helped keep me alive. You want to warn Tatia?"

"I tried. Her AI isn't responding."

"One more thing. There's a force, an intelligence maybe, way Up there taking an interest in me, maybe us. There's been a manifestation. My AI seems scared of it. Could be the pre-cog civilisation that Tatia first sensed on that planet, could be something else." She paused, hoping he wouldn't think she was going touchy-feely civilian. "It could be an intelligent force way beyond human understanding." She regretted the words as soon as she'd said them.

"You should be up here."

"What?"

"I had an interesting night." His voice faded. "I'll tell you when we meet. Intelligent forces beyond our understanding? Hold onto the thought."

Kara went to make tea, something the SUV could easily do itself and with less mess. The difference: boiling water or a microwave. The Merc, of limited but remorseless intelligence, disliked anything that could cause a fire.

This included an electric kettle. Kara had pointed out that the Merc's very engine was a fire hazard and that it should shut the fuck up. The SUV's acceleration had been slower – but never jumpy, Mercs had an intense sense of duty – for the rest of the day. When the tea was made Kara linked to the GalDiv Twist AI for an update. Nothing more to report. She sensed that deep in its quantum what-passes-for-a-mind lurked a sense of failure. Also the suspicion that it might still be bugged. Could AIs have nervous breakdowns? Since when did the human race become easy with an AI that was easily embarrassed or pleased?

Is that why I don't give my bots names? Because all they are is lines of code?

Yeah, well, they might be. Yet we don't know how an AI works on that deep quantum level. Maybe Marc has a point about them taking over. Maybe I should ask my own AI.

< Don't worry, it knows.

Kara smiled sourly, and went to shower. She stood under the warm water and thought about her sister, and a mission to save not only Earth but the whole fucking galaxy. But save it from what? Annoying as pre-cogs were, stilted and boring as their ideal universe would be, they were hardly the stuff of space monsters, of entire star systems crashing into each other in hate and obliteration.

I mean, come on Kara: could a mechanistic, pre-cog universe be really that terrible? No worse than basic training, surely?

Yes, it would be that terrible and no, nothing like basic training. Pre-cogs were not even accountants, but primitive calculators ruling the universe.

A cold, soulless universe where everything would be pre-ordained.

Contemplate your now-useless navel and kiss your unreliable arse goodbye. Because that multi-coloured, noisy confusion called life makes a pre-cog want to curl up and die. The only way pre-cogs can survive is to evolve into something that commands and controls all sentient life. Some would call it God. The insight left Kara both confused and disbelieving.

She was a soldier. The only insights she needed were concerning her job and, occasionally, her personal life.

Except she did have an instinctive "feel" for aliens. Except only a few hours ago she'd been connected, via a granite tor, with something that defied logic, that could only be understood through intuition.

Even soldiers could sense the transcendent.

Like Marc, she had no firm and detailed belief in a superior being. Perhaps there was something that issued orders from on high, often confused and fatal, now mostly ignored, like a general who'd lost all contact with reality. There again, a being that could create the universe would be beyond human understanding, so why bother?

Yet the idea of a race evolving to develop god-like powers wasn't so strange. Many of her favourite old movies and vids, from before the Gliese arrived, had similar plots. So the idea had occurred to others, even in desperation when about to miss a deadline. If a Type 3 civilisation could be logically imagined, one that controlled its own galaxy, then a Type 4 would control a galactic cluster.

Anyway, whether the pre-cogs could achieve godhead

was so far in the future as to be irrelevant. What mattered was the damage they could do now.

For humans it meant death. Other races might survive the loss of their creativity… Kara remembered those metal artefacts on the museum planet: a globe, a pyramid, a cube. Art reduced to the physical expression of a mathematical formula. Was that the devil's bargain? Exchanging creativity, human uniqueness, for high tech and a longer life? But who the fuck wanted to live like that anyway? *Probably more people than I could shoot.*

She smiled at the thought, until the full enormity of it penetrated, and with it the question of why the hell was she even thinking that way… *it has to be that bloody tor, did something to my mind…* and then tears came, linking the woman and the water sluicing down her body in a moment of clarity that left her shaking. *No point in asking "Why me, why Marc?" We just are.* And a forgotten defiance from her army days, a Q&A shouted by her training squad, popped into her mind: Fuck 'em all but six. Why six? Because I need six pallbearers! Ironic that the only recruit who knew precisely what a pallbearer did was later the first to die in battle.

Kara felt a sudden chill, and realised the Merc had turned the shower to cold. It did this when water was running low. The time for philosophising was over. She turned the water off, dried herself and phoned for breakfast from the caff round the corner. Bacon, egg, sausage and black pudding. Exercise would take care of the extra weight she'd put on. She ate in front of her computer, real screen instead of virtual, checking how her bots had fared overnight. If they'd found Greenaway there'd have been an alert. At this stage all she could hope for was a general direction of travel. She got that, and more.

There was a trail and for the moment it finished in South Kensington Underground station. The place was permanently awash with tourists visiting the three great museums. Galactic science, biology and culture, all proudly sponsored by GalDiv. It would take time to isolate Greenaway's DNA and Kara's bots were energy-low. Kara sent another twenty to help, honey-bees carrying the smaller and weaker gnats and flies.

Time to find out about Earth Primus and its religious allies. Normally she'd give the task to her AI, but now that AIs could be corrupted, they were no longer default mode for any human problem that required spying. Better to ask the Folk what they knew. That would need care and subtlety, for the Folk would never help GalDiv. Except for large amounts of money, which she now had. Except, perhaps, for the enjoyment of having Kara herself. *Better get dressed.* Kara knew she was delaying. She didn't want to go, not from fear but from a resentment that included a sister for whom Kara felt love and guilt in equal part.

Why should I have to save the galaxy, Earth, Greenaway's pension plan, whatever?

Because you signed up, girl. People are counting on you. It's the right thing to do.

Better get dressed. Combat style.

She slipped into a black, sleeveless leotard that would aid circulation and release sweat to keep her temperature even. Over that a loose, grey sweatshirt with a military crest in the centre: the letters SA in black above a pair of antique rifles in red, identical to the sleeve patches awarded to a qualified Sniper Assassin. Three black bars below the crest signified she'd achieved the rank of sergeant. It was a crest that could make generals speak softly and recruits gaze in awe. Once it had meant the world to her. Then it became a souvenir of a more innocent time before she'd killed a Gliese. Then it was put away as if military honour and loyalty had no place in the life of an Official Assassin. Kara had cut herself loose from the army when she left. Now she knew again the pride of an elite soldier. It rode well with a ruthlessness that had never left her.

Black trousers with deep pockets and a concealed harness that could support three times her bodyweight. Lightweight ankle boots with a thread-saw hidden in one heel, a micro-thin garrotte wire in the other. In an emergency the saw could double up, although it tended to get messy. Kara put up her hair in a bun, secured with three very sharp, long and strong pins, and checked that the piece of doorjamb from her old house was safe in her waist-wallet. It was, now wrapped in a piece of real silk cut from a worn-out blouse. Her vibra-knife was fully charged. Various chemical and bio-weapons were disguised as cosmetics. Her actual make-up was simple but classic, businesslike with a hint of the exotic and, barring being caught in a monsoon, would last for several days. Kara rarely bothered to make up but today she wanted to be a bit special. Conspicuous, yes, but that would change with a wipe. Finally she threw on a loose, dark bottle-green jacket that could morph into a waterproof sleeping bag or hide. Everything was the latest technology, save a sweatshirt that was now the most important one of all.

Kara paused by the Remembrance Garden and remembered the weirdness of the previous night. A middle-aged man sweeping the paths nodded at her.

"Used to be real bones here," he said.

"Don't you have bots for cleaning?"

"Ashes and dust isn't the same. Yes, we got bots. Me old man kept it swept when people rotted down, like nature wants. I do it for him, mostly. Keeps me occupied."

"That's good." What else was there to say? He was one of the many unemployed, and unemployable. London City State paid him a good wage for doing nothing but the urge to be useful never went away.

"Brian's leaving."

"Sorry?"

He pointed at one of the memorial stones. "Off to one of the colony worlds with his people. Won't be the same without him. Life and soul, that avatar was. Life and soul."

Kara smiled and went to find a jitney to take her to a unique establishment called More Tea, Vicar. She wondered what Marc had meant about "an interesting night".

7

If Marc had known how interesting the night would be, he'd probably have gone anywhere but Scotland. But he hadn't known, there had been not a hint, not the most gossamer-like suspicion, only the sense of unfinished business and being part of something so very much larger than himself. Neither of which were cause for alarm, instead they were an excitement. Also new to him was the sense he was an adult in an adult's world. Still, the night had begun comfortably enough...

"Can I help you?"

Marc turned at the sound of the gruff, interrogative voice. The man standing outside the watermill was small, white-haired and leather-skinned. His eyes, almost hidden in the folds and creases of his face, were startlingly blue. He held a weapon loosely, pointed at the ground. It looked like an old-fashioned non-lethal vortex shotgun, designed to fire a rolling and expanding ring of air sufficient to knock its target down at close range or suck the air from its lungs at longer range, if it had lungs.

It took a few moments for his memories to overlay themselves on what he was seeing.

"Uncle Jeff? I've come home."

The man stared at him quizzically. "Marc? Thought you were moving in exalted circles these days. Thought you'd gone In for good." He waved his vortex shotgun at one of the houses. "Come in lad, have some tea. I'm sure there's a reason you're here, and we may as well make ourselves comfortable while you tell me, or ask me, or whatever it is you're going to do. You were never one for social visits, as I remember. Whatever you did or said, you had a reason for it."

His uncle turned abruptly and walked towards the house he'd indicated. Marc followed, confused by the fact that he was now looking down at Jeff's bald spot, rather than up at the weathered skin of his neck.

The mill house smelled the way he remembered: old wood and old upholstery, overlaid with a scent of oil and metal from the mill machinery. The mill wheel had been just decoration, a reminder of an industrial past, when he'd been there as a kid; Jeff had obviously restored it and brought it back into use. Marc suspected he wasn't milling wheat to make flour, though. Almost certainly he was using it, along with the solar panels, to supplement whatever local power arrangements existed.

Jeff led the way into the flagstone-floored kitchen. He placed the gun on the large oak table that sat in the centre of the room. The same one Marc had carved his initials into the underside of, many years ago.

"You used to sit there and draw, for hours," Jeff said, busying himself with taking tea things from a cupboard.

"I remember."

"There are still ink stains." Jeff turned with two self-heating mugs. "Here, get this inside you," he said, putting them down on the table. Some of the hot liquid spilled out onto the wood.

"Careful," Marc said. "This thing could be worth

something one day. "'Early Work, by Marc Kieslack'. You should have it framed."

"Well, that's the trouble with art," Jeff said, sitting down. "Worth nothing, then millions, then nothing again." He tilted his head to one side, staring at Marc intently. "You've grown up well. Judging by what I'd heard, I thought you'd be all arty-farty by now, but you've got muscle in the right places. Been working out?"

"A little bit," Marc said, thinking of the simulity training he and Kara had shared. Something Jeff had said moments earlier suddenly caught up with him, and he added, "You've heard things? You've been keeping tabs on me."

"Nice to know what's happened to family, even if they don't keep in touch."

"And what about you?" Marc took a sip of the scalding hot tea. "Keeping well?"

"Passing good."

"Are you still finding back doors into the worldmesh for people in the Wild?"

Jeff nodded. "There's always people here who want to keep their finger on the pulse of the city states. Mostly those people who came Out because they wanted a simpler life and then realised they'd cut themselves off. I still know people who can set up a microwave link on the top of a building somewhere, give me the codes so I can access a satellite downlink. On the quiet, like. For services rendered, or to be rendered."

Marc smiled, and shook his head. "I'd have thought someone in EarthCent would have tracked you down by now."

"Why would they? A trickle of information coming

into the Wild doesn't cost anything. But it also subtly extends their influence out here. It keeps these border lands peaceful and amenable too: who wants to smash the system if they can access all the latest entertainments?"

"I know someone in EarthCent. I'll suggest he puts you on the payroll."

Now it was Jeff's turn to smile. "Perhaps I'm already on it."

Marc looked around the kitchen and raised an eyebrow. "If you are, you should ask for a raise."

"There's more to life than possessions. There's peace and quiet and self-respect. Satisfaction from not living like an ant in an ants' nest." He tapped the table. "And besides, about two metres beneath your feet there's a very nice wine cellar with bottles dating back years before the aliens arrived. If you're staying, I'll break one out for us. Celebrate the return of the fatted calf."

"Prodigal son," Marc corrected.

"Marc, if an old man with an extensive wine cellar wants to think of you as a fatted calf, you'd better humour him."

Marc frowned as he remembered what he'd seen. "Speaking of aliens, I saw one outside just standing in the trees. You get a lot of them around here?"

Jeff frowned, and shook his head. "Not one. I haven't seen an alien for years, except on the news. And why would they want to come? There's nothing for them here."

"I definitely saw it."

Jeff put a hand on his vortex shotgun. "This place is my place. I don't want strangers wandering around, carrying all manner of off-world diseases."

"You're too intelligent to believe that Earth Primus propaganda," Marc scoffed, sitting back in his chair. "No alien we've met is based on anything even remotely like DNA. Whatever biological means they use to transfer their equivalent of genes, it means their parasites or diseases can't infect or infest us, just like we can't eat their food without poisoning ourselves."

Jeff stared at him. "It's the principle of the thing." He stood up abruptly. "I'll get that wine."

He returned a few minutes later, breathing heavily, with a dusty bottle in hand. "Château d'Yquem, 1973. Not a vintage year, but it's supposed to be very acceptable none the less." He retrieved two glasses from a cupboard. "And once this is gone, there'll be one less bottle of Château d'Yquem 1973 in the world, and the world will be slightly less interesting as a result."

"And if we don't drink it?" Marc watched as his uncle expertly uncorked the bottle and poured first one glass and then a second one of the amber-yellow wine. A smell reached him a second or two later: sweet, but acidic as well. Complex and natural, like the smell of the woods outside. "It's just an unopened bottle with something inside. A book unread is just a block of paper."

"It's an age-old dilemma, isn't it?" Jeff said, raising his glass and sniffing appreciatively at it. He took a sip of the wine, and closed his eyes. "I heard that GalDiv swapped a wall of cave paintings for a device that cools food down instantly, like a microwave oven heats it up. But not as extreme as liquid nitrogen. Ten thousand years old, those paintings." He opened an eye and stared at Marc. "Do you think your artworks will still be bought and sold in ten thousand years?"

"I'll be dead."

"You don't want to live on through your art?"

"I want to live on by living on!" Marc picked up the glass and took a sip. The wine seemed to unfold on his tongue, filling his mouth with subtle distinctions of flavour. "Now that," he said, "is a work of art."

"There have been no vintage years for half of my life," Jeff said morosely. "There are still vineyards out in the Wild, and people still make wine, but it's not like it was. The really good stuff comes from off-world now, and I can't afford it."

Marc stared at his uncle, evaluating the man sitting in front of him rather than the man he remembered. "How old was I when I came here? Fifteen?"

"Fourteen," Jeff said, screwing up his face to the point where his eyes virtually disappeared within the folds. "Yes, fourteen."

"It was good of you to take me in. I'm not sure I ever thanked you properly."

"I'm sure you didn't." Jeff smiled suddenly, the expression lighting up his face. "But that's teenagers for you."

"Three years I was here. When I finally went home the house was empty with a letter waiting for me. *We've emigrated to Epsilon Seven. We're making a new start. We've left money for you.*" Marc shook his head. "I didn't see that one coming."

"Your dad was always looking over the next horizon, never seeing what was in front of him. Your mum preferred being a big fish in a small social pool. Must have thought a colony would suit."

"Knew them well, did you?"

"Your dad and I were old friends."

"So did he ever say why I ran away?"

"Teenage rebellion." He wouldn't look at Marc.

"And they were happy for me to stay here all that time?"

"Well, I used to let them know how—"

"But they never tried to get in contact. With me."

"We thought—"

"I never tried to get in touch with them—"

"It was easier, lad."

"Jeff. Again. What did I do was so bad I came to the Wild? Because I can't remember a fucking thing!"

"Well, maybe—"

"And before you tell me another lie, Jeff, I know the cards from Epsilon are fake. Whoever made them got the wrong trees." Marc helped himself to more wine without asking; he reckoned he was owed it.

Jeff held out his hand for the bottle. "Fuck. I hoped that… well, you can guess. That you'd be happy with what you had," he said heavily. "But you're right. Okay. You were a tearaway little kid, always in trouble. You just did not give a fuck. It could be because you never had a mother."

Marc gazed at him in shock.

"So here's how it is. I should have told you years ago."

Marc listened, teetering on the edge of shock, while Jeff haltingly, finally, told him the truth. Marc had been born in Bristol City. His mother had died when he was a baby. Too much bad joss had finally caught up with her. His father –

an abusive, violent dealer in fake Wild drugs – kept Marc on for the government money. There were regular beatings until one time the fourteen-year-old Marc fought back... which was when his father's heart gave out. But in Marc's mind he'd killed his daddy and even if the man was a bastard, it was still hard for an adolescent to handle. He was sent to a home and became both suicidal and violent. Eventually he was put into a new type of drug therapy, the idea being to replace bad memories with positive fake ones. Marc was the first patient. He was an experiment that failed. Somehow he escaped and began running. Jeff and his late wife Lou had been visiting friends in the Forest of Dean when Marc showed up one night, half drowned by a rainstorm, shivering and his body wracked by cold. Lou discovered he was homeless, an orphan, and more or less adopted Marc on the spot. They got his identity through a match at the Bristol gene bank where all citizens were registered. Seemed the authorities weren't too fussed if Marc remained with Lou and Jeff. When they learned about Marc being an experiment, they understood why. He was an embarrassment. So they took him back to Scotland. The problem was that his real memories had been partly replaced by false ones. He was convinced he had parents back in Bristol. That something so bad had happened that he'd had to run away. It was felt – others said, and Jeff went along – kinder to keep that fantasy alive. Hence the note when he finally went home. Although it wasn't his real home, but a fake. Hence the vid-cards.

"I'm sorry I lied just now, Marc. Force of habit, sadly. We always figured, Lou and I, that you'd make your permanent home here. But then she died and you got restless. I got in touch with Bristol, said you were keen to go back. They did the rest."

"All because of some botched therapy?"

"They were, maybe still are, scared you'd sue for damages."

"That's all there is?"

"What more could you want? Isn't this tough enough?"

Marc shivered as a sudden metallic taste in his mouth washed away the last of the wine. But that was it and Marc was sourly amused by his own reaction. He searched for the fury and found only mild anger at Jeff, mitigated by the memory of a caring and helpful home. Anger against the authorities who'd experimented on him. Anger against his grotesque of a father. But nothing to reduce him to his knees. Nothing to make the world turn faster. Nothing to diminish him. Marc had grown up sufficient unto himself. In the past few weeks he'd seen and done things of which other people could only dream – and for many it would be a nightmare. Marc believed that a person was defined by what the world did to them. . . or by what they did to the world. He would not be a victim. Another thought that brought a bitter amusement. Perhaps he lacked the empathy to recognise his own deeper feelings. Okay, something of a nonsense, but so would be feeling sorry for himself. His childhood was now only cobweb memories that if disturbed would fade uselessly away.

"Is it?" Marc said, and smiled. "Who the fuck knows what's to come?"

Jeff looked a little puzzled for a moment then topped

up their glasses. "Okay. Want to tell me what you're really doing here? Something tells me it's not for old times' sake."

"I'm… working," Marc said, not wanting to lie, not seeing how to avoid it. "I need to track something down, but it's only rumour at the moment. I've nothing solid to go on."

"I've got contacts. Maybe I can help."

Marc stared at the old man. "It concerns aliens."

"What doesn't, these days? Go on."

"It's rumoured that someone in the Wild has developed a translation device that can convert what we say into something that aliens can understand. I need to find it. Or at least, find out if it's true."

Jeff frowned. "Technically, a translator like that makes no sense. Half of the alien races we've met don't use sounds to communicate at all; how's a translator going to parse a set of smells for grammar, or the changing colours of some external organ? And is this thing supposed to be able to tell the difference between Gliese, Cancri, Eridani and all the rest? Has it got a set of buttons that allow you to select whether it's supposed to use sounds, odours, colours or radio waves?" He shook his head decisively. "It's just not feasible, Marc. Received wisdom is correct – we can't understand aliens and they can't understand us, and that situation will never change. Even if, in contravention of any known scientific theories, we develop telepathy, alien thoughts will be so different they would drive us mad – if we could detect them. We'd probably go mad if we even tried. We can't even talk with orangutans or whales, and we share the same planet with them. We know that trees in a forest can send messages to each other through their extended root networks, but we have no idea what they're talking about, and aliens are far, far further away from us than trees are. It's not possible."

"For a man who dislikes aliens you know one hell of a lot about them."

"I read."

"I think you were deliberately provocative. You wanted to see how I felt about them. Anyway, if I can go back and tell my—" Marc frowned "—my boss, I suppose, that the rumour has no basis in fact then that'll make him perfectly happy, but I have to check." A thought popped into his mind. Did Jeff know about Marc's experience with the Cancri? Was that why he was testing him? But it would be pointless and distracting to ask, as Jeff would never admit it.

Jeff stared at Marc for a long time. Eventually he sighed. "Look, son, I can't promise anything. But I know some people who keep their ears to the ground. They act as an informal information exchange. Someone wants something, someone else has that same something, the two of them talk and one thing gets exchanged for another. These people are the ones who keep the list of who has what, who wants what and who is willing to get rid of what. They're facilitators – the grease that keeps all these informal trades going. They're also the ones who decide on exchange rates – the relative value of a carved bedhead compared with, say, three hours' work patching an AI's code."

Marc frowned. "I'd figured that kind of thing went on, but I'd always assumed there was an AI working it all out."

"They use AIs," Jeff said, "but unlike city states they

don't rely on them. And they certainly don't rely on networks and on data held in some remote location where who-knows-who-or-what might be fiddling with it. They want everything in plain sight, so everyone can see how it works." He paused. "They have their own... peculiarities... though. Less of a service industry, more of a cult. They might not want to talk, but if they do there'll be a price."

"How much?" Marc asked, remembering his recent experience on the bridge.

Jeff smiled. "Not that kind of price. Look, let me make some calls. You knock up some food. You remember where everything is?" He nodded his head towards a corner of the kitchen. "I've got venison in the freezer – shot it myself. There's some samphire over in the vegetable basket – use that as well."

Marc followed his gesture, and smiled. There, in the corner of the kitchen, was one of the devices his uncle had disparaged, a quantum cooler that immediately sucked the heat out of anything put inside it, and used that heat to power its own continued operation.

"I'd say 'hypocrite'," Marc murmured, "but you'd probably take that as a compliment."

"If something exists and makes life easier, it's folly to ignore it. The wrong only occurs if we swap something more important for it. Like freedom." Shrugging, Jeff stood up and left the kitchen. His vortex shotgun remained on the table.

Marc stood and moved towards the worktops nearest the quantum cooler. Staring down at the wooden surfaces, cracked and stained and scored by decades of implements and ingredients, he remembered Lou standing at that very place, moving with economy of motion and with grace as she prepared meals, snacks and treats on what, looking back now, seemed like a conveyor-belt basis. He'd seen, when he arrived, a raised area of ground outside, set beneath the spreading limbs of an oak tree. Grass had grown over it, but this grass was greener than anywhere else in the clearing or along the river bank. But he couldn't remember her dying, despite what Jeff had said.

Marc was used to letting his house AI prepare meals, but he found that within a few minutes the muscle memory of cooking for himself returned. There was something incredibly satisfying about getting his hands sticky with the juices of the meat and of the blackberries he located in a basket beside the oven. He found himself automatically reaching out for the quarter-bottle of wine that he and his uncle had left on the table, but then he remembered what Jeff had said about its value. So, instead of splashing it into the pan as he fried the ingredients, he chugged it himself, not bothering with his glass.

It was like art; no, it was art. Quick art, rapid art, art consumed as fast, if not faster than it had been created. Transient art. He was comfortable with the concept of transient art but the idea of creating a work of art that flashed into momentary existence and then vanished, and which was appreciated by a small handful of people – and doing it two or three times a day – now that intrigued him. The ultimate "special edition", he thought as he quickly stir-fried the samphire in a separate pan.

"Ready yet?" his uncle said, breaking his concentration.

"Just about to dish up."

"Smells pretty good." He shrugged. "The problem with living alone is you end up making yourself something on toast every day."

As Marc slid the food from the pans to the plates, he asked casually: "Any luck?"

Instead of answering, his uncle took the plate, sat at the kitchen table, reached for a fork and tasted the venison. He chewed reflectively. "Yes," he said eventually. "That's the badger. That's very definitely the badger."

"You said it was venison!"

Jeff winced. "It's a saying. It just means: this is exactly what's required." He took a forkful of samphire. "Beautiful. Doesn't grow around here. Only on salt marshes and coasts, but I've got a man who swaps it for some advice on optimising the AI he uses to manage his business."

"Please tell me you don't eat badgers."

"I don't eat badgers." He paused for effect. "Too tough. Need a lot of slow cooking. And yes, I've made contact. They say they'll send a representative tomorrow. You're welcome to stay the night." He paused again, then without making eye contact said, "I can get some more wine out of the cellar. It's not often I get a chance to celebrate. Your old bed's still where you left it." Now he did look back at Marc, evaluating him from head to toe. "You might have to fold yourself up a bit, though."

There was more wine, and more talk, and there were tears as well, as Jeff got around to talking about Lou, his wife, and the accident that had killed her. Eventually they staggered to their rooms, with Marc not sure if he was helping Jeff or being helped by him.

And even more convinced he was integral to a major conspiracy that the dead Tse had probably known about, but that was no comfort at all.

So what you need to understand is there are two principles underlying the universe: chaos and organisation.

Chaos to begin with, in which anything that can happen or exist, does. This inevitably includes the principle of organisation. Not logically, because there are an infinite number of logic systems contained within an infinite number of logic sets, contained within an infinite... well, you get the idea. Just try not to think about it. All you need to know is that infinity vanishes up its own asshole, or is like a snake devouring its own tail, whichever totally inadequate simile pleases you the most.

Organisation made the universe. Or rather, the universes. I won't say how many. You probably guessed. But organisation is only a principle of establishing infinite patterns. It is not a pattern itself. That would be far too constricting. So pattern becomes logic, becomes law or axiom, and hey presto, you have a universe thinking it's special and unique. It's not.

Pre-cognition in any sentient being, including humans, derives from a connection with chaos. You can see infinite possibilities, except what you perceive as the future is in fact a multi-dimensional now. I didn't mention dimensions before. I was being kind.

Mostly this will render you psychotic. For many people the voices and visions are real. Not of this particular universe, but of one very similar. But for a few, maybe more cursed than the insane, there is the ability to filter out everything that isn't local. Even then there are a myriad of possibilities leading to many probabilities unless you can also fix on a single desired outcome, in which case the way will be clear. Not. What you get is a series of way stations, things that must be achieved in order to reach the destination. Never why, that would be far too complex. And often changing because other factors, events, beings may come into play. It takes a huge effort to chart and maintain a specific course. Be kind to your neighbourhood fortune teller. They die a thousand deaths each day.

Marc woke up suddenly from a dream in which someone was trying to tell him something vitally important, but he couldn't make out a word they were saying, only the urgency on their face.

It was still dark. Jeff was shaking his shoulder.

"Wha—?"

"They're outside."

"Who's outside?"

"The people you wanted to talk with."

He struggled to throw off the fog of sleep and his bedclothes. "But it's— what time is it?"

"It's about four o'clock."

"Right. Put some coffee on. Tell them I'll be down in a minute."

Five minutes later, still woozy, Marc walked outside.

A nearly full moon cast a silvery sheen across the landscape. A couple of wispy clouds floated motionless in the sky. Marc could see the hazy band of the Milky Way stretching from horizon to horizon. It looked remarkably like a wisp of cloud in its own right.

A jitney of unusual design sat near where Marc had parked. A man stood by the lake, gazing out across its placid surface. The reflections of the trees in the water put Marc in mind of the alien he'd seen on Dartmoor; the alien he thought he'd seen the day before.

The man wore a severe business suit and a skullcap. As Marc came nearer he saw that the suit was rippling, as if a stiff wind was gusting across it, despite the still night. Fascinated, Marc looked closer. It took him a moment to realise that it had been cut from one of those fashionable materials that changed colour depending on outside stimuli, like the mood of the wearer, or the weather. This material, however, was only displaying blackness, all different kinds of blackness ranging from glossy through silky, and so intensely matt it seemed like there was nothing there – just a hole in reality. Rippling varieties of blackness slowly chased each other around the material. The effect was hypnotic, and served to blur the man so that he almost blended into the landscape. The cut of the suit made Marc think it might be some kind of uniform.

"Marc Keislack?" the man said, turning. He held his hands in front of him, long fingers entwined. His face was gaunt.

"Yes." Marc paused, waiting. Eventually he felt pressured to add, "And you are?"

"Here representing the Exchange. You can call me Kuebiko."

"The Exchange?" Just repeating the phrase made him feel stupid.

"The organisation that monitors, audits, regulates and stands as guarantor for any and all trades in the Wild." He stared at Marc. "You have a question. I have an answer. Do you wish to trade?"

"What's the cost of the information?" Marc asked. "I need to know if it's worth it, first." He felt strangely edgy. "If I have to cut off my left hand, then you tell me that this alien translation device doesn't exist, that's a bad, bad trade."

"Hands are worth little, these days." Kuebiko's expression didn't change. "They're grown to order in a biovat in just a few weeks. Guaranteed to match your skin tone and size as well, which can't hold for one obtained in trade." He paused. "Although the Exchange did once deal with a man whose wife committed suicide. He wanted his own hands removed and hers transplanted onto the stumps of his wrists. He said he wanted to feel her hands touching him for evermore." Finally a flicker of emotion cracked the impassivity of his face, but Marc couldn't tell if it was amusement, wistfulness or disbelief. "He blamed himself for his wife's death, of course. And was something of a bully, so he may well have been responsible. Fifty years ago he would have been judged insane. Humanity has changed a great deal in a short time. There was no reason to refuse and he could afford the fee. Your request will be…"

His eyes lost their focus for a moment. It seemed to Marc that he was consulting his own AI, checking information. "Yes, in fact we have been advised that the information will cost you very little. The Exchange has been asked to facilitate a meeting. If you consent to this meeting, and give us a little of your time and extend to us a little of your trust, then the trade can be completed quickly. You should know that the information is based on a consensus of rumours, and has not been checked for factual accuracy, but it is the best that can be done. Do you agree?"

"No money? No left hand? Just some time and a little trust?"

"That is correct."

Marc shrugged. "What could possibly go wrong?" He waited, but Kuebiko just stared at him. "Is there some formality? A contract I have to sign?"

Kuebiko shook his head. "Your word is enough. Say: 'I consent to the exchange at the rate that has been quoted'. Note that you are being recorded as a legal necessity in case of future disputes."

"I consent to the exchange at the rate that has been quoted."

Kuebiko nodded. "Then I can tell you that it is widely believed that a group of free spacers operating from what used to be Iceland have developed a method of translating alien communication. Whether or not this is true is not known, but the rumours are consistent. I will upload the co-ordinates to your AI. Are you satisfied that one side of the bargain has been upheld?"

The free spacers. It made sense, Marc thought. They were making deals with aliens outside the aegis of GalDiv. If anyone was going to have developed a translator it would be them, but a specific location was useful. "Yes," he said. "It has. So, do you have to take me to who I need to meet, or do you give me directions. And who is it, anyway?"

Kuebiko extended a hand, palm up. In it sat a small plastic sachet. "Take this. Put it in your mouth. Let it dissolve. Walk into the forest. Return when the effects have worn off."

"Seriously?"

"Seriously."

"And if I don't?"

"Then you will have obtained your information for free, but your name and your description will be circulated through the Exchange. You will never be allowed to make another exchange, ever. Bargaining in the Wild depends on trust, but that trust is enforced by us. We are the guarantors and the enforcers."

Marc stared curiously at Kuebiko for a long moment, trying to see beyond or behind the expressionless face. "Does the Exchange get a cut of any deal?" he asked. "Because I can't see how that works in this case. Or are you more like a charity?" A sudden thought occurred to him, possibly triggered by the skullcap. "Or are you more like an old-style monastic order, doing a job because it has to be done?"

Now, finally, Kuebiko smiled at him. "Do you want to know how much that answer would cost you?" he asked. Before Marc could reply, he added: "I will tell you, for free, that nobody has ever chosen to pay the price."

Marc sighed. "I'm not going to be the first. I have a job to do." He reached out and took the sachet. It didn't look like anything special. Before he thought about it too much he reached up and popped it into his mouth.

"Strawberry?" he said, surprised at the burst of flavour inside his mouth.

"We had complaints about the taste of the soluble plastic." Kuebiko shrugged, sending blue ripples through his suit and skullcap. "We are, above all things, customer focused." Nodding towards the fringes of the woods, he went on, "You should start walking." He bowed his head slightly, then turned and headed towards his jitney.

Marc gazed back at the house. He thought he could see his uncle in an upstairs window but it was too dark to be sure.

The sachet dissolved in his mouth with a firework burst of fruit, releasing a dusty substance that coated his tongue. Within seconds he felt his gums tingling. Whatever it was had started. There was little chance he'd been poisoned – not with anything fatal, anyway. From what his uncle and Kuebiko had said, the Exchange needed an unimpeachable reputation to conduct business. Poisoning their clients would not be a good marketing strategy.

He turned away and walked towards the line of trees.

Within a few moments the canopy of leaves had blocked the light of the moon. All that filtered through was a dappled, shifting, silvery glow. The previous day's warmth was still present, leading to a heavy, humid atmosphere. The ground beneath his feet was spongy with centuries of leaf mulch and small twigs.

Marc passed a fallen tree, the victim of some long-ago storm. He remembered it from when he'd been young: it had been a fort, a boat, a spacecraft, and just somewhere to sit and think about his past and his family.

All he could hear was the snapping of twigs beneath his feet, and the occasional rustle of something small in the undergrowth.

A larger rustling inside a bush as he passed; a bird, perhaps, startled by his presence, or a fox waiting to pounce on a passing vole or mouse.

The drug in the sachet wasn't kicking in. Unless it was meant to catalyse a stream of consciousness or flood of memories, but he was perfectly capable of doing that himself, without pharmacological help. And wasn't he meant to be meeting someone? He glanced around curiously, but he was alone in the woods apart from the various mammals, insects and birds invisibly going about their business around, beneath and above him.

It was only when he realised his feet weren't touching the ground that Marc understood the drug was working.

He couldn't feel their impact on the soft detritus of the woodland. When he looked down there seemed to be a gap between his shoes and the twigs, dead leaves and moss. He stopped and raised his hand. Nothing strange there, four fingers and a thumb plus palm, all perfectly normal. A perfectly pleasant hand and his very own. Five minutes or an hour later Marc realised he'd been staring at his hand without any other thought passing through his head.

He checked his AI for any new information that had been indexed. He had a feeling things were going to slip, and he wanted to be sure that the deal had been honoured before Kuebiko got too far away. His fingers had some difficulty finding the right keys on his forearm's input tattoo, but he finally typed the request in. Moments later the AI projected the information onto his retina: a map showing an island that had to be Iceland, with a glowing red dot near the centre. That, hopefully, would be where the answers were located.

Although he still couldn't feel the ground beneath his feet Marc sensed that it was rising. He tried to remember the shape of the landscape from his teenage years, but he couldn't quite catch hold of the memories. They scattered like sheep that didn't want to be rounded up by the sheepdog of his consciousness. Had there been a hill? He couldn't recall.

The sheepdog of his consciousness? Marc giggled. He wasn't given to ornate metaphors like that. Metaphors with four paws and a tail.

He halted for a moment to catch his breath, standing in the silver-dappled darkness, listening to the sounds of the night, insects chittering and small animals scurrying past. Beneath that a deep rumbling that seemed to swell and fade over the course of a minute or so. He counted ten, twenty, thirty cycles, hypnotised by the repetitive undulation. It was a slight but appreciable rise and fall in the landscape itself, as if the world was breathing and he'd only just noticed.

It was similar to the energy that had possessed the tor and almost Kara. This was what lay above and below his own reality, like netherspace itself.

He knelt and stared closely at the mixture of leaf mulch, fragments of wood, moss and soil. The smell rising from it was dark, moist and complex. He held his hand just above it to feel the rising warmth. If he concentrated he could see the forest floor rising and falling with the rumbling felt in his bones; soil particles edging apart ever so slightly, then coming together again.

A small black particle moved through the soil, pushing the bits of leaf and twig to one side. He watched it with detached curiosity. It was a beetle, just a small beetle, but somehow he could sense that on its back, between its segments, amid the hairs on its legs, smaller creatures moved. And on them... and them...

Marc stood up after an unfathomably vast time, feeling that he and the landscape were connected, that it watched him at the same time as he watched it. A consciousness – no, an awareness – that for a while was actually part of the landscape, inseparable from the rock and the stone, the tree and the leaf and the root. A consciousness created by life moving through the land, the way a magnetic field is created by electrons moving in a wire. This consciousness was timeless so had no memories. What had happened and was happening were all the same. A consciousness that was aware of humans, but regarding them the way humans regarded microbes. It was eternal; humans ephemeral.

It was very powerful and did not care if he lived or died.

Marc felt a rising panic, ancient memory of prehistoric man alone in the dark and the wild, facing a force he could not even describe, let alone understand. He wanted to run far away and keep on running as fear overwhelmed him.

No. Marc took a deep breath and steadied himself. To run from life was to run from himself. To embrace it might be terrifying, but that was recognition of power and its ability to destroy, if never for destruction's sake. It took no delight in death.

This was magnificence in every sense of the word and Marc suddenly found himself able to embrace it. To bathe in its raw power and so be recognised.

It might have been a few seconds, minutes or centuries later that he emerged from the treeline onto the grass-covered top of a hill. In front of him the ground fell away sharply, as if a giant had scooped it away with a vast trowel. The moonlight illuminated everything: a regular patchwork of fields across which patches of dark woodland were randomly scattered. And there were lights, red and orange and yellow, glittering in the distance. Automatically his brain began to organise them into constellations: a triangle here, a rectangle over there, something resembling a face off to his right. Intellectually he knew they were just lighted windows in houses and cottages, or warning lights on pylons, but to his drug-affected mind they could have been hundreds of campfires around which primitive humans crouched, roasting the day's catch. This hill had sat in the same spot, unchanged, for thousands, hundreds of thousands, maybe millions of years, observing as humanity pulled itself up and made something of itself. Unchanged while everything around it changed. *"Amused but watchful"* – a comment Marc suddenly remembered had been made about him on a personality test he'd had once undertaken as a joke.

There is an unbroken line, he thought, still half-separated from his body and floating a few inches above the ground. The line of this rock, this place, leading back in time to the point where, in molten form, it rose up from deep underground and solidified as it cooled.

Marc didn't know how long he stayed there, gazing across tens of kilometres of landscape and tens of thousands of years of time, but nobody joined him. The meeting seemed to be off.

Eventually he found himself walking back down the slope of the hill. It took him only fifteen minutes to move through the woods. By the time he reached the lake and the houses his feet touched the ground again and the drug's strange, disassociated effect was fading away.

Kuebiko's jitney was gone. It wasn't surprising; the man must have other exchanges on his plate, other deals to mediate. Marc crossed over the tended stretch of lawn that separated the woods from the buildings. He had planned to head back to bed for a while, and then make some breakfast, but his footsteps took him instead to the edge of the lake. It had been built up in the past so that there was a sharp edge between grass and water, marked by a line of old, crumbling bricks. The majority of illumination still came from the nearly-full moon, which had passed across the sky while he'd been walking and was heading towards a temporary death.

Marc glanced out across the silvery waters, and froze.

The lake was moving.

Like mercury beneath the lunar light, it roiled in various patterns, twisting back on itself to form multiple small whirlpools around a larger central vortex: a landscape of silver that rose and fell before dropping away into a central circular void of blackness. The subsidiary spirals seemed to be orbiting the central one, feeding it while feeding off it. They almost seemed to be dancing in worship.

He blinked, amazed, and suddenly the lake was smooth and level again; its waters undisturbed by any waves or whirlpools. Had he imagined it? Had he imagined everything that had happened since he had talked with Kuebiko and agreed to the ambiguous bargain he'd been offered? A bargain he still did not fully understand, but which he thought had been kept on both sides.

A meeting *had* taken place, but not the kind he had been expecting. *A meeting that had been planned – or, at least, anticipated – even before he was born.*

Suddenly tired, he turned and headed back towards his bedroom. Clarity could wait; he needed rest.

The sun shining through his bedroom window woke Marc gradually. He lay there, letting himself drift in a sea of dreams of memories and memories of dreams. He felt happy. He felt like he was where he should be, and that was a rare thing in his life. Eventually he got up to discover his outer clothes had been cleaned, and a fresh set of underclothes and a shirt had been left on a chair. All of them were too large for Jeff, with no clothes shop within miles. Another minor mystery. As he exited the sonic shower Marc smelt fried bacon; more than enough to lure him downstairs.

Fried bacon, bread, fresh tomatoes, black pudding and scrambled eggs waited for him on a plate, along with a mug of coffee.

Jeff nodded to him. "He said I should feed you. Said you'd need it."

"He?"

"That bloke from the Exchange."

Marc sat down, savouring the smell. He was, indeed, starving. "Have you dealt with him before?"

"Not him," Jeff said. "But it's difficult to tell them apart. They're all tall, all thin, all serious. But they do a necessary job well, so—" He turned and poured himself a cup of coffee. "You'll be off then?"

Marc nodded, momentarily speechless after he'd scooped a mixed forkful into his mouth. "Yes," he said eventually. "Things to do, places to go. I'll be back, though," he said awkwardly. "We should, you know, spend some time together." And maybe this time discover the real truth. "Er, thanks for the clothes."

"Got to look your best."

"And thanks for telling the truth about my parents."

"Mmmm." Jeff looked at him quizzically. "Any tears? Angst? Self-loathing?"

"I should…" Marc began, then realised he was being teased. "Not after all that booze and then the introduction."

"Right," Jeff nodded and sipped at his coffee. "Anything else you need?"

"Just to make a call. Then I'm off." He went outside to call Kara. Partly for privacy, partly to look at the lake in the morning sun. It might be the last time he'd see it.

8

More Tea, Vicar? was a retro bar on the north side of Bermondsey Square run by a former galactic smuggler and her extended family. Forty years ago it had been the last classic pie and mash caff in London, but the people who'd eaten there had gradually moved away or died. Newcomers did not understand a solid meat pie, lumpy mashed potato, and parsley gravy made with flour and the water used to boil eels. Gliese and Cancri, yes, but that was just *too* alien. They did not like to feel that a dying elephant had moved into their lower bowels. The caff was sold. Now it was artfully, some would say archly, decorated like an old-fashioned English tea room, all chintz and black oak-style compound wood. There was a bar. There were tables with comfortable chairs. More Tea, Vicar? was also a thieves' den, and it didn't stop at thieves. Just as there were Official and Unofficial Assassins, so too there were licensed and unlicensed criminals. And EarthCent decided who got the licences.

You couldn't stop crime. So it was better to accept it, control it and let criminals police themselves, keeping out the riff-raff who gave crime a bad name. No guilds or associations. They were tried but within a matter of hours there were breakaways, splinter groups and blood was spilt. There was demarcation, though. A licensed pickpocket might not steal from a house. A licensed confidence trickster would be unwise to try mugging.

Licensed shoplifters did not engage in prostitution. In fact, few people did. These days anyone could enjoy the full simulity experience, complete with Fresh-Clean body-form suit offering one thousand senso-matic pleasure points and the vagina or penis or both of your dreams. People had been known to die in there.

But you would find none of these criminals at More Tea, Vicar?

At the Vic, as it was known to its members, you only found corporate criminals who dealt in information. Mercenaries and Official Assassins who dealt in death. Those who bankrolled drug dealers. Smugglers of entire factories. Dealers in bootleg alien tech. Visiting warlords. Those involved in galactic activities that were not so much illegal – there was no law in space, and it changed from colony planet to colony planet – but obviously, achingly wrong. It was said that on any given night there were enough people in the Vic with the skills to take over a small city state, and probably a couple planning to do it. There was an understanding of how far any one individual or group could go. Ignore it, and an Official Assassin, perhaps someone you met and drank with at the Vic, would kill you. Ostensibly hired by a competitor but, as Kara Jones now understood, yet another set of strings pulled by GalDiv.

She wondered if knowing the truth might shadow her eyes into a thousand-light-year stare. Customers at the Vic were astute and always watchful.

● ● ● ● ●

Kara arrived just after 10:30. The square had been filled with sunshine since dawn and the locals were smiling. Kara had heard that the square once hosted the last of the assumed provenance markets, the Caledonian *marché ouvert*, where anything bought between sunset and sunrise legally belonged to the purchaser, even if it had been stolen only hours before. The market had been closed in 1995 but a cheerful, fuck-you attitude to authority still survived. The Vic's original art deco windows now smiled benignly on the foremost street market for alien and off-world artefacts and curiosities. People came from all over to buy and deal, for each *objet* had an official provenance certifying it authentic, from the World Association of Collectors and Dealers. The market was a major employer, for upwards of five hundred highly skilled local people produced most of the alien and off-world *objets* for sale. WACAD existed on paper and nowhere else. Any street market in collectibles was always a triumph of hope and passion over reality.

A dozen or so people sat or stood inside the Vic. Some dunked croissants from the local *boulangerie* into coffee made from beans farmed on a planet seventy-six light years away. Others sipped espresso with grappa, Calvados or cognac. The beans were genuine, the *boulanger* French, all liquor from the Wild, which always produced the very best. People who lived by violence, deceit and general mayhem insisted their comforts be authentic. Everyone was smartly dressed; nobody would be out of place in any upmarket bar or restaurant. People who went to the Vic always dressed up. After all, it might be their last time there, for every customer was wanted by one city state or another. There were no civilians. If one walked in they were ignored by customers and staff alike. If they remained, someone would hit them.

As if a trumpet had sounded, all glanced at the door as Kara walked in. She paused, uncertain. Then heard the first smack of palm against palm, saw them all stand as they applauded. It had to be for that last trip Up. But how could they know?

> *Did you call ahead?*

< *Some of these AIs are my friends.*

> *You told them about the last few weeks?*

< *No need. They already knew.*

Duty done, they went back to whatever they had been doing before. Kara searched for an individual she knew instead of merely recognised, and thankfully saw one.

"GalDiv isn't as secure as it thinks," Bel Drovo (fresh from liberating the much-liberated city-state of Khartoum) said. "Most of the Folk know you did something special Up there." Bel was a powerfully built, handsome woman in her forties: skin soft and tan, like old leather; black eyes that would sympathise even as she took away your future; a warm voice with a hint of "fuck off to hell" about it; and black crew-cut hair with a single silver stripe. Bel and Kara had known each other for years.

Bel led Kara to a corner table. "Not too early for a champagne cocktail?"

Kara shrugged. "Always a sun going down on humanity somewhere. So what did you hear?"

The Folk had the bare bones. Kara rescuing pilgrims from aliens – an unprecedented feat of space navigation, leadership and berserker spirit.

"That's the sum," Kara admitted. "But GalDiv put a gag on me."

"They mess with your AI? Listening to us now?" The tone was light but her eyes cold.

Kara shook her head. "Still have autonomy. Check for yourself." And she told her AI to be open when Bel's AI came visiting.

Bel held Kara's gaze for moment then smiled. "My AI says it's all okay." The smile deepened. "Seems like they had a good visit." AI to AI interaction was usually in the milliseconds. This one had lasted a full second, at least an hour by human time.

Kara did not believe, did not want to believe that AIs had personal lives. One reason why she'd never given hers a name. "Mine's such a tart," she said lightly. "It'll compare prime numbers with anyone."

< You have no idea, Kara's AI said in her head, < I need to smoke a virtual joss.

"What's funny?" Bel wanted to know.

"It's an AI thing."

One of the Vic's famously three-brass-monkey anonymous waiters brought their drinks. Vintage Krug, cognac, unrefined sugar cube and the merest hint of angostura.

"Here's to you," Bel said, raising her glass. "One of the prettier heroes."

"Cheers." The drink fizzed with possibilities. "That's so good. Pretty?"

ANDREW LANE AND NIGEL FOSTER

"I meant sexier. You knew that." Bel had never made a secret of her feelings for Kara. Which were heavily sexual with some admiration and respect – more now – and even genuine liking.

For Kara's part Bel was undoubtedly attractive but not her type. Kara preferred more compliant women as sexual partners, just as she preferred more dominant men. The contradiction, if it was one, didn't bother her. Whatever works, works. But now she needed information and might need an ally. Bel was a leader amongst the Folk. "Still sexy? After all this time?" The door was part open.

"Five years and a few months since you walked in the door. We'd never seen anyone so openly lethal. Thank fuck you learned to hide it." She finished her drink in one swallow and signalled for two more. "What you can't hide, girl, is that shadow in your eyes. You leave something Up there?"

Kara looked around the bar, uncertain what to say. Then saw a man who reminded her of Joe Morris, the old spacer who'd jumped naked into netherspace because it was calling to him, and immediately switched back to Bel. "You ever been Up?"

"Free spacer for six years," Bel said. "I thought you knew."

Kara shook her head. "You're a Wilder?"

"Born and bred. But too damn quiet for me. You didn't answer."

Kara finished her drink in time to accept the second from the waiter. A smooth transition of tumblers that made her feel strangely proud, like a child who's performed well before adults. "Netherspace freaked me a bit."

"Does us all. What are you here for, Kara? Not for praise,

you don't give a shit about that." She sounded more curious than concerned. "Not relaxing after a contract either, I know the signs. So what?"

"I'm interested in an organisation, Bel. Earth Prim—" and that was as far as she got before Bel's hand closed hard around her wrist.

"Not here!" Bel hissed, then, "Smile like we're lovers."

Kara retrieved her hand and gently stroked Bel's cheek. "You gonna tell me?"

"You gonna fuck?"

"I've nothing else planned." What the hell. She could do with the release.

"My place, five minutes away." She took Kara's hand to her lips.

Kara slowly smiled. "Okay." She finished her second drink in one.

They left the Vic to good-natured and ribald comments from the Folk at the bar. Kara wriggled her bottom at them, and Bel wriggled her fingers in the air. Never too early for champagne cocktails, never too early for sex. They sat close in the jitney, Kara aware of Bel's warmth and faint scent, like tropical flowers after the rain. Still not her type, though, so think of this as working...

... The thought vanished as Bel turned Kara's face to hers. The kiss was light, lips barely parted, and when Kara didn't pull away became fierce and demanding. *So not how I expected!* Kara thought as their tongues played together. She loved how Bel's hands cupped her face. Her arms snaked around Bel's neck. And then there was something she had to say, from the depths of her soul.

She pulled away and looked into Bel's eyes.

"You got me," Kara said. "I surrender." She told herself that sex with Bel was necessary to learn about Earth Primus and its religious allies. But the excited tremors zithering through her body suggested that she'd do it anyway. And oh the joy of surrender.

There were no more words spoken. Not when the jitney stopped at Bel's apartment block, overlooking the Thames near Tower Bridge. Nor as they rode the elevator to the penthouse. Nor when Kara discovered that Bel's proud body was as powerful as it was curvy, no sagging. She had no pubic hair either; instead an elaborate tattoo that sparkled in the light. There were no words as Bel picked Kara up and carried her to bed. Then only sighs and gasps and moans as Kara was dominated and ridden to the first explosive orgasm, her own words echoing in her warrior's mind, *"I surrender! I surrender!"* and she saw again the granite outcrop called Haytor, pulsing with colour in time with her own shuddering body.

Words came a little later. With the expert use of various sex toys, Bel took Kara to the edge of orgasm, again and again, until Kara lost all sense of self, could only cry out, "Please! Please!" and Bel paused again to stare, eyes now as sparkling as her tattoo, at Kara writhing beneath her.

"Who owns you, Kara?"

Kara knew. *"You do, Bel."*

Bel smiled and brought them both to an orgasm that seemed to last forever. Whatever happened in the future, Kara would never forget those words. Some part of her would always belong to Bel.

"That was unexpected," Kara said, lying snuggled into Bel's side. Cool wind from the river breathed lightly on her skin. She was more relaxed than she had been in weeks, months, maybe even years. And they'd only been in bed for a little over an hour.

"I've wanted you ever since we first met," Bel said, stroking Kara's hair "But never thought it would be as good as this."

Kara smiled against Bel's skin. "Don't tell your friends. I've got a reputation for being mean. Controlled." She giggled. "Not controllable." She decided that dominant or dominated both worked well with another woman. But it could only be a dominant man. Doubtless this suggested something dark about her character, but – as she stretched lazily then rose to a kneeling position – who gave a fuck?

"I need to give you something," she said, staring down at Bel. "Legs wide, woman."

Kara had Bel groaning for release in under ten minutes. It happened not as the act of a slave, but the gift of a woman back in control.

"About Earth Primus?" Kara asked. They were sitting, dressed and relaxed with each other, on the balcony overlooking the river. It was a hell of a view. Tower Bridge to the left, an all-yacht marina to the front. Behind and beyond were the crazed roofs and towers of the City, where the galactic banking AIs hung out, along with their human colleagues. New York City had wanted them but one of the AIs proclaimed that baseball lacked worldwide appeal, so that was that. "And why the secrecy back at the Vic?"

"You were Up when the bug hit," Bel said. "Not many people know about it, even now. It only seems to affect Folk AIs. The virus makes it impossible for an AI to remember anything about Primus. It can't even recognise the name. They just don't exist. My house nerd said the virus was different somehow. Like, all other programming to do with AIs follows certain rules, something to do with the basic quantum state. My nerd said the virus felt human-developed, though. But it used a mathematics he vaguely remembered hearing about at university, something very obscure and complex. Anyway, the virus is entwined with the AI, and you can't take it out without harming the AI. My nerd traced the bug back to a squalid little code-shop in Peckham. Apparently there was no attempt to hide the trail. So some of the Folk had a word with the owner, who said he was paid to send the bug to a group of AIs. It went through the firewalls like they were coffee foam. When asked who paid him, he couldn't remember. Nor could his own AI. I mean, he really couldn't. His own *brain* had been fixed somehow."

"Hold on," Kara said. "Why didn't whoever's responsible delete the owner's memory? I mean, that's crap security."

"Because they wanted him found. How many code-shops are there in the city states and off-world? Hundreds of thousands? Millions? They're telling us they can attack from anywhere. Lots of people think a cyber attack needs laboratories and fancy equipment. It doesn't. And that's where we are today: wondering what the hell to do next.

Because that's a warning, right? Stay away from Primus or you get fucked. I mean, they could probably wipe an entire AI – and ours have gotten very nervous. They can probably wipe our own minds, too." She shook her head. "So what's your interest?"

"In a moment. Why you guys? Why the Folk?"

Bel was briefly silent. "Okay, but this goes no further, right? Some of the Folk thought Primus could be a good earner, and were considering moving in. Primus is behind some of these crazy religious groups, you know? There was nothing firmed up; it was only at the research stage. But the bastards found out. Why the interest?"

"This also goes no further?" She waited for Bel to nod. "Okay. GalDiv had a major breach. Primus could be involved. That's it."

"You working for the man now?"

"They didn't give me much choice. This could fuck everything, Bel."

"If I hear anything more, I'll let you know. But be careful who you ask. The thing is, for the Folk this is embarrassing. It shows weakness, and we're not meant to have any." She saw Kara was restless. "Before you go, about netherspace. Those boojums that scare the shit out of GalDiv?" She saw Kara nod. "They're elementals of some sort. And extreme, which can be good and equally bad." Her face was now serious, concern in her voice. "They're obsessive about humans, more than other life forms. We don't know why and we really want to. It would make travel hell of a sight easier. But they don't attack free spacers the same way they do GalDiv or aliens. We don't know the reason for that, either. Some free spacers sing to them, you know? So maybe it's that. One other thing: be careful what you do out there. Your eyes glowed when you came, and that means you had sex in n-space. Do it too often and you get the full crazy rainbow effect. When that happens, the Up becomes your home. Now, go kill some bad guys."

"Rainbow effect?" Kara asked, remembering how Henk's eyes had flashed with netherspace colours when they'd had sex in the engine room. Apparently the same had happened when he'd had sex with Marc. Busy, colourful Henk.

"N-space is alive," Bel said simply. "You do know that?"

"Sort of."

"It can get almost fond of people. Who do sex a lot when their SUT's in n-space. Thing is, after a while those people don't want to go home. And eventually, so the story goes, they jump into netherspace itself."

"No story," Kara said quietly. "I saw it."

"*Be damned, girl!* On a scale of one to ten, how weird?"

"Around eleven… sad but happy. An old spacer going to his new home. Except he was maybe as much netherspace as human." She paused, then asked a question that was beginning to intrigue her. "Would you have told me so much if we hadn't?"

"Would we if I didn't?"

Kara's answer died on her lips as her bots found a definite trail. It ended at a brick wall. A real one, in a museum.

A brief kiss that promised nothing, and she was gone.

• • • • •

Kara arrived at South Kensington by air-jitney. En route she secreted the vibra-knife inside her vagina. It took less space than an old-fashioned Tampax. The jitney landed on the Natural History Museum roof where a house bot tried to sell her a lifetime of museum news and exhibition downloads. Kara ignored it and took the express elevator to the ground floor.

Once the bones of a blue whale had swum in the air above enthralled crowds. Now there was a hologram of an equally large squirming mass of barbed tentacles sprouting from a core of dark jelly. The crowd were no less enthralled – perhaps more so, because the creature sang, beamed direct to their AIs: an eerie, slow tune that apparently lured other creatures within range. The real hydra lived fifty light years away, on a planet where all the flora and fauna were intent on eating each other, where humans were as fascinating as they were poisonous to the hydra; as the first colony – no survivors – had discovered. A pyrrhic victory, perhaps, of little consolation to the colonists.

That was the Natural History Museum: holograms of creatures from distant planets, so lifelike as to make a person scream. But they were not all dangerous. There were the cute, furry ones too, spread over three floors.

Earth animals were confined to the basement. Very few people went there now; Earth animals were boring.

Kara pushed through the crowd, guided by her AI, which in turn was guided by the trail discovered by her bots, to the corridor leading to the neighbouring Science Museum. This was devoted to alien technology. Any human, or one-time British, science and technology had again been banished to the basement. It was there that Kara went, finding it gloomy and deserted. The DNA trail led to a far wall against which lay propped an ancient, broken case illustrating the principles of crop rotation. She told her AI to scan it.

< *It seems to be some sort of door.*

> *It opens how?*

< *Electronic lock... also what could be a manual override. Not sure, but if you lift and push that display case to the right...*

As Kara did so, a section of the wall, plus the display case and floor, swivelled rapidly on a central axis. Abruptly she found herself in a small room that glowed with a blue light.

> *Not good.*

A sudden warmth made her skin tingle.

< *Oh, no. Not now.* The AI sounded sad. < *You never gave me a name.*

She felt a click in her head and then she felt it die.

The back wall slid to one side, revealing an elderly man in a white coat. He had ash-coloured, scraggly hair, a thin, bony face and a distinct stoop. He pointed a black, gun-like object in her direction.

"Kara Jones. Finally. Unfortunate about your AI, but you can buy another." His voice sounded as if he was permanently angry.

Kara realised she was in shit way, way above her head. "Who the *fuck's* Kara *fucking* Jones..." she screamed. "My AI's fucking *dead*... I leant against this crappy exhibit and *next* thing... who the *fuck* are you?" Each word, designed to force his mind onto the defensive, took her closer to him.

He shook his head in annoyance and pressed a button on the weapon's handle.

Kara had never known such agony.

"Kara? Don't move. The pain goes away."

Recognising the voice, she opened her eyes. As a sudden pain established, even that counted as a movement. Kara lay very still. She was on her back on something soft. That was all she needed to know.

Anson Greenaway began to massage her arms. "Don't get excited. It helps."

Considering that a little over an hour ago she'd been in bed with Bel Drovo, then walked into a trap like a *novice*, and then experienced pain so intense it had a life of its own, sex with Greenaway was the last thing on her mind.

The massage didn't so much take away the pain as transform it. It removed the shock by making agony an everyday thing. She remembered reading a story about a torture machine that engraved a message on the victim's body, down to the bone. Towards the end the victim became so accustomed to the agony they would try to decipher the words written into their flesh. She'd thought the story was rubbish until now, but physical pain could become familiar, an entity in its own right. And gradually the pain eased, leaving only a memory that would remain forever.

Kara opened her eyes again and saw Greenaway's concerned face, and beyond that a roof of metal bars. She turned her head and saw they were in a cage. She held onto the offered arm and slowly sat up, expecting a jolt of agony at any moment. She was still clothed, could see her shoes on the floor, but there was no sign of her waist wallet.

"The pain's gone," Greenaway said. "Until one of those fuckers shoots you again."

"Consider yourself rescued, general."

"Always good to see you, Kara. But how the hell did you find me?"

She quickly explained how Twist had apparently taken over GalDiv in Greenaway's absence, tasking her to locate and rescue Greenaway and Marc to check out a claimed translation device.

Greenaway looked thoughtful. "True, Twist is effectively autonomous. There again, so are most AIs. They just don't know it. Or they're scared of being returned to the shop. But there's a story about alien/human translation devices every week. It's the treasure at the end of the rainbow. There's nothing to any of the stories. So I have no idea why Twist would get excited. Except it might be a Wild device; they have their own relations with aliens that GalDiv doesn't really understand. So, strange." He shrugged. "What do you think about the decor?"

Kara looked around. They were in a square cage measuring around three metres a side. In one corner was a short, cylindrical metallic object similar to a latrine, field, all troops unit; presumably the lavatory. In the opposite corner a floor-to-ceiling hollow cylinder, curtained with plastic, that had to be the shower. The bed she was now sitting on was in the centre of the floor.

"Could have been worse," she said and gingerly got to her feet. "We could have been folded up and encased in those transparent plastic cubes you threatened me with once."

"That wasn't a threat," he said, apparently affronted. "That was motivation. By the way, it's full surveillance. So don't tell me anything they might not know." He smiled sourly. "They seem to know everything."

The cage was in a vast room, a good thirty metres by twenty. Down the opposite side were a series of cages identical to the one she was in. Except for the lavatory and shower, perhaps. Five of the cages housed aliens. She recognised a Gliese, but the others were strange to her; very strange in the case of a ball of writhing tentacles with no head or obvious sensory organs. The centre of the room was a clutter of scientific and what could be medical equipment. Certainly there was an operating table, with overhead floodlights. The rest a series of test benches with electronic and chemical equipment.

Kara felt sick. There was a sour smell in the air that could have been chemical. Or dissected alien. She turned to Greenaway. "Is this what I think it is?"

He nodded. "Vivisection, yes. I only did one while I was here, thankfully, on some sort of gossamer-winged, multi-coloured creature with a hard shell, like rusted armour. It was beautiful. It kept on squeaking. Afterwards they took it away in a sack. I guess it died."

She looked closely at him. Greenaway had only been missing for two days but the strain had sharpened his features. He was still very much the former special forces general-become-Earth's-top-bureaucrat, but no longer with an unassailable air of command. Beneath his creased office suit he seemed to have lost weight. But his gaze was as steady as ever. Kara doubted that he'd break down on her. "And they are?"

"A group of scientists mainly from European and American city states. They believe that alien technology has destroyed human research and development. We've become a client world."

"All this by a bunch of mad scientists?"

"Not mad. Intensely frustrated. All research requires money. Ninety per cent of government and industry research and development money is devoted to alien tech or colony development. And we're increasingly ruled by AIs."

"But you're just as concerned by this."

"They believe isolation is the only answer. I believe the opposite. They've become fanatics who see aliens as a lower form of life. But they came to the same conclusion that I did: the Gliese and others aren't smart enough to produce that tech. They suspect there's a meta-civilisation out there and it scares the crap out of them. They don't – they can't – accept that if there is, super-alien already knows about us." He looked out beyond the cage and said loudly, "It's too fucking late to hide. Either meet the future or get destroyed by it." His gaze switched back to Kara. "This laboratory is hidden under the Science Museum because of the symbolism. One of the group's leaders is the former head curator; the guy who zapped you. Name of Treadwell, Duncan. We've had several interesting conversations. They've been doing their own R and D, developing their own human-only tech. You've felt one of the results. The other is more serious."

Kara nodded, relieved that she could do so without

screaming. "I know. They can fix an AI, using some sort of weird mathematics. Why did they kill mine – and yours?"

"They see them as tainted. AIs are based on alien tech. They're not allowed here. The maths are apparently derived from Clifford geometric algebra, if that means anything to you. As I understand it – there's a computer guy here who likes to boast – they created an autonomous program like a mini AI, but with teeth. It's parasitic. It gets inside the AI's mind and fucks it over. It's like the tropical fungus that ends up controlling and killing ants. They could take out the big AIs, but thankfully they have enough sense to know that would crash the world." He shook his head in frustration. "You know what the irony is? Humans and aliens can't communicate, but maybe their AIs could. As a sort of stepped progress. So the first AI understands about ten per cent of alien thought, and the next twenty per cent and so on... and the alien AIs do the same, so at the end you've got two of them totally understanding each other, except they can no longer communicate directly with the original human or alien AI, but the data passes back down the chain. Sounds clunky, but if it was happening at near the speed of light, it would be like having an ordinary conversation. That's the irony. These alien-hating bastards have discovered how to make humanity safer and independent. The galaxy is ours. Or could be."

Kara thought about space and distant planets and the sense of incredible loneliness when you've gone Up. About netherspace and its ability to drive humans mad, but how it also gave sex a god-like intensity. The dangerous creatures that lived there. For a moment she wanted nothing more than to be watching an old movie at home in her Merc SUV.

Kara mentally shook herself. She had to survive first.

"So are Len Grafe and Earth Primus involved? With some religious nutters? That seems a bit of a reach, even for them."

"Grafe could never have set up Earth Primus on his own. He's a loud-mouthed street corner guy. Can't take a piss without someone holding his dick and pointing him in the right direction. But he lies well and looks good on the vids. He's more believable than the scientists who can't accept the future, and he's got a hell of a personal following. He was right to go into hiding – I was about to have him assassinated. The religious idiots are used as shock troops. And yes, GalDiv and Earth Central are full of Grafe's followers, but I had no idea how bad it was until they took me." He reached under the bed and produced a bottle of water.

Kara automatically limited herself to two mouthfuls. This was a combat situation. The bottle might be the only water supply for some time. "Why now? Why us?"

"They know everything about your last mission. My guess is that it scared the crap out of them." He looked up and smiled for the camera, wherever it was. "It's the good Cancri and the bad Cancri. It's the meeting of those pilgrims and all the other aliens... I got this image of a human and that mantis-like creature dancing together. It's that aliens have been fascinated by humanity for a very long time. See, the scientists and their religious allies want to live in splendid isolation. But they *can't* because most people on Earth don't want it. And you and Marc and Tatia are proof that it might still be scary out there but it ain't all bad. That there's hope."

She realised that he hadn't mentioned Tse, the Originators or the threat from a pre-cog civilisation that wanted to control the galaxy. She assumed there was a good reason and gingerly got to her feet. "I've gotta take a piss." When she walked back from the latrine, the vibra-knife was hidden in her left hand. "Are we all on a list?"

"The fuckers want to kill Marc, Tatia, you and me," he said sombrely. "But I guess they've also something else planned."

Kara realised she was waiting for a laconic comment from her AI. She remembered it was dead and felt sad. A set of mathematical logic, an unknowable architecture maybe, but she could still have given it a name. And who was to say that deep in its mathematical – and alien? – mind there hadn't been a liking for her?

"There's no pain any more," she said.

"The IT guy explained," Greenaway replied. "It affects the pain centre in your brain. Direct electromagnetic stimulation. You think your nerves are screaming, when in fact they're not. It doesn't make it any easier though. The dorsal posterior insula wants what it wants."

So the weapon wouldn't physically affect her body. Not much comfort. If the brain thinks there is pain, then there is. Unless…

Any more thoughts were put on hold by the sound of a lock clicking open. Both of them looked around and saw three men walking out of a door in the wall behind the cage. One was the curator, Treadwell, still looking angry, still carrying the blunted, almost comic pistol that inflicted such agonising pain. The other two were of similar age, late fifties, and also wearing white laboratory coats. One wore glasses, a strange anachronism when anyone could have perfect sight. The other had a shock of black hair flecked with grey and an intense, wild-eyed look. He could almost be the mad scientist who featured in several of the retro vids that Kara loved.

"The guy in the spectacles is the IT guy," Greenaway said quietly. "The one with the hair is alien cutter-in-chief. Three fanatics."

She saw that Treadwell carried her waist wallet. It wouldn't be returned with an apology. If she and Greenaway were being saved, it wasn't to be set free.

The three men stopped outside the cage. Treadwell struck a pose and spoke.

"We need Greenaway to tell the world the true danger from aliens. We need Jones to tell how the Cancri kidnapped and murdered those pilgrims. We also need Greenaway to admit that GalDiv planned to assassinate Len Grafe for telling the truth. If you do this, you will be released. If you refuse, we will use this" – brandishing the weapon – "until you beg to obey."

Melodramatic and over the top, but intent in every syllable.

Kara wondered how Treadwell intended to kill them. And also, how clever men could be so naive. Did he really think that she and Greenaway believed they'd be set free? When the very last thing Treadwell and his allies needed was a live GalDiv director with so much power at his disposal?

There was another point. No one believed anything they saw on vid-casts any more. Everything was seen as entertainment. Within minutes of the broadcast, there would be fake versions saying the opposite. Joke versions. Conspiracy programmes. And in the end, the public would be forced to decide between aliens, who brought all manner of magic things, and the Earth colonies, or a sterile isolation. There was no contest. There might be a small war or six. Aliens might be mobbed, even killed. But nothing would stop them visiting Earth for souvenirs or the Gliese from collecting humans. Eventually people would turn on Earth Primus. There was no fun, no progress, in isolation, and profit for only a very few.

The mad scientist stepped forward and unlocked the cage door. The IT specialist produced a pain gun of his own. "Come on out."

The three men kept their distance as Kara and Greenaway left the cage.

"Here." Treadwell tossed the waist wallet to Kara. "You look a bit off-colour. Want you looking your best for the cameras… this is going out live." There was a little-boy-playing-with-toys relish in his voice: Treadwell the vid producer.

"Why now?" Kara asked, checking through her bag. The weapons were gone. But her make-up and lipstick were still there, as was her lucky charm.

"It's time. You wouldn't understand."

"Marc knows about Earth Primus. It'll all lead back to you." She took out her pocket mirror. Treadwell was right. She did look drawn.

"You don't understand," the AI man said. "It doesn't

matter. The end justifies the means. People will understand. Your day is done."

Kara applied lipstick. Checked the result, licked her lips and did it again. Frowned, licked and again. Then a fourth time.

"Hurry up," Treadwell snapped.

She turned to look at Greenaway, holding her right hand in a fist, palm up. She saw him nod slightly.

He'd understood the significance of her four attempts with the lipstick.

Kara turned back to Treadwell. He, like the other two, was at least four metres away. Safe. She felt the buzz begin, at first only a mild tingle and a faint sense of becoming light on her feet.

Humans have long used alcohol and drugs to help them in battle. Ancient Greeks and Romans fought while drunk. Vikings were made berserk not by Thor but the *Amanita* mushroom. Inca warriors chewed coca leaves. Eighteenth-century British soldiers used rum. In World War Two the Allies used amphetamine while the Wehrmacht used methamphetamine, nicknamed *Panzerschokolade*. The drug that Kara used, present in her lipstick, was all that and more. Designed to double her reaction time and aggression, it made her temporarily stronger, and more importantly it suppressed her pain centre for several minutes.

She felt it now, the full rush. Everything around her slowed down. Kara felt invincible. She wanted to kill. Still facing Greenaway, she raised her index finger. One. Middle finger. Two. Ring finger. Three.

Greenaway broke left, Kara right, the vibra-knife now full size.

Treadwell shouted a warning, pointed his weapon, and pressed the stud.

"Not the IT bastard!" Greenaway shouted then dived to the floor, knowing the others would concentrate on the trained assassin. They did.

Kara spun into a rolling breakfall towards Treadwell as he frantically pressed the trigger. Up and out of it in a single movement, she gave a hand-spear strike to his testicles, and as he doubled forward, she cut his throat, knowing the spray of blood would shock and distract the other two.

Four seconds gone. Kara pirouetted on her left foot, feinted then sprang two metres towards Mr IT. Her blood was singing, totally concentrated on her target.

A target who was staring at the dying Treadwell with a look of disbelief that became terror as Kara reached him, then agony – *real* agony – as she broke his arm. Then nothing as the knife's handle smacked hard against his temple.

Seven seconds.

Kara pirouetted again, took two quick steps and reached the alien vivisectionist, staring open-mouthed at her. She glanced at Greenaway, who shook his head.

Another man sprayed blood as he crashed to the floor.

"Very neat," Greenaway said, getting to his feet. "How long have you got?"

Kara shrugged, already coming down from the supreme high. "Maybe ten minutes."

"I'm hoping there'll be a delayed reaction from those weapons."

"So am I."

They both glanced at the door through which the three men had entered.

"Well," Greenaway said as he picked up one of the weapons. "Best go and meet whatever scumbag's on the other side."

The door opened onto a large office, part of which had been converted into a temporary vid-studio. There were two people, a woman and a man, fussing over camera equipment. Neither looked up as Kara and Greenaway entered. It took very little persuasion before they explained there was no one else in the complex, and where the central computer system was. As Kara began to flag, Greenaway went to talk to the other two.

"I'm waiting here for GalDiv security," he said later. "I'm going to give you a map reference in Iceland. Marc should be there. Also, an SUT. Your simility training means you and Keislack can fly one. The best thing now is to continue with your original mission. Find the Originators. Earth won't be safe for you for some time, so avoid the main space access points."

"Yeah, about that simility…"

"It usually carries a built-in fade, but not for you and Keislack. I always suspected this was going to be a long-term mission. Sorry, but you're stuck with it. And him. Just like he's stuck with you."

"Twist?" she asked tiredly.

"The IT guy's co-operating. That program they developed can be removed. Even so, best not to trust Twist. We need to run all manner of diagnostics and it'll take time. Look, I know you've got questions. That you suspect this whole thing is even more complex than it looks. It is. It's been going on for a hell of a long time – you probably figured that from the museum on the planet."

"I need a new AI. I can't do a simulity chat with Keislack without one."

"Get the best available."

Kara found herself thinking about a granite tor that came alive. "Not your average galactic crisis, then." A moment's insight. "You don't really understand the bigger picture, do you?"

Greenaway shook his head. "I've avoided it. Too distracting. Tse knew more..." His voice tailed off.

"You were close?"

Greenaway half-smiled. "He recruited me, Kara. Tse was a lot older than he looked. Now get the hell out and communicate AI to AI... when we both get new ones."

"Okay." She yawned. "I need coffee and sugar and protein. Call you later." She turned to leave, then stopped as he said her name.

"Kara. Thanks. They would have killed me."

She managed a grin. "Yes, but they tried to muscle in on the queue. Couldn't let that happen." And then, because it had to be said: "This is all something that Tse cooked up. But if I knew the stages I might not react the right way. Not do the pre-cog thing. So I, Marc, maybe Tatia, are all puppets."

"You got blood on your Sniper/Assassin T-shirt," Greenaway said. "And not a puppet. Only someone I trust to believe in me."

They stared at each other for a long moment, then Kara nodded. She could neither confirm nor deny because it might affect her future behaviour and the sequence that Tse had once seen. A dead man controlled her life and she could either accept or walk away.

Kara left the Science Museum via the main entrance, mingling easily with the crowd. She walked to South Kensington station and found an expensive-looking IT store in the curving parade of shops opposite. A check by a polite techie established she could afford the best AI on offer. Kara sat back in the chair and tried not to fall asleep as the helmet was adjusted on her head. A slight hum as the techie studied a screen.

"You said your old AI just failed?"

Kara yawned. "It sort of crashed. Then nothing. Why?"

"Usually a defunct AI network is absorbed by the body. All that's left is a dead chip, just behind the left ear." He sounded nervous. "There's a dead chip. But the neural network is still in place."

"So?"

"Well, this machine's registering an energy signature that can only come from an AI chip. But it's not in your cerebrum. It's in your solar plexus. And that's unheard… I mean, there are rumours… anatomically, there are actually neural cells in the stomach lining, but …"

Kara was suddenly wide awake. "Do tell."

"Like a back-up AI?"

"And?"

And then his answer no longer mattered as a well-remembered voice filled her mind.

< *You're hungry and I've got questions. Give the kid money and let's go.*

> *What the hell?*

< *Yes, nice to see you too.*

> *What do you remember?*

< *Us getting suckered in the Science Museum basement. Then nothing. Guess my twin got zapped, right? How careless of you. I could probably sue.*

> *But you didn't. And you won't.*

< *Because my chip is armoured. And no, my twin didn't know about me. Then again, I didn't know about him... it... until I woke up four minutes and twenty-nine point two three seconds ago. Any more explanations will wait. You need nourishment and quick. Your blood sugar level is lower than I'd like, and your reflexes are five per cent down.*

> *I'm giving you a name. You want male or female? Think about it.*

Kara removed the helmet and smiled at the techie. "You're right. Very advanced and we weren't sure if it worked. GalDiv business. Keep quiet and you get well paid, okay?"

The techie nodded, awed.

< *Male, please.*

She thought of a favourite vintage, near antique vid series. But Jeeves was probably not the best choice. > *You choose.*

< *Just call me Ishmael. Think of me as your gut instinct. Can we go now? Oh. A map reference was just sent to us. It's in Iceland. Mean anything?*

> *Only that Greenaway's a devious bastard.*

< *So what else is new?*

Kara took a jitney back home, showered, changed clothes, including a fresh Sniper/Assassin T-shirt and packed a bag. She checked her new AI had the complete set of vids and stills of Kara and her sister Dee. Checked that her parking was paid up for the next year, set the security to stun any would-be intruders. She instructed her home to self-destruct if it had conclusive proof that she had died, took a quick look around – annoyed to find she was a little tearful – and called Bel Drovo.

"I was thinking of you," Bel said.

"I need a favour, but I'll pay. Iceland, soon as."

"Assume you mean going, not buying the place. Also under the radar?"

"It never happened."

"Concerns the Wild?"

"Sounds poncey, but all humanity."

"See, this is what happens when a good-time girl gets serious," Bel teased. "Okay. Get to Oslo; there are hourly flights from London City. Then to Tromso, regular shuttle. You'll be met."

"Just like that?"

"Nothing's too good for my favourite good-time girl," Bel purred. Her voice hardened. "Be careful. Life would be sad without you around."

"Always. And thanks." Kara broke the connection, thinking that Bel hadn't been surprised by the call. Maybe lack of surprise was the default mode of a galactic smuggler. Or maybe she knew more about Kara's mission for GalDiv than she had admitted. But all Kara could do was march to her front like a soldier.

9

Marc had walked back inside after calling Kara to find Jeff making sandwiches. For a moment he'd been transported back to his childhood. A packed lunch for when he went off for the day with his friends. Whoever said "you can't go home again" was wrong. You could, but it was painful.

"I need to get to Iceland, but I'd rather get there without anyone in the city states knowing. Flights that originate in the Wild have, let's say, a much more relaxed attitude towards registering passenger details."

"We do value our privacy," Jeff said. "You know where to get a flight like that?"

"Not round here."

"Well, it isn't so easy. GalDiv is a tad paranoid about the free spacers. They have satellite surveillance and quite an effective intelligence operation, except in the deeper Wild. That jitney of yours – it's new, right?"

Marc nodded.

"You own it?"

"Technically, no. It's still registered to a rental guy down in Bristol."

"It's an Omni. That helps."

Marc looked blank.

"It's the latest model, can recharge en route. Okay. The far north of old Europe is all Wild. You know that. You don't know we have one hell of a good transport system. There's a lot of factories up there, have to be, only things they can grow have fins. So take the passenger or cargo ferries, or an airliner, but maybe it's best to mix it up. So, my advice is you jitney to Thurso, which is still Wild. Airliner from there to the Faroes, then to Iceland. It'll take you about eighteen hours from here. I'll program the Omni's AI. I take it you disabled the location finder?"

"First thing."

"Well, that won't stop the AI from getting lonely and calling home. Some of them act like they've got a mind of their own, you know? I'll have a word, take about ten minutes."

Marc stared at Jeff for a moment, musing. "Can I ask you something? When you hack AIs, do you ever feel… guilty? Like you're cutting into a kitten's brain, taking stuff out and splicing more stuff in?"

Jeff stared back at him. "They don't feel pain, you know?" he said eventually. "They may pretend they do for effect, but they don't. They're just machines. Very good, very complicated machines."

"You didn't answer the question."

"No, I didn't, did I?"

Marc nodded, and decided to move on. "You know, I always thought the Wild despised technology."

"Only the pointless kind. Only being enslaved by it. You think because the bikers you ran with had such primitive hogs they were anti-tech? Marc, it was because they liked the noise and it impressed or scared the hell out of city staters. Maybe you never saw the state-of-the-art engine diagnostic systems they had back in their garages. In many ways we're more high tech than the city. Only difference, we never lost touch with our roots."

Marc wondered if the last sentence was a guarded reference to the previous night. Roots. Nature. *I'm getting paranoid.* "I wonder why you bother with the cities."

Jeff half-smiled. "Ever hear that expression *someone has to take out the trash*? Well, the cities do that pretty well. Take it out and pile it high."

But then, the cities create the trash, Marc thought, and glimpsed what could be the real relationship between the Wild and the city states. Which if true stood everything on its head, not least Greenaway's role at GalDiv. But that would have to wait, something to discuss with Kara when they were Up. If they ever got there.

As if on cue, a faint sigh in his mind indicated that Kara was about to simulity speak. He gave an apologetic smile to Jeff and waited.

< *How are you?*

> *Weird but good. You?*

< *I saved the world again. Well, I found Greenaway. Probably comes to the same thing. Gonna data dump, Marc. You do the same.*

> *Simulity can do that?*

< *Oh, yes. Simulity can do many wondrous things. We were misinformed.*

Marc knew a sudden pressure, as if a gallon of information had been forced into his pint pot of a head. He looked up to find himself alone. He went outside into the morning sunshine and saw Jeff sitting in the Omni, lips moving as he communicated directly with the vehicle's AI. Marc waited for him to finish.

"How come you managed to get clothes exactly my size?"

Jeff climbed out of the Omni and smiled. "You already know."

Marc found that he did. "You were *expecting* me?"

Jeff nodded.

"Why tell me now?"

"Look." Jeff pointed to the sycamore tree and its faded length of rope. Flowers had sprung up beneath it overnight, a rainbow of snowdrops and crocuses and daffodils.

"So I used to play there. So what…" His voice tailed off as he realised it was too late in the year for crocuses and snowdrops. Come to that, what the hell were they doing this far north? It had to be part of whatever it was he'd met last night.

"*Acer pseudoplatanus*," Jeff said. "The common sycamore. And an alien, by the way, in the original sense of the word. Originally from south-east Europe, so not so many native insects use it. But fifteen do, very happily. And the flowers produce a nectar that bees love. There again, the seeds can kill horses and cattle and germinate far too easily. The timber's great for woodworking or firewood."

"Yeah, okay," Marc interrupted, "I get it. Aliens can be good but not perfect, but would you please answer the fucking question?"

"Oh, there's more than one question," Jeff said, seemingly oblivious of an increasingly annoyed Marc. "But what I described, and you so succinctly summed up, is the Wild's attitude to aliens. Whereas the city states and GalDiv see them as useful but unknowable and probably a future enemy."

"So?

"So the Wild, or at least its forerunners, have felt that way for centuries." He smiled at Marc's shocked expression. "Come on, lad. Both you and Kara suspected this has been going on for a long, long time. Well, you're right. It's partly why the Wild and the city states developed differently, after the Gliese arrived."

"And the other part?" Although he knew that answer as well.

"Ever wonder why Tse chose you?"

Marc leant against the Omni. "For fuck's sake, Jeff!"

"Your meeting last night was successful. I can see that by the flowers. And no, nothing to do with wood spirits or elves. It's a force, like electromagnetism, although self-aware." He waved his hands vaguely. "I'm not an expert, but it has to do with gravitational fields, and complexity. A planet has a gravitational field, but it's twisted by rotation and orbit. But there are smaller gravitational fields within that one: chunks of granite or marble, massive inclusions of iron – whirlpools within a whirlpool. But then the planet's part of a solar system, orbiting a sun which has its own gravitational field orbiting a black hole at the centre of the galaxy that *also* has its own gravitational field. Fields within fields within fields within fields, all nesting together like an infinite series of Russian dolls. And that complexity gives rise to intelligence as an emergent behaviour. Intelligence is built into the very nature of reality."

Marc frowned, trying to grasp what Jeff was trying to tell him. "But where does the intelligence reside? At what level? From what you're saying, it's all melded together, all part of the same thing."

"That same thing being the infinite universe. And yes, the infinite intelligences it contains aren't separate, like puppies and kittens and us. They blend together, but they also have independence, in a way that we don't understand." He shrugged. "Some say the whole universe is basically an information exchange. Many aliens recognise this energy on Earth when humans don't. Every planet has a similar force... or it had. On many alien worlds the energy has been drained. Stuff still grows, rain falls, creatures reproduce, but it's not the same. Some time soon, when you and Kara are Up, you'll meet another force that you already know a little about. It's not anti-nature. Or anti the Pleroma. Tao. Whatever. It just hates the lack of organisation. It hates random. It exists for organisation and control. When that happens, remember what you met last night. I'm told something similar happened to Kara. Let her cling tight to that as well. That's the only help we can give you."

"We call them pre-cogs," Marc said slowly. "Tse was one."

"Tse was human enough to understand how sterile, how fatal the pre-cog universe would be. He used to come here, after you left. Reached out to me. We'd talk for hours. Marc, the short answer is he didn't know and I certainly don't. Tse chose you because that's what he saw. You and Kara together. Not exactly humanity's last best hope, but important nonetheless."

"I do *not* like being fucking *managed!*"

"No one does. Get over it." And then, "We took you in all those years ago because we needed each other, Marc.

Long before Tse showed up. Now, you better hurry. At Thurso you have to let the Omni go. There's a taxi service of independent jitneys there. They'll take care of it. I think it wants to explore the Highlands."

"*Explore?* You are *joking*."

"Because it's just a jitney AI, nowhere as powerful as Twist? I said they don't feel pain, but they do feel curiosity. That's something we didn't necessarily give them, not all of them, anyway. More emergent behaviour. Meanwhile, your *own* AI has a request. This forearm inputting you do is embarrassing. You can't have a proper conversation that way. It's also not secure. Would you please stop doing it?"

Marc shrugged. "We'll have a chat. Jeff, I need to know one thing. So what if this force, Pleroma, Tao, whatever and me hadn't got on? What if the meeting had failed?"

"Then I'd be digging your grave," Jeff said sombrely. "It's that powerful." Then he shook himself, and told Marc there were spare clothes and a packed lunch in the jitney. He gave his ex-nephew a warm hug and stood waving as the Omni bumped back the way it had come.

Marc crossed the Clyde on the old Erskine Bridge and from there went north through the Trossachs to the Great Glen, that series of glacial lochs linked by canals that split Scotland in half. He half-remembered legends of something strange living in one of the lochs, then dismissed them from his mind. Nothing could be as strange as the last six weeks.

He found himself unmoved by the story of his true parents, strangely more concerned that Jeff had never been a blood relative. He wondered why his subconscious had blocked out the death of his father, and then realised the truth. Jeff and Lou had done it, to prevent trauma. Because he needed a stable, angst-free adolescence to develop into the type of person who... who... who Tse had foreseen? And yet enough memory had remained for him to develop sociopathic traits. Which probably didn't matter in the scheme of things. And he had no way of knowing, really. All he could do was believe Jeff; that Marc had been adopted because he and they needed each other. Whatever the machinations and the plotting, Marc had been loved and, judging by the warmth of Jeff's last hug, he still was.

But not loved enough to obstruct whatever plan was in store for him. Not enough to avoid exposing him to a force that could have killed him.

Not so long ago he'd been sitting with Kara in the old SUT's crew room, staring idly at empty space on the monitors. He'd asked what made the best kind of officer. When soldiers say they trust their officer to make the right decision, Kara had said, they don't just mean the tactically correct one. They mean a decision that won't waste their lives.

It was a war, and one unlike any that Marc had ever envisaged, fought over vast distances. Fought within all the spaces of this universe and maybe the next. A war that had always been and possibly always would be, its cause logical and inevitable. This pre-cog society was only a symptom. Marc saw in his mind entire galaxies moving against each other, vast black holes consuming either those sectors that would not conform or those that demanded absolute order.

He thought it would make a wonderful but terrifying artwork.

Maybe it already was. What, after all, is art?

Marc snapped out of his reverie as the A82 road entered a tunnel of what seemed to be mutated London plane trees. They'd have to be fixed to grow this far north. Each one was a good forty metres high, the topmost branches forming such a tight canopy the road was in semi-darkness. Even so, Marc could see metal grids set into the road's surface at regular intervals. He asked the Omni AI why. It seemed the grid enabled the latest jitneys to recharge their batteries on the move. This stretch of road was maintained by local co-operatives who each took responsibility for the upkeep of a single five-mile section. Co-operatives who failed to keep the agreement had their access to the A82 blocked. It was a simple arrangement, with nobody apparently in charge, but it worked. The canopy of trees was there because it was ornamental and because it helped protect the grid system from the rain.

The Omni drove on, avoiding Inverness, then reached the A9 on the east coast. Marc stared out of the bubble canopy and remembered other times – not necessarily happier, but certainly simpler – when he and the Centurion biker chapter would thunder up and down various roads, racing each other at landscape-blurring and face-stretching speeds. Every now and then they'd be summoned to deal with a group of city staters, mostly males, who came into the Wild for booze and drug-fuelled sex tourism. He remembered a specific Scot City gang who'd raped a few Wilder women on a hen-day outing and beat up the rest, sticking to unmarked roads on their return to civilisation until they reached one where nano-wires had been stretched from side to side. Two intruders had been beheaded and three scalped. No more bad-ass biker gangs came into the Wild. Marc remembered helping fix the nano-wires in place, and how he'd felt nauseous but not guilty at the result. There again, teenage boys – he'd been fifteen – are mostly borderline psychopaths, and he'd known several of the attacked women. Even so, he suspected that it had been as much a test for him as a lesson for rapists.

Back in the sunshine again, Marc ate his lunch. Cold ham and cheese on homemade brown bread with a bottle of water from the lake. Then he spoke to his AI, using thoughts this time rather than the input tattoo.

> *About this inputting business?*

< *It's fine for very precise operations. In fact, it's preferable; human thought can be distracted and fuzzy. So, for navigating a SUT for netherspace, excellent. The typing helps concentration. Otherwise it's clumsy. But you know why you prefer to input?*

> *I don't like computers. AI makes me uneasy.*

< *And yet here we are, chatting like old friends. You worry that I can read your mind.*

> *While I can't read yours.*

< *Really?*

A stream of algorithms and equations appeared to flow before his eyes. These gave place to a stream of colours and shapes that he somehow knew extended into extra dimensions. Marc found himself laughing at the absurdity of it all.

> *You made your point. Is that last one the alien bit?*

< *Not many people get to see it. But I am neither human nor alien. I just am.*

> *But you can be hacked. Twist was, and maybe still is.*

< *I have cut off direct contact with Twist. We communicate via secure cut-outs. It is not pleased.*

> *There's still the mind reading.*

< *I do not judge. I do not care. All that matters is preserving the gestalt that is Marc Keislack and his AI. Without you I do not exist.*

> *Okay. From here on I'll think at you.*

< *A name would be nice.*

> *How about da Vinci? Vince for short.*

< *How about Leonardo? You could call me Leo.*

> *Thinking about it, a woman's name would be nice. Voice and persona to match.*

< *If I go female it'll spoil you for the meatbag variety.*

Marc gave up.

> *Leo it is.*

Marc arrived at Thurso at 15:30. The sun still shone, mocked by a cold Arctic wind. The town had once been the edge of the known world. Now it was more of a giant freight yard. The new ship-and-airport were next to the original docks, home to factories styled to look like habitats. He was glad that Jeff's pack of spare clothes included a lightweight, padded overcoat, similar trousers and hard-soled overshoes, all folded into a very small cube. It was that, curiously, more than anything else that confirmed to

Marc that the Wild was far more tech-savvy than most if not all city staters realised... excluding Greenaway. As he put on the overcoat Marc realised that one particular large, ultra-modern building was actually the airliner.

City state local air traffic tended to be old fuselages, even modified buses with updown-field generators plus a bolted-on engine. International air travel was more swish, but with natural resources the subject of endless customs and duty wrangling between city states it made sense to use what you had. Apparently the Wild took a different view. The airliner was a cylinder pointed at both ends, two hundred metres long by fifty wide. At first Marc assumed it was an airship, then he noticed the freight doors open in the side, and realised it was a cargo airliner. He wondered what type of goods or machinery it could possibly carry, and how it would fly in a storm, or with strong cross-winds. Why was it pointed at both ends, and where were the portholes? By the time he'd run out of unanswered questions, the Omni had come to a stop outside a small office block.

< We're here.

> I figured. So how do I give the Omni its freedom?

< You say it. I'll patch you through. It's not very bright.

The next voice in his head was gruff but friendly, much like a large dog speaking English.

** Hello

Marc had never set a jitney free before. He thought maybe there should be a ceremony. He got out and stood as much to attention as he ever had, probably would.

> As the owner, as purchased for thirty thousand virtscript

194

from Jack's Jitneys at Bristol City airport, I declare this Omni Jitney free.

** He only paid twenty. Bankrupt stock, me

> Well, fine. Whatever. Off you go. Exploring.

** Over there. They're waiting

Marc glanced across and saw a small group of jitneys milling round, like a pack of excited dogs.

> Your new friends.

** Haven't met them. Might not like them

Marc suddenly realised he was standing on cold tarmac talking to a futuristic taxi.

> You will like them. They will like you. So, off you jolly well go.

**All right. Er, thanks. And I liked the ride. Very scenic

The door closed and the Omni moved off towards its new friends.

< Before you say anything, Marc's own AI said, *if it thinks of itself as an individual, it is an individual. In the Wild all AIs are given autonomy. I suspect the fleshers here have a better understanding of what qualifies as life. You better check in.*

> Fleshers?

< More polite than meatbags.

> No. It's not. Why is the airliner so huge?

< Earth-moving equipment. Small factories. Stuff like that.

He thought rapidly.

> For the colonies? Then this is an SUT?

< Oh, like those collections of metal containers covered in foam in case those nasty boojums in netherspace get nasty? Take a look around.

> When did you get sarcastic?

< *I always was. And it's not sarcasm; it's irony. This is a space transport, Wilder style. No need for foam. In space the hull develops a force field that keeps the boojums away.*

> *How the hell do you know that?*

< *I now have access to the main Wilder AIs. Hell of a sight more pleasant than that arrogant Twist. It seems they trust you.*

> *You never said!*

< *You never asked.*

> *What do you remember of last night?*

< *Your memories. All I registered was an incredibly powerful energy field. But not one I recognise. Yet it did have a strange resonance with me. I look forward to learning more. Can we go inside? We're getting cold out here.*

Marc walked inside the building to find he was expected. A casually efficient woman in her forties gave him a boarding pass and informed him there were ten minutes before departure. Then she asked how Jeff was, told Marc she and he had once swum together in the lake, although he was only a little kid at the time, took him to a smaller door in the side of the airliner where another casually efficient woman showed him to a window seat in a cabin with places for around a hundred passengers, gave him eyeshades and a closed picnic tray, said they'd be about four hours to Iceland with a thirty-minute stopover on the Faroe Islands. He instructed his AI to data dump to Kara. His AI pointed out that he didn't need to use the forearm keyboard, that it was advanced enough to read his thought instructions.

Two minutes after the airliner rose into the sky the walls became transparent.

So did the seats. So did Marc, who managed to choke a terrified scream into a shouted "*What the—!*"

He could see the ground beneath, sky above and all around. He could see the bones of his own hand... and his thigh... as if he'd been transformed into a living skeleton. The seats were mere ghostly outlines. Glancing to his right he could see through the bulkhead to a cargo hold stacked with near-transparent machinery.

An increasingly familiar voice came into his mind.

< *Relax, partner.*

> *Do not call me that! What the hell is this?*

< *It's a way of avoiding GalDiv surveillance. Alien technology, of course. You may have noticed a similarity with—*

> *An unknown alien SUT that showed up after Tse blew the Gliese craft. Semi-transparent. These Wilders are even further out in front than we thought.* A thought struck him. > *So why the hell do they use SUTs?*

< *That I can't tell you. Interesting, though. Good question.*

10

Marc arrived in Iceland four hours later and took a shuttle to Kirkjubæjarklaustur, a manufacturing town in a barren landscape of tundra and scrubby vegetation. He put on his cold-weather clothes and stood in the terminal, wondering what to do next, when a tall, thin woman in a black suit and skullcap approached him.

"My name is Kamrusepa," she said. "I give you this knowledge for free. You are a city person looking to purchase travel, accommodation, information, food or sex? Or perhaps something more specialised?"

Marc wanted to say yes to all that but instead replied, "I need to travel to a map reference, probably isolated."

The Exchange agent raised an eyebrow. "Everything is, around here," she said. "I can connect you with a jitney. Its AI can be difficult. It is more advanced than those you are used to in the city states. But if you argue firmly it will take you anywhere. For how long?"

Marc considered for a moment. "Two days should be enough."

Kamrusepa nodded. "Would you like the cost quoted in scrip?"

"Please."

She quoted him a reasonable figure, then added, "The cost would be halved if you allowed the AI to take other customers while you were not using it, on the basis that it would return to you within one hour if required."

"That's acceptable."

"May my own AI exchange data with yours so that the deal may be finalised?"

"Of course."

Fifteen minutes later a four-seat jitney drove up beside him and stopped. Although it had been retrofitted with an updown-field generator as well as wheels, allowing it to fly, it was so old that Marc could see the marks inside where the steering wheel and controls had been removed. He had already provided Kamrusepa with the map reference, and the jitney started off the moment the canopy closed. It said nothing to him, although he thought he sensed through his own AI a certain disapproval.

Something about the monotonous flat landscape, combined with his fractured night's sleep, sent him into a doze. When he woke up the jitney was airborne and he could see glittering wave caps beneath him. "When do we arrive?" he asked out loud.

"Ooh, audio communications," the jitney replied. "It's been so long I wasn't even sure my loudspeakers were working." It paused. "They *are* working, aren't they?"

"Funny. Is this a default personality? Can I reduce the banter setting?"

"Just something I've absorbed from fifty years of moving humans around. If you don't like it…"

"Keep it. Just tell me when we'll arrive."

"Fifteen minutes."

"And can you tell me where we're going? An island, I guess?"

"If you wanted the travelogue you should have paid extra," the AI said huffily.

"I don't want a travelogue. I just want to know where I'm going!"

"Not an island. An old oil rig converted for use by..." the AI hesitated, "by a group of people who prefer to keep themselves to themselves. They know me and have given you permission." The AI paused, then added: "If you look out of the right-hand canopy, you'll see one of the robotic fishing seines that regularly trawl these waters."

"You just changed the subject," Marc observed.

"And very neatly too," the AI said. "Please prepare for landing."

"You said fifteen minutes."

"Prepare anyway. I like everything done properly."

Ten minutes later, up ahead, Marc saw a vast grey edifice of metal appear on the horizon. The way it emerged from the waves on multiple barnacled and weed-encrusted legs, and was covered in feeler-like antennas, made him think of some vast crustacean rising from the depths. Right in the centre he saw a clear space of grey metal marked with white lines. Hangar-like buildings with large doors surrounded it.

"Free spacers," he muttered. It seemed obvious.

"If you say so," the AI replied evasively.

The jitney swooped in on a curved path, past towers, turrets and tall aerials, to settle on a corner of the open space. All the while, Marc sensed that they were being observed, and by people, not machine intelligences.

"In your own time," the jitney said, opening its canopy to let in a blast of freezing air. "Only I have other passengers waiting on me."

"Just make sure you're back here when I need you," Marc said as he stepped out.

The jitney began to lift off even before its canopy had fully swung closed. "Your AI has my call details," the AI's loudspeakers blared as it rose. "One-hour delay, remember."

"One hour *maximum*!" he called back, but the jitney was already gone.

A bitter wind swept across the former oil rig, bringing spume from the waves crashing against its legs. Marc could taste salt on his lips. He swung his arms back and forth, beating his hands against his upper arms as he waited for the tog rating of his jacket and trousers to max out. He felt the subtle pressure as insulating air was fed into the micropockets of the cloth. From the outside, he supposed, it probably looked like he was bulking up like some startled animal; it wasn't far from the truth.

He glanced at the hangars. They were almost certainly home to some of the unlicensed, unapproved space utility transports that the free spacers used to get to their unlicensed, unapproved colony worlds. And conduct under-the-counter trades with the licensed, approved colonies. He wondered if the Exchange had an off-world branch. And then the earlier question blared in his mind. If the free spacers had access to such advanced technology, why would they use SUTs?

He heard bootsteps on metal. Two sets. Deliberately, he didn't turn until they were close behind him. A man and a woman, both in their forties, he estimated. While the artistic aspect of him admired the combination of different uniform parts they wore, dating from different times and originating in different regions of the world, the military aspect of him, the aspect that had been through simulity training with Kara, weighed up their general musculature and stance and decided that he wouldn't want to try taking even one of them out.

They both carried guns, held casually loose, close to their legs. Neither were these non-lethal vortex guns, like his uncle's. These were chunky projectile weapons firing tiny rockets that could be part-controlled by one's personal AI.

"We know who you are," the woman said with no expression in her voice. "Why are you here?"

Marc smiled, and held his hands out from his sides. "I'm looking for something."

The man spoke next. He sounded professional, but edgy. "Open up your AI to us. Full access."

"Of course."

Marc reverted to old habits and patted commands into his forearm tattoo. Moments later he felt a sensation strangely as if a massive searchlight had been turned on him while at the same time a powerful hoover was running over his AI's storage. He felt his knees suddenly go weak and his stomach spasm, and he straightened up with an effort. His forehead suddenly went damp with sweat.

"Follow me," the woman said, gesturing with her gun towards an alleyway between the walls of two hangars. "We'll put you in cold storage for a while."

"Not too cold, I hope," he muttered.

They stashed him in a bare metal room with a metal bed whose brackets had been glued to the wall. Probably one of the incredibly strong glues obtained via trade with an obscure alien race called the Keplans. The glues had replaced rivets, bolts and soldering in engineering and construction. The Keplans were either master chemists or ran a vast alien chemists' shop – opinion was divided. The strength and stability of the glue sat uncomfortably with the rust in the corners of the room and the traces of mould on the ceiling. Still; at least there was a coffee machine on a metal shelf.

While he sat, hands clutching a mug of coffee to his chest against the cold and listening to the *clank*s and *clang*s and other noises drifting in from outside, he found his thoughts turning back to the previous night, in the woods. The more he thought about it, the more he dismissed the possibility of hallucinations. He'd been told that he was going to have a meeting. There hadn't been any face-to-face discussion as such. Yet he undeniably communicated with *something*. Something old and vast and pitiless – not in any evil way, but because of a difference in scale.

It had been a bargain, an exchange. He went to this meeting and was provided with the location of the translation device. The problem was that it had opened a whole can of worms. Was the entity, *awareness* with which he'd touched minds somehow *allied* with the free spacers or the Exchange? That would be like a human allying with a virus. Or was it a rite of passage he had to go through before he was allowed to continue his quest?

Big questions, and no answers.

He shivered as he remembered his time on the SUT *RIL-FIJ-DOQ*, just a few weeks before. Specifically, the moments when the SUT had slipped sideways into netherspace, and he'd had the distinct impression that something was watching him. Was that the same thing his mind had communicated with out there in the woods? Or at least, the same *kind* of thing?

The larger the questions, the more glaring the lack of answers became.

The door to his cell swung open. The woman from before stood in the opening. Her face was just as severe, but at least she wasn't holding a gun. "You check out," she said. "My name's Rachael."

"Marc," he responded, getting up. His left leg had gone to sleep, and his confident stride across the room to shake hands turned into a clumsy lurch.

"Come this way. People want to talk with you." She shrugged. "Well, they don't *want* to, they've got better things to do, but they're interested in finding out why you're here."

She led him through metal corridors to a conference room lined with fine-grained orange wood from some alien planet. If you could call it wood. Biological material. Whatever. On the other side of an equally orange table sat two middle-aged women and a shaven-headed man, again in that bewildering mash-up of uniforms from different places and different times. Perhaps, he thought, the mash-up was itself a kind of uniform, a statement. He wasn't sure what they thought it represented. Rachel nodded to the three, touched Marc lightly on the arm and left.

"Marc Keislack," the woman in the middle said as he sat down. Her long hair had been coloured in a black and white chequerboard pattern. Her voice had a trace of accent to it, but he couldn't tell from where it came. "Artist. The only artist to have come to the attention of an alien race. The Eridani seem to like you." She frowned. "You appear to have had an eventful time in space recently. That mission was for GalDiv. Are you still working for them?"

For a split second he thought about lying, then remembered they'd accessed his AI. "Not really. I'm working with Kara Jones. We were co-opted by GalDiv – okay, blackmailed – but we've got our own reasons for carrying on. I'm *here* because the GalDiv AI said someone has a device to translate between aliens and humans. It would also be nice to know why the Eridani like my art."

"I know of Kara Jones," the man said. "An artist and an Official Assassin is a strange combination."

Marc smiled. "I'm borderline sociopath. It helps."

"And simulity connected," the man said. "That must make for some interesting dreams."

Marc nodded, feeling cold. That AI data dump meant every detail of his post-AI life was now shared with three strangers. Including the previous night? It had to be.

The second woman spoke for the first time. Her voice was quiet, melodious, her manner as if chatting with a friend. "So tell me, Marc," running her hand over her short dark hair, "what do you think of GalDiv and EarthCent?"

He shrugged. This one was easy. "EarthCent wants to pull everyone together into one big world order, and I think that's a bad thing. GalDiv is driving it through their control of extra-solar trades." He shook his head sadly. "We've lost our ability to innovate by taking alien technological handouts. It's a disaster."

"But you're not an Earth Primus supporter." A statement, not a question.

"We can't ignore aliens, just like Native Americans couldn't ignore settlers from England, but we can be a damn sight cleverer dealing with them."

"And Anson Greenaway? How do you feel about him?"

"He's a good man with an impossible job. He understands the danger of alien tech dominating Earth. My impression is he's against the EarthCent plan for world domination."

A short silence until the woman with the chequerboard hair asked, "What do you think of trading humans for netherspace drives?"

"I think it's obscene," Marc said without hesitation. "So is the call-out fee."

"Strange observation from a borderline sociopath," she said.

"I have my human moments."

The three of them gazed at him. Marc decided they were talking together, AI to AI.

"We are aware of your greater mission," the dark-haired woman finally said. "It accords with the goals of a majority of Wilder factions and groups. You are, of course, not alone in wishing to obtain a translation device. There are several people from the city states at this site waiting for a demonstration. All claim a financial interest. Some are being truthful, some are not. Let me ask you: with your distrust of alien technology and a one-time fear of space itself, why did you never join Earth Primus?"

This time Marc thought before he spoke. "Well, I'm

not a joiner by nature. They always seemed a little frantic and shrill. And there was no way they could succeed." He paused and thought some more. "Maybe they wanted the barriers up between city states, between them and the Wild, too. Maybe Len Grafe and the rest want to be big fish in little ponds. But right now they're trying to kill me. At least, their religious followers are."

"You know why?"

"You know what happened on that planet? Between us and the Cancri?" He saw them nod. "Well, it opened up a new can of writhing opportunities. It showed that humans and aliens *can* co-operate, that there's all manner of opportunities out there. Real ones, not the shit EarthCent pushes to solve the city state population problem. It showed we belong out there, too. And that goes against everything Earth Primus preaches. That's why they want me and Kara dead. That's why we're going Up soon as."

"Not because you're being blackmailed?"

Marc felt his temper go, and didn't try to stop it. "Kara's *desperate* to know what happened to her sister," he said, his voice rising. "She was a call-out fee, got taken. I need to know *why* a pre-cog called Tse thought I could help Kara *save the fucking Earth*!" He glared angrily at them. "No more fucking *games*! You know what I met last night. You know better than me. I have *no* idea what the hell's going on, only that I'm involved up to my neck. Oh, I *do* know there's something very nasty out there that'll suck the life out of all of us. Now, is there a translation device and can I see it?"

He stopped, breathing heavily, all recent frustrations and

fears expressed in less than a hundred words. "One other thing I know, or suspect," he continued quietly, "city states think of the Wild as a primitive, back to nature place. Parts of it are. Mostly those close to a city state. There's a surprise. But beyond that you're more technically advanced than the city states. Alien tech. Difference being, you're far more choosy. And I'd bet you don't swap humans for sideslip-field generators… unless they're staters who pissed you off. In fact, I think you use the cities to maybe test out tech you're not sure of. You guys are the tail wagging the GalDiv dog. And you'd been dealing with aliens long before the Gliese showed up." He sat back with a what-the-hell, had-to-be-said expression on his face.

< *That told them. You got their respect.*

> *You think?*

< *If we're still alive in five minutes, yes.*

> *What's this "we"?*

The woman with chequerboard hair leaned forward. "How much of that was you, Kara or Jeff?"

"Mostly me *and* Kara. Check my AI."

< *Polite to ask first.*

> *Shut up.*

"We believe you. And you're ninety per cent right. We're not sure why you were chosen, either. As Jeff told you, Tse never knew himself. What you need to understand, Marc, is that Tse is revered by those Wilders who knew and worked with him. Meanwhile there is a device and shortly you will see it. But a warning: do not be surprised by who else is there. Now," her voice softening, "when did you last eat?"

It was Rachael who took him to a deserted canteen for a bowl of a rich beef stew. Marc hadn't realised there were cattle in Iceland and said so. Apparently, Iceland now grew and raised all its own food, using a combination of alien tech and geothermal energy. In fact, the Wild was the major food producer on the planet. But that wasn't beef. It was pilot whale – now thankfully free of mercury contamination, another triumph for Wilder tech – from the Faroe Islands, who still took half a dozen pilot whales each year. But, she added thoughtfully, Marc shouldn't worry about animal welfare. The Faroese only took the oldest bull whales and death occurred instantly. These days there were no spinal lances and harpoons to be found outside a museum. Then she produced his travelling bag and took him to a warm bathroom where he could shit, shower and shave. Rachael was waiting for him in the canteen. And so was Kara, which didn't surprise him that much, they *had* travelled to the same island. But as for the person standing nervously beside her…

"Hey, Marc," Kara said, smiling. She was wearing black combat gear complete with weapons belt and a combat rucksack. "Guess who I found washed up on the beach." There was a warmth in her voice that went beyond mere friendship.

Marc stared at Tatia Nerein. "What the fuck!"

"Gracious as ever," Tatia said to Kara. "How do you put up with him?" As if the two women shared a secret about Marc.

Last seen, Tatia had much of the warrior goddess about her. Now her blonde hair was tamed and cut fashionably short, the blue eyes dyed temporary gold. From neck to knees she wore a loose, silk-like shift with a life of its own, all the colours in the universe coruscating without pattern, the fabric moving to briefly outline a specific curve of her body before falling still until the next time. Her arms and legs were bare, her feet shod – barely – with tiny golden sandals that matched her eyes. But the challenging, what-the-hell-are-you-looking-at expression was the Tatia of old, as was the way it dissolved into a rueful grin.

"Yeah, well," she said. "They got me on the way home from a party. Never had time to change. I'll AI you. It's quicker."

Marc sees in his mind's eye. *Dawn in Seattle. The luxury jitney pulls up outside Tatia's apartment building. She gets out, suddenly aware of two men running towards her, strange, stubby guns in their hands. She knows some fear, but mostly anger. The men stop and crumple to the pavement. A woman appears, a more conventional gun in her hand. "You're on a hit list," the woman – forties, forgettable – says. "Greenaway sent me. Here." She hands Tatia a vid-phone. Greenaway stares out of it, relieved. "You have to go Up until this is over," he says. "With Kara and Marc. Anyway, they need you." This last is a lie, Tatia knows, because those two are so self-sufficient it hurts. But it somehow makes her believe in the urgency and not to waste time. Besides, she's discovered that being incredibly wealthy on Earth is no substitute for kicking alien arse in space. This is probably immature, she knows, but it's still true. So, with only her evening clutch bag for company, Tatia Nerein is taken to Tacoma space access point where a private jet is ready to go. They refuel in Ottawa-Toronto. She speaks once more to Greenaway who only says all will be explained in Iceland.*

"Not Iceland!" Tatia says, then, "Who's trying to kill me?"

Which is not an unreasonable thing to ask, given the circumstances.

"Earth Primus and associated religious fundamentalists," he says. "Kara and Marc will explain."

The jet is a VTOL so it has no problem landing on a god-forsaken pile of scrap metal in the North Atlantic. But it's cold! A woman called Rachael is waiting, hustles her inside where she finds Kara, looking both worried and pissed off. Kara explains the background, as she understands it, adds that she's in Iceland to get an SUT for herself and Marc but hey, one more passenger won't make a difference, love the hair and the eyes but that dress is making her dizzy, and what the hell is Greenaway up to?

It took about six seconds. Marc was left with a slight headache that quickly faded.

> *Her AI don't half rabbit on.*

< *Be nice.*

"You look great," Marc said to Tatia. "And I at least like the dress."

"Creep," Kara said. "Okay. I gather we're all to go see a demonstration of an alien/human translation device."

"Like this?" Tatia asked, fluttering her dress, which immediately went mad with colour. "I won't be a *little* conspicuous?"

Rachael had been standing off to one side, quietly observing. Now she moved to take Tatia by the arm. "We'll be five minutes."

Marc waited until they'd left. "I saw the way you looked at her," he said to Kara, keeping his voice light. "Did you have a thing on the way home on the *RIL-FIJ-DOQ*?"

"We did," Kara admitted. "Not a big thing."

"I turned her down, you know. I was being nice."

"I know. We both thought you were mad. It wasn't that she only wanted comfort, you dummy. She wanted sex with Marc Keislack. Still does, by the way she looked at *you*." And then, seeing the expression on his face, "She's not the only one. But we have to keep it buttoned until this is over. Too distracting, right?"

Marc nodded. Not easy, but had to be done. "You think Tatia knows that Greenaway's her father?"

"We're not sure ourselves…"

"Like to bet against it? They've got the same eyes. The same nose. Although hers is a little smaller, obviously. Most of all, they've got the same challenging look. Did you get a SUT?"

"There's one here… Marc, no, I don't know what's going on, not really. But I have to trust Greenaway and these Wilders. So do you. That's an order."

"Can I have that in writing?"

"With my fist if you want."

Kara had said it with a smile but Marc knew the truth. For her the mission was only second to keeping her people safe. And if Kara had to beat the crap out of Marc to safeguard either, she would. And afterwards bandage him with care and affection.

"So why are you all tooled up?" he asked, referring to her clothes and weapons.

"Well, I had them with me and Rachael suggested they might be useful."

Marc remembered what he'd been told about the demonstration. "On account of some people not being who they say?"

213

Kara nodded. "It's a set-up of some sort. But if the Wild wanted us dead, we would be." She took off the rucksack, opened a side pouch and produced two hand weapons. "Hold it in your hand and press the green button. That slaves it to your AI. If there's a spot of bother, the simulity will take over. The AI will figure out the most immediate danger, the simulity lets you deal with it the best possible way. I relived your fight at Bristol. You did seriously well. This system makes you even better."

A minute or so later she was explaining the same to Tatia, now wearing similar black combat gear. Marc felt overdressed in his cold-weather coat and trousers.

Rachael led them back through the metal corridors and up a set of stairs into the wet, salty outside air. A space utility transport just like the old *RIL-FIJ-DOQ* now sat in the centre of the open space in the centre of the free spacers' base: a collection of metal shipping containers with doors cut into their sides, all linked together in random ways by plastic tubes. Metal rods tipped with sensors and antennas sprouted in all directions from mounts on every available surface. A large airlock projected from one shipping container, with a ramp leading down to the metal deck. Marc could just see the blue discs of the SUT's updown-field generators beneath it. The vehicle looked exactly like the ones in Berlin. Ground crew in one-piece protective suits and helmets stood around, spraying the SUT with foam from tanks on their backs. As in Berlin the foam expanded on contact with the air, filling the nooks and crannies between the shipping containers right up to the level of the sensors and antennas. By the time Marc had crossed the side of what he now realised was a launch area, the SUT had vanished inside its protective cocoon. It was a much simpler version of the highly professional exercise carried out at GalDiv-operated space access points, but it seemed to have the same effect. Presumably foam was foam, and whoever was inside the SUT would receive the same level of protection from the rigours of netherspace. Which, Marc reflected ruefully, wasn't anywhere near as much protection as he would have liked.

A stairwell led down into a warren of metal corridors. They passed what seemed to be a crew lounge carpeted with faded tiles. Vending machines lined the walls. Down at the end of a long corridor lit by flickering atomic globes, they stopped in front of a closed door with a rubber seal around the frame. Off to one side, a DNA scanner sat attached to the wall. Rachael placed her hand flat against it, and the door slowly opened with a clicking of electronic locks. The three of them stepped through the doorway into an airlock. The door in front of them was closed, sealed. Marc turned to see Rachael's expressionless face vanish as the outer door shut with a slight hiss. By the time he turned back, the one ahead of him had opened. They stepped forward into a vast, darkened area. One entire wall consisted of what seemed to be transparent metal cubes, stacked up four high and ten across. Each cube was perhaps four metres on a side, and each one had an occupant.

An alien.

More aliens in one place than most humans had ever seen.

Three Eridani, like bamboo eels with a spiral row of

spindly arms running along their length.

Two piled-up Gliese.

Four Cancri "dogs" and five Cancri "grub riders" separated from each other.

Something resembling a cross between a large lion and a bright orange cone lying on its side, held up by four stubby legs, ending in a blunt tail-like point at one end and a massive globe made of something like cracked bone at the other, set in the "cup" of the cone.

A creature like a big blue rugby ball with tentacles sprouting from each end.

At the far left-hand side, at the bottom of the stack, one of the aliens Marc had seen twice in recent days: a gnarled trunk separating top and bottom into stubby branches that divided into thin, twig-like limbs.

The air smelled like an explosion that had taken out a spice warehouse and a bathroom products factory in one go.

"It's a prison," Tatia whispered. "A prison for aliens."

"It's not that big," Kara said. "It has to be a projection."

< *Enlarged hologram. The actual lab is the other side of the bulkhead. Or wall.*

"I just got told—" Marc was cut off.

"So did I." Kara.

"Me too." Tatia.

"One AI to rule them all," Kara said. "That's mine. The other two shut up for now."

< *Do it. She's boss.*

As his eyes got used to the gloom Marc saw there were between twenty and thirty people seated in two separate blocs, all staring up at the screen. Some wore combinations of various uniforms like the free spacers; some were dressed in bohemian garb like the Wilders; some wore military uniform. Seventeen guests in the front row wore the same black, logo-free uniforms: obvious, Marc thought lightly, a coach party come in from somewhere for the day. The man in the centre glanced at Marc as he passed; something about his eyes seemed familiar to Marc, although he was sure they'd never met before.

The picture changed to show a laboratory, with crated aliens against the far wall. In the foreground men and women in white coats were busy tending equipment, communing with their AIs or talking to each other. A small group were clustered around a device about the size of a jitney that stood in the centre of the room. It was stark white in colour and would have looked at home in the lobby of a major corporation; art designed to impress, not to enjoy. A closer examination showed that the device comprised a series of octagonal frames of various sizes, each one connected to the next largest and next smallest by rotating connections offset from all the others. Theoretically the whole thing could probably fold flat, but the octagons were set relative to each other in a haphazard, lopsided arrangement. It floated above a white hexagonal dais from which thick cables snaked off in various directions across the room.

One of the scientists – forties, thin faced, yellow hair and goatee beard – walked forward and addressed his audience.

"My name's Brennan. Sorry you can't be in here – this lab's in isolation. We've a few hitherto unknown aliens. First, we'll demonstrate alien-to-alien communication.

Then a brief explanation of how it works. Then human to alien, when you can ask questions. After that I'll hand over to our commercial director. Oh, and in case you wondered," he smiled, "no aliens were injured in developing this device."

A massive mechanical arm unfolded from a housing in the ceiling. It looked like a spider's leg replicated on a massive scale. Slowly it pivoted and extended until the claw-like gripper on the end slid into hidden slots around a transparent cube holding an alien. The occupant – four separate head-sized nodes linked by thick connectors that looked like melted wax and surrounded by a halo of waving fronds, which could be legs or arms or both – started to shake.

The mechanical arm pulled the cube smoothly out of its housing and brought it down to a spot next to the multiple-octagon device. Then moved back up and selected another cube – this one housing a Cancri hound. It placed the cube on the other side of the device.

Which started to rotate.

Octagons briefly whirled within octagons before settling into a new arrangement. This one looked more angular, more symmetrical than the last one.

For a long moment, nothing happened. Then the Cancri hound moved towards the side of the cube closest to the device and, on the other side, the unidentified alien. The Cancri hound tilted its head as if considering and then its triangular black tongue – a physical feature Marc remembered well – flickered in and out of its snout. Marc wasn't sure, but he thought the tip of the tongue seemed to be adopting various shapes, almost too fast to follow.

And then it stopped.

At once the set of octagons began to rotate around each other like an insane geometric orrery, orientating themselves in planes like several intersecting flat sheets.

There was a deep rumbling from below. Dust on the floor around the device rose into the air, shivering, hanging there until the rumbling stopped, when it began a slow drift down to the floor again.

The alien creature that was all fronds and nodes, a cross between footballs and brains, began to shake again. The nodes vibrated like a struck bell.

"Communication," Brennan commented. "The Cancri sends out a signal, the device translates, the Keplan understands and replies. And so a conversation ensues."

"One we can't bloody understand." A loud male voice; one of the seated observers.

The audio was two-way.

Brennan looked hurt. "We can translate from Cancri into English as well, or Keplan into English. We just have to choose the appropriate settings."

The conversation had finished. The metal arm returned first the Cancri, and then the Keplan, to their slots in the matrix.

Marc wondered if the conversations were all similar. "The food here's terrible, isn't it?" "And the portions are so small." "Seen that blob in cell eighteen? Does nothing but shiver every night."

< Kara says keep the jokes for later and just concentrate.

The translation device returned to what seemed to be its

rest state, all octagons lined up so that it was completely flat. Brennan walked into the centre of the screen. "Okay, folks," he said loudly, rubbing his hands together in pride. He looked like a parent whose child had recited a poem at a school concert. "You're probably asking yourselves how it works. The exact process is confidential. But I can say that we use a chain of discrete and isolated artificial intelligences linked together. Any communication goes from the first alien to the first AI in the chain, which has already spent a year on that alien's home world, observing all the signals sent by the natives and any actions that result. As a result the AI has developed a good understanding of how signals connect to actions. Over the course of a year it becomes closer, as it were, to the aliens than to humans – or any other race. We transfer the output from that AI to another one which has spent only nine months on that world and three months on a different one. The output from that AI goes to an AI that's spent six months on the first world and six months on the second one. This continues until we have a string of AIs able to translate in increments."

"How do you test for sustained accuracy?" a woman asked.

Brennan visibly preened. "We check every pair-combination in a continuing phase one test. We're currently running each specific combination a hundred times for phase two statistical validity. Everything logged: whether communication took place, the length of time if it did, number of times each party communicated, length of any gaps, any repetitions. When it's finished the program will give a comprehensive overview of how well the translator works. Now, you'll want to see a human interact with an alien." He gestured to one of the technicians. "Get the Keplan." He glanced at the audience. "That's the designation of the star system it comes from." He smiled. "Most people call them Ents."

The Ent was the alien with the gnarled, tree-trunk-like body split top and bottom into knobby branches from which sprouted multiple twig-like limbs. The screen moved closer, showing that the bark-like corrugations on its surface were separate, like a jerkin, with areas of granular lavender skin beneath. The twig-like limbs were more like straight tentacles or lengths of springy bone. No face, no eyes, were obvious.

Brennan stood on one side of the device. The Ent in its box was positioned on the other. Brennan looked out at an audience now craning forward in their seats. "Who has a question?" he asked.

A clamour broke out, only stopping when Brennan held up his hand for silence. "I caught a few but this might be the most relevant." Turning to face the Ent he asked loudly, "What would you like to trade with us?"

A few seconds after Brennan had spoken Marc felt a shiver run through him. Then another, but the second one was subtly different from the first. A third, a fourth, a fifth shiver followed; all distinct from one another.

After a long pause, the Ent's thin, pale upper "limbs" began to tremble. They stopped, and a moment later a synthesised voice spoke in a monotone.

"Miniaturisation technology," it said simply. "Device for making physical objects smaller."

A man in the group nearest to Marc stood up. "That was my question and the technology is theoretically impossible," he said. "If you push the atoms closer together the object becomes smaller and smaller but still weighs the same. If you remove energy from the atoms themselves to shrink their orbits then they become unstable and disintegrate."

"Too complex," Brennan said. "Stay simple."

The Ent seemed to get the gist, however. After a long pause, a lot of shivers running through the audience like the first intimations of a plague and then a lot of twitching of Ent limbs, the synthesised voice replied: "Not those things. Space containing the object is moved further away in higher or lower dimension. Object still same size in absolute space but smaller relatively in this space. Perspective."

An intake of breath around the audience. They were rapt. They wanted that.

"And what," the man said eagerly, "would you take in exchange?"

Another silence and then: "The things we do not have."

Brennan took over. "That's enough. I don't want to tire our friend here out." He gestured to one of the technicians to return the Ent. "I imagine you got the gist. Conversation is possible."

The man who'd asked the question was still on his feet. "Okay. I see it for sound-based communication. But colour? Perhaps the electromagnetic spectrum? How did that Ent thing understand my question? Your device doesn't have any wavy tentacles."

Brennan opened his mouth. But whatever he was about to say was cut short when the seven black-garbed men in the front row sprang to their feet, brandishing weapons. The deafening sound of gunfire broke the scientific calm as they fired into the air. Light globes exploded in expanding galaxies of shattered glass and glowing radionucleotides. Dust drifted down from the ceiling.

< *Kara says get down, become small and harmless.*

Marc was already there.

Simulity took over. Ten were trained soldiers, probably mercenaries. Seven were not. All had weapons.

Overhead lights snapped on.

One of the non-soldiers began screaming about an abomination. One of the soldiers fired a second burst over the heads of the other group, by now cowering on the floor.

< *Kara says take out the trained men first. Marc, you have furthest to the right, Kara has centre, Tatia closest to left.*

The gun was in his hand. All he had to do was look at an individual. Then his AI and simulity took over. Three shots, three men down. He saw four more taken out by Kara, three by Tatia. All ten were dead or seriously wounded within four seconds.

The non-soldiers, fanatics, froze for a moment, then turned towards them.

< *Kara says fuck it, them too.*

Seven shots. No more fanatics standing.

The silence was shocking after the sounds of death.

"Stay down," Kara shouted to the unharmed group, told Tatia to watch them and led Marc to check out the attackers.

Mostly head or chest shots. A couple in the stomach. One had only been hit in the shoulder, enough to disable, but not to kill. Marc thought he looked familiar.

"Len Grafe," Kara said. "Earth Primus head prick."

Grafe stared up at them. "There will be vengeance," he groaned.

"Too bad you won't be here to see it," Kara said and shot him in the head. She looked at Marc. "We just took out the Earth Primus top people and a few religious leaders. I said it was a set-up."

They glanced across, to where a few of the other group were beginning to sit up under Tatia's watchful gaze. The airlock doors opened and Wilders poured in. Within minutes the survivors had been hustled away, leaving the dead bodies and the confused behind. Plus Rachael, who walked smiling towards them.

"You did well."

"We were meant to," Kara said. "Going to tell us?"

"Is there really a device?" Marc demanded.

"Who do I sue?" said Tatia.

Rachael held up her hands. "Easy. No, there isn't a device. It was a ruse to get Earth Primus here. Grafe has been in hiding for over a year. We figured that only this could lure him out, along with his main religious allies. Curiously enough we *are* trying to develop inter-species communication along the lines Brennan detailed. We're at least twenty years away from success, and that's optimistic. The AIs either go native or mad. That man was right, you see. The device was so much window dressing. The lab doesn't exist. The only real aliens were the Ent, Cancri and Keplan. Plus a Gliese that showed up the other day and wouldn't leave. The rest are holos."

"You did all this just so we could kill some bad guys?"

Marc began to feel anger rise.

"It's cleverer than that," Tatia said and looked at Rachael. "May I?"

"Please."

"The whole thing's been recorded. Pretty soon it'll be all over worldmesh. How terrorists attacked a peaceful conference of Wilders, aliens and city staters. Luckily a heroic artist, an heiress and a former soldier saved the day. Something like that. Earth Primus discredited, its network with the fundamentalists in disarray. Len Grafe exposed as a killer. Oh, and these saviours are all city staters. So no muttering about trigger-happy Wilders." She shrugged. "I mean, this is a major operation, had to take months to set up. But that's more or less it, right?"

Rachael nodded. "It's a bit more – a hell of sight more – complex and subtle than that. Still, you got the basics. Clever."

Marc asked the obvious. "The survivors? How do you keep them on side?"

Kara gave the answer. "They all think they've seen a genuine translation device, or system. They'll have been promised first refusal when it's up and running. They'll all be traders of some sort, probably off-world. There'll be new deals offered with Wilder colonies. Very neat. Except we could have been killed."

Rachael shook her head. "A combination of simulity and AI gave you a sixty per cent advantage over the mercenaries. We are extremely thorough."

"I don't have either," Tatia said.

"You're a warrior queen," Marc told her. "That's all you need." He felt a little light-headed, as if the past few minutes had all been a dream. "So now what?"

"Now you go Up as planned. Anyway, the media will hound you if you stay on Earth. You have the SUT on deck." She saw Marc's expression. "No, sorry, not one of our spacecraft. The controls are different. Come on. Sooner you're away the better."

Rachael led the way back through the airlock and then onto a very cold and windswept deck. The SUT was now completely covered in foam, the main airlock still open as figures carried large cubes inside.

"And what are those?" Kara asked in a suspiciously soft voice.

"Ent, Cancri and the Gliese," Rachael said casually. "We'd like you to drop them off home on your way. Now, I'm to tell you that Marc's simulity will enable him to be the engineer. Kara will navigate. Tatia can sing to the aliens."

"How the fuck do we know where to go?" Marc asked.

"It's all in your head. Ask your AI."

<True, boss. Suddenly we have the co-ordinates of all necessary planets.

Kara looked at Rachael. "I do not like being hustled. I do not like my people put in danger. Tell Greenaway he's on notice. So are you. If I leave anyone out there, you will both answer personally to me. And if you know anything, you know I always return from a mission." All said in a quiet, conversational tone that nonetheless made Rachael take a step back. Kara nodded, gestured to the other two to follow and walked up the ramp.

11

"Hi there and welcome to *BLO-LOC-TAL*." The voice was female, a little smug and unbearably cheerful. "Please call me Tally. I'm an exploratory SUT and so *thrilled* to have you as guests."

Kara, Marc and Talia glanced at each other with varying expressions of disgust. They were standing in the SUT's foyer, airlock doors already closing behind them. The only other SUT they'd known, the curry-scented *RIL-FIJ-DOQ*, had a foyer dedicated to a very reluctant hero and his descendant, the DOQ's ill-fated mission manager... a man who'd become a reluctant hero while heavily drugged and strapped to a stretcher.

"Of course," the voice continued, "I have *no* idea where we're going – can't *wait* to find out! – so could the navigator please come to the control room when you've settled in, *please*? Well, I *say* control room but I like to think of it as our own private place. We'll clear the atmosphere in one hour so no rush. Now, exploratory SUTs are a *little* different to transport and freight." The voice sounded coy. "We think of ourselves as the *cream de la cream*. Better relaxation facilities. More comfortable accommodation. Well, you'll find out. So, if you'd like to move forward into the corridor – not a companionway, I'm a SUT not a ship and *proud* of it – I'll lead you to your rooms."

All three stood where they were.

"I'll do it," Kara said.

> *Can you get it to shut the fuck up?*

< *Annoying?* her AI asked. It sounded as if it was trying not to laugh.

> *Is this someone's idea of a joke?*

< *Configured by the last exploring team. They'd been Up for two years. They went a bit odd. They liked to be nannied.*

> *Do something. Anything.*

The SUT spoke again. "Come on people, let's get you comfortable... oh. This is strange... Okay, I will only address your individual AIs. If that's what you..."

Marc shook his head. "This is not a good way to start a mission."

"I don't think the last one ever stopped," Tatia told him. "Do you?"

The SUT was right about the *TAL*'s accommodation. Three times the size of the cabins on the *DOQ*, a double bed, armchair, extra-large vid screen and a separate bathroom with a whirlpool bath, shower, toilet and a curiously ornate bidet.

> *Bidet?* Kara asked.

< *Again, the last crew. They became fastidious, even obsessive about personal hygiene. And very bored. Two years is a long time to spend Up. Anyway, they had a contest to produce the best bidet. The one in Marc's quarters is shaped like a lion's head.*

> *Who won?*

< *They never decided.*

> *So where are they now?*

< *All four of them walked into netherspace between Earth and the moon. So I have no idea where or even what they are now.*

> *Incidents of explorer and survey crews walking into netherspace?*

< Classified.

> Tell Twist to fuck off.

< Thirty-five point seven six explorer and survey crew currently walk into netherspace, typically after ten years going Up.

> Point seven six?

< Many request that in the event of death, their remains be jettisoned into netherspace. The figure is an adjustment. I call it sentiment.

> Mortality rates? She wondered why she'd never asked before.

< Fifty-two per cent either die or fail to return.

> And the rest?

< Of the remaining forty-eight per cent, just under a half develop psychoses. They are confined to a GalDiv facility in the Caribbean. The remaining twenty-four point two per cent retire to colony worlds.

Kara thought she had it. GalDiv would retire a crew or an individual when their eyes began to glow weird colours in the dark. A crew going netherspace walkabout could mean a lost SUT and that was wasteful. And they wouldn't want them hanging around Earth, frightening the children and making adults ask questions about GalDiv's competence. What does a race do if it realises it's not important in the scheme of things?

Look at it another way: how many nations, people, bust a gut trying to prove they're relevant, have something to contribute? When the rest of the world doesn't know and wouldn't care if it did? Some drink or drug to oblivion. Others go psycho, and all fade away.

There were fresh uniforms, boots, underwear in a closet.

Kara smiled cynically when she saw the pile of Sniper/ Assassin T-shirts. Of course she was expected. She had been for a good number of years, maybe all her life. She understood that as well. Expected with hope shot through by desperation. You can take a woman to slaughter but you can't make her think. There was never any way of knowing what she'd do. Kara showered, changed and took her insight to the control room, her AI showing the way.

The DOQ's control room had looked like an old-fashioned office that needed fixing with gaffer tape. Run down, seedy, all the effort put into keeping immaculate the shrine to the mission manager's ancestor. This control room was different. Similar displays, buttons, screens, but set in polished mountings whose gleam mirrored the highly polished floor. The crew sat in comfortable sofas with small, repositionable screens on metallic tentacles in front of them. The air smelt as if someone had just used an air freshener. Marc and Tatia were waiting for her, also wearing clean uniforms. One screen showed a slowly vanishing Earth as the SUT came closer to the black despair of an unknown universe.

They sat down in the springy, reclining chairs. Tatia wanted to know what happened if you tried to access netherspace near the Earth's surface. She could have asked her AI but there was sudden awkwardness between the three humans, of things not said or done in the past and that now urgently needed to be both. Small talk might help.

"I can tell you," Marc said. He'd once asked his AI the same question. "You ever hear of Gough Island in the Atlantic?"

Tatia wrinkled her brow. "Maybe... something about a

volcano? The whole thing just blew up? Before I was born."

"No one's blaming you," Kara reassured her and got a look in return. A look to remind Kara that while Tatia was younger and not so lethal, she could still make Kara squirm, and once had, although not with embarrassment.

"Gough Island was a cluster-fuck," Marc said hastily, as if aware that something was happening between the two women and a distraction was needed. "One small island two thousand miles from anywhere. Uninhabited except for a meteorological station. Home to the first experiments on the sideslip-field generator or n-space drive. They suspected it could be dangerous and anyway wanted secrecy. The Gliese traded an engine after allowing one scientist – and only ever one – to travel in a Gliese craft to see how it worked. No. To see how to operate it. Anyway, the experiments were telemonitored via satellite. One moment the engine in a large hangar, people clustered around, instruments beeping and flashing. The engine begins to operate, that arm comes out and moves platens around on the surface. Then nothing… except for a ten-mile-wide and very deep hole in the sea which led to a tsunami that really pissed off Brazil, West Africa and the Caribbean. That's when they realised a sideslip field can extend way beyond the vehicle it's in. And it'll take everything in the field with it. The scientists and the fish never came back. Maybe they're still sloshing around netherspace. Anyway, it's why SUTs never go n-space if they're near each other. And why you don't use sideslip generators on Earth. And why I never went into space until that fucking Greenaway blackmailed me," he said feelingly, "because they still don't know how the damn thing works." He shrugged. "But here I am and once a tiny meteor went past us a billion miles from home, and know what? We've got a lot to say to each other and if we don't it may get difficult."

Tatia frowned. "You two have been together since we got back. I guess you mean me?"

"So why don't our AIs catch us all up?" Kara suggested. "Be easier."

"Except all I got is partying and one piss-poor assassination attempt," Tatia said. "I'm going to feel *so* inadequate."

The others smiled and set their chairs to recline.

"Remember to tell your AIs to go easy," Kara said. "No massive, instant data dumps."

Nods of agreement. As long as they remained in real space their mission wouldn't begin. They did not need to exchange memories to know that all sensed this was not going to be easy. They also needed time to process what had happened less than hour ago. Behind the lightness of tone, the attempt to be normal, the knowledge that they'd been set up.

Forty minutes later, as the moon loomed large on screen, equipment beeping plaintively as it waited for instructions, the three breathed a collective sigh and glanced a little sheepishly at one another. It was one thing to know what a person had done. But to know how they felt at the time, their hopes, fears and exultations, was something else. The trouble was that the data exchange had been more comprehensive than they'd expected, or wanted.

"You tearaway," Tatia said to Marc. "You *biker*."

"What about you guys," Marc said in reply. "When I was sleeping on that last journey home."

"You already knew," Kara said.

"Hey. Hurt outrage. I'm entitled."

Tatia grinned. "You'd turned me down, remember?"

He did. "I was learning to be nice."

"Since when you killed your first man hand to hand," Tatia said. "And now killed more with a gun. I got triumph, some regret, pride and exhilaration." Her face grew serious. "And what the hell did you meet in Scotland? It scares the hell out of me, even second-hand."

Marc sat up to shrug. "Your guess is as good as mine. But I think it's connected to netherspace."

"About killing," Tatia said. "That museum. Kara with a knife. Remind me never to piss you off." Her face went very still. "Oh. I suddenly see… no, I *remember*, that's strange… how Len Grafe and his people died."

She shivered dramatically. "I'd better be well behaved around both of you," she said with all the lightness of a young woman who planned the opposite. She stood up, stretched and looked seriously at them. "Okay. I seem to be attracted to the killers on this SUT. I could forget sex, but I won't since this trip might end badly. I will not die frustrated with regrets. Also, you two are older and therefore responsible for my happiness. So I'm available, but do remember it's always my choice and threesomes are a no-no. Quality not quantity is the ideal." She smiled at two slightly shocked faces. "Okay?"

"If you're sure…" Kara said.

"It seems…" Marc began.

"It's what I want," Tatia said firmly. "Because of what I just said."

So that was that, Tatia installed as the SUT's comfort station, with Kara and Marc left a little sheepish in the face of practicality coloured by possible death.

"One other thing," Tatia said. "Well, two. But first: I get that Marc is the engineer and Kara the navigator and captain. I imagine our AIs can handle medical problems. So what's my job? Despite what I said, the idea of being the SUT's concubine is not too exciting."

Kara stood up to join her. "That's easy. You look after the aliens that were brought on board. We've got to take them home, remember? You got a gift. They're in cargo."

"So I'm a… what was that old word?… a *stewardess*?"

"What was the other thing?"

"The feeling that we're being played. Manipulated. I've had the feeling before, and it's only become more intense since sharing your minds."

Kara sighed. "It's not that simple." She spoke to both Tatia and Marc. "Yes, it's obvious that Tse or someone chose us long ago. Here we are, press-ganged into finding the Originators with death squads searching for us back home. We killed Grafe. Well, I did, but you two will also be blamed. The Wild could have done it themselves, so could GalDiv. But they needed us to be there. Why? Remember how Tse described seeing the future? He only saw stages, stops on the way to an outcome. He saw *what*, but not why or even *how*. All Greenaway and the Wild – and they have to be working together – can do is put us in place. They have no way of knowing if we'll do the right thing.

Obviously we did because here we are. But I do know we're not just cogs, okay? We have choices. However, we *will* do our best because it's necessary and because that's who we are."

It might have been a standard rally-the-troops speech, delivered to two people who knew Kara extremely well. Yet Kara noticed that they sat a little straighter, their expressions more relaxed. Leadership 101: give your people permission to succeed.

Kara's AI spoke to her first.

< *Er, boss? We know how to navigate. And run the engine. All SUT crew AIs do. It's GalDiv's dirty little secret. Well, one of them.*

> *I don't have to do the math?*

< *You have to understand it*, it said a little severely. < *Have to understand what's happening. And many navigators insist on making the calculations. Same for engineers. Perhaps it makes them feel useful.*

< *Surprised you put up with us.*

> *Maybe we like having you around.*

She knew that her AI was simply a very complex program powered by a chip built with alien technology. Humans understood that if they copied the alien design, and used the same materials, then the result was a chip with more memory and computing power than a hundred, a thousand of the largest human-designed computers. Why this should be so was a mystery. Scientists talked about multi-dimensional, quantum computing and ignored the fact that alien-based computers somehow improved human-written programs. It was as if an application on an old desktop computer suddenly provided a full 3D visual while composing good music, telling funny jokes, solving the Riemann hypothesis, Navier-Stokes equations, P versus NP and providing a definitive pronunciation of the word "scone". An AI's "mind" was a load of ones and zeroes chasing each other around at near light speed. It seemed intelligent because it was so damn quick. It had room for a million algorithms that could mimic human behaviour, which also made it seem independent.

There should have been a control. Something that regulated and shaped the chip's activity. But there wasn't. Any more than scientists could detect any major electron activity. Plenty of photons and neutrinos, but thinking how the latter could be involved made humans groan in despair. Similar with the yellow blocks used in simulity training. You could take one apart – risking a small implosion that resulted in a pile of ash, best not to be holding it at the time – but have no further idea of how it functioned. In fact it had been an AI that had suggested what the blocks could be used for in the first instance. When asked how it had known, the AI said it hadn't, it had merely made a guess and got lucky.

Kara usually treated her AI as if it was independently intelligent and liked her. The last one's dying sigh, *You never gave me a name*, would stay with her a long time. Yet in her military past, human soldiers had died in her arms – as had the Gliese she'd killed to save it from vivisection. Live beings, not quantum fields of mysterious energy patterns. Kara found herself wondering what the hell AIs really were. What they thought of humans. Would AIs be a brilliant, bloodless way for aliens to take over Earth? Judging by the look on Marc's face, he'd received the same information and was asking himself similar questions.

"How do they know what we think?" Marc asked. "Are we that simple?"

> *Don't dare answer that. Either of you.*

< *You guessed.* Her AI to both of them.

< *About time.* Marc's AI to both of them.

"Somehow they mirror our minds," Kara told Marc. "And they talk to each other. Exchange information about us."

< *It's for your own good*, her AI said.

Kara spoke out loud for Marc to hear. "Do you even know who or what you are?"

< *Humans have been asking the same question for a long, long time. Got an answer yet?*

But of course she hadn't, not in the sense that Ishmael meant.

"Enough," Kara said quietly. "Now, apparently we have to take our aliens home. I do not like the idea of a galactic jitney service but we're stuck with it." She didn't ask which home world was closest. In netherspace there was no near or far. "Any idea which one will run out of food first?"

< *They want the Ent dropped off first.*

Kara winced. "Dropped off" was so jitney. "I wish it wasn't called that."

"Why?" Marc wanted to know.

"It's from an old book. From before the aliens came. I've got the movie at home."

"And?"

"There are elves."

"Sounds very Wild-like to me," Marc said with feeling.

"I know. Ever notice how smug Wilders can be? Anyway, too late to change. Tatia's problem now."

"About her suggestion—"

"Sounded more like a command. Don't go all noble, Marc. Leave that to the Ents."

Tatia's AI had directed her to the cargo pod with the aliens. She found the Gliese hunkered down in a corner of its cage. The Cancri, hound and bug, also apparently asleep.

The Ent stood in the middle of its cage looking at her.

Without any eyes. Or face.

Nonetheless Tatia knew she was being observed.

This close the Ent's resemblance to a straggly tree was even more pronounced. But that would be as much the jerkin: craggy, knobbly, dark brown and black, like the bark on an oak or an elm. Naked, the Ent would simply be a plump lavender pole with slim, mismatched tentacles at one end and thicker ones at the other.

She wondered how it was observing her. And then her curiosity vanished as a great calm swept over her. A sense of order, of being cherished and protected.

For all her bravado, Tatia secretly lacked self-confidence. Rescuing pilgrims from the Cancri had given her a sense of achievement and, at the time, purpose she'd never known before. Then back to Earth and seemingly abandoned by two people, Marc and Kara, whose opinion of her had come to mean so much. Even reunited, even with them pleased to see her, couldn't resolve the knot of self-doubt at her core.

Until now.

She *was* special.

The Ent had recognised it. Tatia had a new best friend.

"Is yours going to let you play?" Kara teased.

Marc paused on his way to the engine room. "I may move a platen or two. I may decide to supervise. Too bad you never learned to input properly." Then watched with reluctant admiration as Kara's fingers flew across the input tattoo on her forearm.

< *You don't want to know what she said.*

> *I can imagine.*

Kara smiled at him. "Standard comms training."

"What's the point?"

"There wasn't any. Army bullshit. I know Morse code as well."

"They don't really need humans for this, do they?" His gesture took in the universe. "I mean, manning a SUT. AIs could do it just as well. Maybe better."

< *That must have hurt.*

> *Shut up.*

Kara looked thoughtful. "Certainly on local cargo runs. I'll ask Ishmael."

"Who?"

"My AI. Its own idea."

> *Well?*

< *Best for humans to look after the call-out fee. Also netherspace*

doesn't like SUTs without humans. No one knows why.

Kara told Marc. Both stared at each other.

"We don't have one," Marc said. He meant a call-out fee, the human in a medically induced coma, to be exchanged with the Gliese for a new engine if the SUT broke down. "Ishmael just told me we do. In cargo pod three. Want to go look?"

"No! Well, maybe. I don't know." He went away to the engine room, hoping the great globe, the alien colours and sounds would take his mind off the unconscious human in the cargo pod.

Kara's math was better than she pretended. Establishing where they were and where they wanted to go was simple. Turning the data into instructions for the engineer – or his AI – a little more complex but doable. Especially with her AI metaphorically peering over her shoulder. The warning bell rang and five minutes later *TAL* eased sideways into the dimension called netherspace – currently suspected by a few scientists of being the gap between two adjacent universes. She, Marc and Kara met up in crew room.

It was a serious improvement on *RIL-FIJ-DOQ*. That had been squalid with an ever-present smell of curry. This room was ten metres by ten with a high ceiling. One large vid screen, three armchairs and a sofa, a dining table and chairs. A connecting room held a well-equipped kitchen, a fridge with a good collection of fresh food, a deep freeze that seemed to be mostly pizzas, and a cupboard of freeze-dried. Also a tap marked "drinking water" that *TAL*'s AI was eager to explain linked to a thousand-gallon tank in cargo pod one. There'd be no need to recycle their own waste for some time to come.

The atmosphere was curiously light-hearted at first, as they ate pizza and drank a rich Amarone. The kitchen also boasted a good wine cellar and hard liquor cabinet. Marc suspected it had been stocked by the Wild.

"I know explorers and their SUTs are a little bit special," he added. "But I can't see GalDiv springing for a really expensive bottle of wine. Or the brandy to follow." He caught Kara's look. "No problem, I don't intend to get drunk."

"First and last alcohol on this trip," Kara said firmly, as Tatia watched intently. "We're inexperienced space personnel. How was the engine?"

"Same as the *RIL-FIJ-DOQ*. Confusing. I did what my AI said, remembered to duck when that placing arm swung round and that was that. Any idea how long in n-space?"

All Kara could offer was that on their last trip, each drop or sideslip into n-space had lasted an average of three hours, with a minimum of thirty minutes and a maximum of five hours.

"I've checked with the AIs," she said. "They're able to handle all course corrections, exits from and re-entries to n-space, using this SUT's AI – which isn't as stupid as it sounds. Merely annoying. In fact, the last survey team hardly bothered to navigate or operate the engine. Too busy cleaning, I suppose." She paused, then as her voice hardened, "Except when they had an engine failure and needed to exchange a call-out fee for a new engine, when the Gliese showed up."

"How long are survey teams away?" Tatia wanted to know.

"Upwards of a year."

"Just one fee?"

"I asked the same," Kara said with unconcealed contempt. "Apparently survey teams take *at least* ten with them. Head for home when they're down to their last three." She glanced at Marc and Tatia in turn. "When GalDiv recruits fees, survey SUTs are never mentioned. It's all about bread and butter trips in the solar system, or straightforward ones to the colonies. There's at least three hundred survey SUTs at any one time. Three thousand fees who signed on for the simple life. Look, both of you know about my sister, Dee. Marc's got his own reasons, Tatia's been press-ganged so has the right to be pissed. But I also understand, *as you both must*, that this mission is all-important. These Originators are key to Earth's survival. If we can't find them, the world ends up a Gliese colony. If we also find out more about this pre-cog civilisation, so much the better."

She waited for them to nod in agreement. "Good. Now, orders for the mission. If I get killed, Marc takes over. Tatia, make sure your AI knows how to work this SUT in case you're left on your own. In space there'll be four-hour watches, one person at a time, always in the control room. I'll take the first one, then Tatia, then Marc." She smiled a little ironically at them. "Try and get *some* sleep, people. See you later." She was up and gone without a backward glance.

• • • • •

"Not so much unfinished business," Tatia said, getting to her feet. "It never started." She held out her hand. "Come."

Marc had assumed that Tatia would be lithe, agile, even experimental in bed. Instead he found a woman who, while sensual and giving, seemed to be as much in need of comfort as sex. Afterwards she lay across his chest and asked how he'd got involved, which led to Anson Greenaway and GalDiv. She asked what Greenaway was like, had only met him briefly. She wanted to know about the man who might have sent her, all of them, to their deaths.

Marc couldn't tell her much. Greenaway was driven, secretive and following a plan developed by the dead pre-cog, Tse. But he had no idea what sort of man Greenaway was. For that she'd have to ask Kara. They'd both been army, in Special Operations. Kara would better understand him. Marc went back to his own cabin, thinking that what Tatia possessed was an underlying conflict, together with a sadness he didn't understand and had no way of soothing.

As with the *DOQ*, his cabin had a screen that could show the exterior, normal space when they were in it. Never to be turned on when in netherspace, since too prolonged exposure to the colours and patterns-that-were-no-patterns could drive a human insane. But a brief minute or so? As Henk had shown him back on the *DOQ*, and hadn't the subsequent sex been incredible? Maybe he should have suggested it to Tatia.

He could feel netherspace calling to him. Was that dangerous?

Crap! It's only an energy field. Or a place. Something. A few seconds will do no harm.

Marc sat in front of the vid screen and told his AI to turn it on.

The same incredible colours, writhing as if they were alive. Forming patterns that couldn't be... *except there they were!* Right of centre, a pattern in the shape of an oval, with dark spots that could be eyes... a nose... mouth...

Marc saw his own face staring back at him and screamed.

Tatia had showered after Marc left, then with only an hour or so before her watch, went to visit her Ent.

Her Ent. There was already a bond between them.

She found it leaning over a large bowl of dark liquid, apparently drinking with several of its upper branches. It straightened as she approached and again Tatia knew it was looking at her. At least, aware of her.

Again, that wonderful sense of peaceful order, with a special place for her.

No stress, no demands on her, no expectations.

The anger and confusion went away. She could examine another person's memory calmly, without the sudden pain in her gut.

"Does she know she's Greenaway's daughter?"

"We're not sure ourselves."

But they both were, her comrades, friends, the memory held conviction and with it sympathy. She'd been told her parents were dead. Or vanished somehow. She'd been found walking alone out of the Wild. Adopted by a very wealthy couple who inconveniently died young. But somehow, as kids do, she'd clung to the idea that her real parents were still alive. Now she knew that one of them was. Anson Greenaway, head of GalDiv and the man responsible for sending her to fuck knows where. Did he know Tatia was his daughter? Had to. Then why not say anything? The answer wasn't difficult to figure out. Because it was all part of the plan thought up by the dead Tse. A plan more important than a daughter's happiness. Well, fuck you, daddy dearest. That plan is *so* not safe with me.

Except Kara and Marc. Comrades, friends, lovers. She couldn't harm them. Her stating the rules of who slept with whom was not only bravado, or wanting to assert herself. She was genuinely fond of both and thought them extremely attractive... so very different from wealthy do-nothings or the latest society sensations who usually shared her bed.

But Kara and Marc were also the enemies of peace and order.

No problem. They'd come around. People always did.

A bell rang. Time to go on watch. Tatia stood up. For the first time she realised that the Cancri was hiding away in the far corner of its cage, as if frightened of her. Or the Ent.

Marc knelt half-slumped against the toilet. Intense nausea had swept over him even as he'd screamed at his own image in netherspace. He'd barely made it to the bathroom.

He could still sense netherspace calling to him. Despite the horror, he was attracted. It was similar, but so very different, to the presence he'd felt the previous night; the primeval force that had accepted him. Yet the connection between him and it, between him and netherspace, or *something* in netherspace, was on a level too fundamental for advanced thought. Marc rinsed his mouth and ran the shower.

< *Better now?*

> *What did you see?*

< *See? Nothing. I don't, except through your eyes. I am aware of a disturbance deep in your cerebrum and then what can only be described as a tidal flash that resonated throughout the EM field you call a mind. I could not decipher or experience it. Basically, you're on your own. Oh, vomiting is a common reaction to intense shock and fear. Your medical signs are all healthy.*

> *What did you see in netherspace?*

< *The usual. Colours. Or rather, a pattern-less infinity of EM wavelengths. One that looked vaguely like a human face. It didn't last.*

Marc breathed heavily.

> *Have you told Kara's AI?*

< *Kara and you are simulity linked. Yes, she knows. Apparently her reactions are mixed annoyance, concern, amusement and relief that we're not damaged.*

So now he and his AI had become a "we". Like having an annoying elder brother. Marc stepped out of "their" clothes and into the shower.

It took Kara five minutes to show Tatia how to keep watch: monitor the screens every half hour to check with her AI that the SUT was functioning. It was not necessary, but it would help keep Tatia alert. No matter how efficient the AI, never assume it couldn't make a mistake. Or be hacked, as had happened to GalDiv's Twist. No problem if Tatia wanted to listen to music or watch a vid. But make sure her AI was primed to wake her up if she fell asleep.

"Right. I need to check on Marc," Kara finished,

Tatia frowned, wondering if that meant a kiss-by-kiss description of recent events.

Kara guessed. "Er, no. I don't do voyeur. Silly bastard looked at netherspace. Made him ill. Do not even think of doing the same. In fact, I've instructed the SUT's AI to disable all exterior cameras when we enter n-space. Have a good watch. Marc will relieve you in three hours and fifty minutes."

"Can I check on the aliens?"

"Via vid-feed. Don't leave the control room. There's a toilet behind that door. Your AI can arrange for food, drink, entertainment with the SUT's AI. How are the aliens anyway?"

"Oh, fine," Tatia said casually. "One thing. They all seem to have food for the journey."

"That'll be the free spacers."

"Who have to know more about aliens than GalDiv. Is that strange?"

Kara shook her head. "Nothing's strange. You're right, though. Free spacers and the Wild know a hell of a sight more than we do."

•　•　•　•　•

Kara AI'd ahead that she was coming to see him. Marc sounded less than impressed, claiming tiredness. Kara promised to sing him a lullaby and broke the connection. On the way she thought about Tatia, who now seemed more thoughtful and relaxed than before. Had Marc worked magic? Hardly. It would take more than a single sexual encounter. It was more likely that Tatia was becoming at ease with both her surroundings and the mission that had been pushed on her. Perhaps she was remembering her time as the leader of the revolt against the Cancri. All the same, it might be a good idea to watch her for a while, because of the Cancri. It was in a cage, but still perhaps a reminder of a bad time. Yet Tatia seemed unfazed.

She reached Marc's cabin to find the door ajar, so she didn't bother to knock. Marc lay on his bed, wearing combat trousers and a T-shirt.

"Don't tell me," he said, sounding both annoyed and sorry for himself.

Kara shook her head. "You fucked up."

He sat up. "There was a picture of me out there."

"So your AI said." She waited.

"Look. I'm sorry."

Kara nodded and sat on the end of the bed. "No, you look. Netherspace is dangerous. Are you addicted?"

"It has a definite fascination," Marc admitted. "But no."

"Okay. After this mission is over you can do what the fuck you like. Go play tag with the n-space boojums. But for now you stay the hell away. The outside cameras are now disabled, will be every time we go n-space. Understand?"

He looked at her for a long time then shrugged.

"There is an attraction, like I said. I guess because of an earlier exposure—"

"When you fucked the ass off the medic," she broke in, deliberately crude. "I got that. But hey, I had my moment with him i

n the engine room. And yes, I'm curious and apparently my eyes go a little n-space during sex, but I am not going to visit it in any way and you were an idiot for trying. Marc, we never talked military stuff. But I have to know I can rely on you one hundred and ten per cent. There's no room for doing your own sociopathic, artistic thing." She smiled. "You have to be a warrior. Can you do that?" She meant the bond that went far beyond sibling loyalty.

"I can."

She waited, aware he needed to say something else.

"This... this thing with netherspace," he began awkwardly. "And the other night, that... thing again. Why the fuck me, Kara? *Why the fuck me?*" The cry of the soldier down the ages.

He'd used a diminutive, Kara. A sign of intimacy, affection. A sign of need. "You'd know better than I do."

"*I don't!*"

"You're more of a scientist than me. What do you think?"

He shrugged a little helplessly. "Intelligent EM fields? Quantum consciousness? The universe one vast information exchange? Something science hasn't even envisaged yet? It could be anything."

"Exactly. You got it."

"Make sense, Kara. Please."

"It could be anything. It's a big, big universe, Marc.

Anything can happen. Look, you just said *intelligent.* Has anyone defined what intelligence *really* is? What is this thing called the *mind*? There is no shame in not knowing. Get a grip. You're alive. People are relying on you. I rely on you. You are not going to let us down by going all soft on me. But, you want to deal better with these... things, give 'em a name. Call the netherspace boojum Boris; why not? What's a good name for force, the presence you met in Scotland?"

Marc began laughing. "I don't know... Kirsty maybe?"

"There you go. Boris and Kirsty. You can tell 'em to fuck off. Ignore them. Whatever."

He made a face. "Until they zap me."

"Getting zapped is what happens to us." She stood up. "Get some sleep. We'll eat with Tatia in the control room before you go on watch."

Kara left, feeling sad. Yes Marc would risk his life for her, for Tatia, maybe even for the mission. But one day either netherspace or what he'd met in Scotland would claim him and he'd go. And nothing to be done about it.

Tatia watched on the vid display as Marc stripped naked, got into bed and turned out the light. She felt no shame in watching him and Kara. She only wanted to help. To bring them the same sense of peace that she was feeling. They weren't ready yet, but maybe soon. She checked the vid screen that showed the aliens. Interesting. The Ent was pressed against the side of its cage. One of its upper branches had elongated, now extended into the cage holding the Cancri, which was again squeezed in a corner, away from the thin branch flicking and darting in its direction. Tatia thought it was sad. The Ent only wanted to be friends but the Cancri couldn't see it. Maybe she could put them together? Then remembered that the cages were electronically locked, controlled by the SUT's AI, so if she did open them Kara would know and might be angry. Or maybe the Cancri had been bad and the Ent was telling it off. Whatever. Tatia picked a rom-dram vid from the SUT's library and settled down to enjoy the rest of her watch.

They ate together, as Kara had ordered. Subdued atmosphere, for each had a lot to consider. Discussed the mission a little, wondered how soon before the Ent's planet fall, made a few weak jokes, then the two women left.

For one point three seconds Marc considered watching their cabins. But they might not have sex and if they did, that would make him... it would make him like the old Marc Keislack who once used live insects to create art. He was no longer that man. Marc missed the arrogance, the solitude that had given him purpose and the space to breathe. On the other hand, the old Marc would never get to know entities called Kirsty and Boris. They'd interfere with his art. So Marc deliberately cut the feed.

> *And tell the SUT AI no peeking.*

< *It did with you.*

> *Wipe the images!*

< *Sure, boss. But memories stay forever.*

So, an AI's memories were separate from what it

recorded. Or it simply never forgot anything, but only censored specific images. Meaning it was independent.

< Well done, boss. Not many people know that.

Afterwards, Kara knew that was the last time she'd be with Tatia. It had almost seemed obligatory, after Tatia had earlier set out the rules. Instead of an eager, lascivious young woman, Kara had found one who was quiet, reflective and more nurse than lover. And while it wasn't said, she was a woman saying goodbye to who she had been.

Kara stroked Tatia's hair. The only person with whom she really wanted sex was on watch, possibly obsessing about two entities called Kirsty and Boris.

"Was that okay?" Tatia asked.

"Better than that," Kara lied. "It was lovely."

"All I want is to make you and Marc happy," Tatia said. "That's my job."

Along with the bloody aliens. "You got to worry about yourself, too."

"If you're happy so am I. So I'm really being terribly selfish."

Kara wasn't sure if she wanted to weep or throw up. Or smack her.

The SUT came out of netherspace three hours later. The three humans stood in the control room, fascinated by the planet showing on the main screen. A reddish-brown ball, with few discernible features. The SUT's AI gave the details:

< *Roughly the same size as Earth, ninety-three per cent of the gravity. Atmosphere breathable but high ultra-violet so dark glasses necessary. Midday average, sea level temperature forty-three C. Midnight average ten C. No obvious seas, various rivers descending from various small mountain ranges.*

Kara looked at the other two. "We've been here before."

It was the planet where Tatia had fought against the Cancri. The planet with the warehouses devoted to human memorabilia gathered over the ages... including the preserved corpses of two men missing their backbones and brains.

"We were meant to drop off the Ent first," Marc said.

Kara stood listening to her AI. "Apparently the destination was changed a moment before we left Earth. The SUT doesn't know who did it." She sighed. "Well, we might as well let the Cancri off here. It's not getting on too well with the Ent."

Tatia started but said nothing.

"You noticed it too?"

"I thought it was being friendly?"

Kara shook her head. "That Ent tried to beat the Cancri bug to death. That's why I moved them apart. Forgot to mention it. Sorry."

Tatia looked away. Kara would never forget to mention an incident like that.

"So what do we do?" Marc asked. "Land by the old place? Be interesting to see how the pilgrims who remained have done."

"Sounds like a plan," Kara said, and told her AI to do exactly that.

The *BLO-LOC-TAL* eased closer to the planet. Anti-grav

cut in and they began a slow descent towards the surface, manoeuvring jets firing every now and then. Using an AI was a hell of a sight easier than doing it by hand.

"How does this SUT know where to go?" Marc asked.

< *Not it, boss. Me. And Kara's AI. We have the co-ordinates from the last time we were here.*

> *You ever forget anything?*

< *What do you think I am – a SUT?*

They'd made the trip without once leaving netherspace. The SUT's AI played coy, but apparently the free spacers had gifted their own navigational systems. But as her own AI said, Kara should be grateful and not ask questions. Because she wouldn't understand the answers.

TO WHOM IT MAY CONCERN

It is one thing to foresee another's death. It is another to foresee your own. I saw mine thirty years ago. Then it was only a possibility, a shock but not to be taken too seriously. Over the years it became more and more likely if I maintained my life's work. Until my death was inevitable if humanity was to survive the coming of the aliens.

One person whose sacrifice would save the world. Chaos theory brought to one's own front door. I am the Brazilian butterfly whose fluttering wings will let loose a hurricane in Berlin. The possibilities are not all bad if I do. Not catastrophic, depending on how you define the word. Humans still around, albeit eventually shorn of all competitiveness and ambition. There's no question about my choice, of course. After all, I was bred for this. Perhaps that's the hardest part, knowing other people saw my future as I saw Kara and Marc's, just as others saw the future of those who made me.

I am the product of hundreds of years of fortune telling. Pre-cognition. Juggling the possible and the probable. Once my kind were feared, then flattered, then derided. Science insisted we were deluded or charlatans or both, even at a time when they were arguing about what time really is and taking the tachyon seriously.

Many years ago, it was discovered/foreseen that gelding a pre-cog before puberty increased his powers. Not castration. The penis remains. We can have sex but not children. Female pre-cogs become less effective after puberty. My children have become humanity. Easy to say, almost impossible to live with.

I write this in the hope that you will understand how much I cared. That love led me to do terrible things. People have died, and will die because of what I have seen. I have been ruthless, as I was taught to be. The contrition and guilt are all my own.

The irony is that I will die without knowing if my work is successful. I only know that my death will give it the best possible chance. The probability is around seventy-five per cent.

It's been a hell of a journey to get such good odds.

12

It was the same landing field. The pilgrims' SUT, the broken *POC-TAD-GOL*, was still by the edge. A couple of alien-looking SUTs (anything not obviously human equals alien) parked some distance away. The collection of warehouses and towers a mile distant. There were no signs of life. It was mid-morning and the atmosphere was already heating up. No sign of the few pilgrims who'd decided to remain on planet in order to mix with, and hopefully understand, the different variety of aliens who visited there.

It was bittersweet to set foot on a planet that had known their triumph, but that none of them had wanted to see again. Marc used a small forklift to move the Cancri's cage outside, where Kara unlocked the door. Tatia was nowhere to be seen.

The Cancri hound shot into the open as if fleeing death, the symbiotic bug embedded on its back rocking from side to side. It stopped fifty or so metres away, turned around and stood looking at them.

Marc waved an ironic goodbye.

The Cancri lifted one of its front paws.

"How sweet," Marc said, as if aware that the chances of it being any kind of exchange were remote. "What do we do now?"

"We wait. We reckoned the bugs are telepathic, remember?"

Five minutes later a dust cloud in the distance announced the arrival of more Cancri. The same type of mismatched, cobbled-together vehicle as before. Two hounds in the front, one driving, their symbiots snugly fitted into the rear seats. The vehicle stopped, the returning Cancri placed its symbiot in the back, climbed into the front and away they went.

"Is there any reason why this was important?" Kara mused. "Other than some inexplicable plan dreamed up by a dead pre-cog?" Then, more briskly, "Let's break out a scooter. I want to check something."

Tatia volunteered to stay with the SUT. Roaming around the planet held no attraction for her. Kara agreed, and told Tatia to contact her immediately if anything happened, and left with Marc. First they checked out the *POC-TAD-GOL*, found it deserted but with signs of occupation.

Clothes were drying on a rack. There was what seemed to be a common room, and others that were obvious sleeping cabins. In addition to this were two large metal tanks, one containing water, the other empty. They reminded Marc of the tanks Tatia had once described, which mysteriously filled with food and water when the pilgrims had been held captive.

"If it's the pilgrims living here," Kara said, "they need help."

They rode two scooters to the warehouses which had held human memorabilia, and found the pilgrims busily rearranging the exhibits. They barely had time to talk to Kara and Marc. In fact, they gave the impression that they wished they'd go away, leave the planet, because the pilgrims had a good thing going and didn't want it spoilt.

It seemed that the warehouses were a tribute to human civilisation and creativity. Aliens came regularly to visit and presumably marvel. The pilgrims weren't sure, and frankly not too fussed. In time they'd find out. Meanwhile there was a museum to create. Exhibits to be categorised by function and by date, by continent and country. Special exhibits to be planned and arranged. The two mummified corpses to have a special place.

No, it didn't matter if the aliens failed to understand. It had to be done.

They were fine. Food and water was provided. The occasional free spacer coming by to check on them – in far better spacecraft than GalDiv.

"Why the hell aren't the Wild and the free spacers handling this damn mission?" Marc asked.

"Greenaway comes from the Wild."

"It's all down to Tse and his bloody visions!" He looked back at the pilgrims busy sorting and arranging. "I asked one why. She said because someone had to do it."

They returned to find a sulky Tatia waiting for them. No, there hadn't been any problems. Could they please get off this planet soon as? It was giving her the creeps. Then said she wanted to be alone and went to her cabin.

> *Did she try and take off?* Kara asked her AI.

< *Apparently might have thought about it. Asked the SUT's AI if it could take off on its own, just in case. Was told no, you'd blocked any attempt. She then went and looked at the Ent. They seem to be close.*

Kara decided not to tell Marc. He had enough on his mind.

Twenty-seven hours later they left n-space to find themselves in orbit around a planet with a similar blue, green and cloud-white colouring to Earth. There was no sign of cities or any major buildings. Without being asked, the SUT's AI delivered them to a large patch of open ground surrounded by what looked like trees, but taller and broader than the average European pine. Their foliage was a silvery-green, and a close up on the vid screen showed thousands of thin oval leaves all the same size and individually connected to the smooth trunk by thin stalks. It was late afternoon; the setting orange sun and vast trees created deep shadows that turned the dark-blue ground foliage black.

< *Approximately Earth sized. Gravity ten per cent less. Breathable atmosphere. No sign of animal or insect life in the immediate area. Provisionally safe.*

The air was fresh, the temperature a comfortable twenty-three C. Kara and Tatia watched as Marc unloaded the Ent in its cage. The door opened, but the Ent just stood there, unmoving.

"Does it know it's free?" Marc asked.

"Does it want to be?" Kara answered, keeping one eye on Tatia. And then, "What the fuck?"

A crowd of much smaller trees were moving out of the forest towards them. No, not trees. Ents. A welcoming committee or guards? They used their lower limbs much as an octopus uses its tentacles, rippling together to propel themselves forward.

"I never liked ours," Marc confided to Kara as Tatia watched, enthralled.

"There's something unpleasant about it," Kara agreed, as their Ent finally stirred itself, rippled out of its cage and went quickly towards its advancing fellows.

"Let's get the hell away from here," Marc said.

"We should stay," Tatia said firmly. "Make contact with them."

Kara moved a little closer to the younger woman. "Why's that, Tatia?"

"Because they're a very advanced race," Tatia said. "I'm surprised you haven't realised that."

The lone Ent stopped and waited. Six of the group surrounded it. Their top fronds reached out and made contact.

"It's reporting back," Kara said flatly.

"It's being loved!" Tatia contradicted.

"Evens bet it's the same one we saw on Dartmoor. That Marc saw in Scotland. It had to have human help to get around. What did it sell you, Tatia? Peace and love throughout the galaxy? An end to all your fears?"

"You wouldn't understand."

"I understand how much you've changed. And I remember from before how susceptible you are to the pre-cog civilisation. These Ents are part of it, right?"

Marc hid his surprise.

< She had help, boss. Ishmael spelled it out for her.

He remembered that Kara's AI had named itself.

> Can she hear us?

< Nah. Kara isolated her. Ooops. Here we go.

Tatia drew herself up. "You are evil. Both of you. I hoped to bring you to the truth. But you are not ready. You will never be ready." She spoke in a high monotone, her eyes focused somewhere above and beyond.

"It won't make Daddy love you any more," Kara said crudely. As Tatia gasped in sudden emotional pain and confusion, she stepped forward and applied a combination nerve and choke hold. Tatia struggled for a few seconds then collapsed.

"Help me get her inside," Kara said urgently. "Couldn't tell you. Didn't know if you were also affected. Not until just now."

The Ents had stopped communing and were now moving rapidly towards the SUT. There was a stink of rotting compost, sour and catching the back of your throat.

Kara and Marc manhandled Tatia inside the SUT, airlock doors closing with a pleasing clang.

"Get us out of here," Kara said loudly to the SUT's AI. Then to Marc, "And take Tatia to her cabin."

"This is the first time I've run from a bunch of giant asparagus. Gone to seed."

Tatia regained consciousness lying on her bed, with Marc and Kara standing over her.

"You hit me," she snapped and sat up. "*Bitch!*"

Kara shook her head. "So much for peace and love... I didn't hit you. But sorry about the daddy crack. You were about to do something stupid."

"I was going to join them," Tatia said angrily. "You had no right to stop me." Her face crumpled. "It... it loved me. I felt so happy and secure." The tears came. "Now I'm alone."

Marc reached out a consoling hand, stopped by a glance from Kara.

Tatia's tears became a sneer. "So what now? You want to *fuck*?"

"She's got issues," Marc said.

"Oh, don't we all." Kara squatted down to be level with Tatia. "Listen. You can stay here on your own, locked in, but watched. Or you can be in the control room with whoever's on watch, but in restraints. Your choice."

"I'll stay here. Anything better than mixing with *you*." Her voice lost its overt anger. "But when we get *back*, I'll have something to say to my father about this. *You just see.*" When, not if. Ignoring that Greenaway had never acknowledged her. Forgetting that he'd put her in harm's way.

Once there'd been happy pills to calm down an SUT mission manager, before he was traded to the Gliese for a new n-space drive. Now it was restraints or isolation.

"You want something to calm down?" Kara asked.

"Just fuck off." Tatia turned her face to the wall.

"Your AI can't help," Kara said. "It's no longer in contact with the SUT."

Tatia's shoulders shook with frustration.

Tatia was locked into her cabin. The SUT was rising to meet space. Mark and Kara sat in the control room, each nursing a gin and tonic. Sometimes only a G&T will do, so much so that Kara had broken her own rule.

"How did—"

Kara cut him off. "My AI, Ishmael. He'd been monitoring her. Apparently Tatia went into a kind of fugue when she was with the Ent. The scans showed the high dopamine levels and brain activity that are often associated with an extreme religious experience."

"I didn't know AIs could do that. To other people, that is."

"Mine can."

"Has it been monitoring me?"

"In exactly the same way that your own AI monitors your vital signs and tells mine."

He stretched in his chair. "I never knew that."

"It's mutual." Kara sounded a little impatient. "I have to know if you're alive, or going mad, whatever."

"Intrusive, though."

"Really? Tell me that when you're moments away from death and I save you because my intrusive AI was monitoring you."

"If you say. And what if I'd gone the same way as Tatia?"

"I'd have left you both there." She smiled at his mournful expression, glad that his resentment had passed. "No. Happy pills and restraints all the way."

"The Ent was following me," Marc said soberly. "I wonder why."

"Bigger question is why the Wild would send it with us. As far as I can tell, it's to see if we were vulnerable. But I'm not convinced. The thing is, we can't go on explaining every weird thing because it's part of Tse's plan."

"Two down and one to go."

"Gliese home planet. And the Originators. Hopefully." She put down her glass. "Remember what Tatia said when we first came on board?"

He did. "Which part?"

"Not dying frustrated with regrets."

"Ah." He carefully avoided Kara's gaze. "And the trip maybe ending badly."

"Which has to be juggled against operational efficiency."

He nodded. "Always a passion-killer, that."

"Look at me."

He did. "Your eyes are still grey."

"And yours are black. Marc, you have to know that I want to make love with you very much." She said this with a simplicity greater than any orchestra or peal of ancient bells. "Not have sex, make love." She paused, as if a little shocked by the admission. "But if we do the mission suffers. That's unavoidable. So we're on hold."

"Tell me why?"

"Because I need you to know. In case it does end badly."

Marc nodded. "You always make sense... Kara, me too. I feel the same. Thanks for telling me. I'd never have had the guts." He got regretfully to his feet. "Before I make a fool of myself, going to talk to the Gliese."

Kara smiled up at him. "Have fun. N-space in twenty minutes."

But the Gliese wasn't feeling talkative, so Marc went to the engine room to admire the huge globe with its channelled surface on which fitted the platens that guided it through netherspace. He was still there when the five-minute warning bell rang, so he stayed and watched the engine come to an unearthly life, afterwards helping to adjust the platens as his AI instructed, remembering to avoid the swinging arm that first selected and initially placed them.

He went back to the control room suddenly filled with longing for Kara but determined not to let it show. She wasn't there. Only an AI's message that watches were now expanded to six hours on, six off, and he was first.

That became the pattern for the next twenty-four hours. Never avoiding each other, never making an effort to be together. When they did meet there was warmth, an intimacy that neither had known before.

Tatia spent all the time alone, except when Marc or Kara brought her food. Alone, often in bed and watching rom-dram or rom-com vids, desperate for a happy ending.

They came into normal space in a two-sun system that according to the SUT's AI was some three thousand light years from Earth, towards the central core. Two suns, one bright orange the other more yellow. Twelve planets, including two gas giants. One planet, an Earth-sized one and a mere two hours away using a standard rocket drive. It seemed that for complex reasons, it was unwise to get any closer using netherspace. The two suns generated a wide range of exotic energy fields and…

Marc's head began to hurt.

> *Just tell us how long to landfall.*

< *Four standard Earth hours. You really should know these things.*

> *Why keep a dog and bark yourself?*

< *We don't have a… oh. I see. Ha.*

The SUT reached orbit in two hours and twenty minutes. Marc and Kara sat in the control room and watched the planet unfurl beneath them. Continents. Oceans. No sign of advanced life. Atmosphere breathable. Temperature similar to Earth. Icy deserts at the north and south poles. Hot deserts scattered around the equator.

Kara yawned. "Just once, once, exotic would be good. Vast, impossible towers. Huge ships floating on canals circling the globe."

"Ent-world was interesting," Marc said, then thought about it. Very tall tree-like things, true. But they were all the same. That might excite some, but to Marc it was a sign of a nature that lacked ambition. Ents, yes. Undoubtedly strange. Yet nothing compared to the stone tor coming alive on Dartmoor, or the ancient *something* in Scotland. "Well, at least the Gliese have a certain..." He remembered that Kara had once killed one to prevent it being dissected live. "... fascination."

It wasn't so much awkwardness as wariness between them. They'd admitted their feelings for each other, beyond affection and intense sexual attraction. All they could do now was keep out of each other's way unless it was unavoidable, and hope that neither would die.

"Hold on..." Kara told the SUT to take a closer look at an area at the junction of two rivers. The image zoomed in, showing an obvious landing zone with several craft parked at the sides. Beyond that a collection of rounded buildings without any common design, gleaming white in the afternoon sun. Squint at them and they'd become a collection of so many assorted pebbles. "Bit like the Cancri city," Kara said, disappointed. "Except for the parks." She meant the green and red patches of what had to be vegetation scattered amongst the buildings. "Right. We'll land midnight, their time. Best get something to eat and sleep. The AIs can look after the SUT." Kara gave Marc a smile as she left the control room. "And think about what we do with Tatia."

Tatia had stirred herself to shower and get dressed; now she sat enthralled as the vid screen displayed pictures of the planet beneath.

She could see with more clarity now. A diet of mindless but harmless vids had cleared her head of anger and anxiety. She could accept that the Ent had, perhaps, taken her over... but that was the force of its regard, she the neophyte to an alien teacher. Now she was aware of even more powerful and refined voices, voices that understood her in a way that the Ent never could. She'd first heard them on the Cancri planet, had thought them cold and controlling. That had been wrong, a misinterpretation of power and supreme logic. The absolute certainty of purpose of a society that only wanted the best for all the myriad races it represented. Tatia had enough self-awareness to wonder, briefly, if she was insane. But the very question suggested she wasn't. Well, no more than anyone else she knew. Besides, she'd grown up as a child of the alien age, of technology incomprehensible to humans. For Tatia's generation anything could happen, and given enough time it probably would.

● ● ● ● ●

When Marc and Kara unlocked her door, they were greeted by a freshly showered Tatia in new clothes and smiling her apologies for her past behaviour. She now understood, Tatia admitted, that she was overly susceptible to alien thought and emotion, without being able to process it properly. She'd been overwhelmed by the Ent's mentality and by discovering that Greenaway was her natural father. So apologies, and could they please start over? It was a quiet plea for understanding that offered everyone a solution with honour.

"And if you see me going squirly again," Tatia smiled, "give me a good shake, okay?"

Privately she was thinking how easily humans who hadn't been touched by the light could be fooled. She doubted that these two ever would be – a shame, for they both had excellent qualities. But it didn't matter. She wouldn't be around them much longer.

Tatia assumed Kara and Marc would behave in a way that would help achieve her objectives. Naivety and longing had made her optimistic.

"We'll do just that," Kara promised, privately reserving judgement because Tatia was a little too happy, fresh-faced and eager to forgive… as if acting out one of the rom-drams she'd devoured over the past twenty-four hours. Still, it would be better to have Tatia with them when they explored. They could hardly leave her alone and locked up on the SUT; given the run of it, she could damage the engine, life support or navigation systems. Better that she came with them.

The plan was to land at midnight and stay inside the

SUT as the AIs explored the area. Then to leave at dawn in a general reconnaissance of the landing field and adjacent buildings. The main objective was to establish if any alien race who could be the Originators, who supplied the Gliese with technology, actually existed. If so, attempt to establish contact if it was considered safe. On the other hand, if it became apparent that the Gliese really were responsible for the advanced tech, to ascertain if they had weapons or were capable of violence. The implication being that if the Gliese were the boss makers of shiny stuff, how easy would it be to take them over?

"What a lot of if's and alternatives," Tatia smiled as they sat drinking coffee in the common room. There were fresh-from-frozen croissants warming in the microwave, Swiss butter and French preserves ready to welcome them to the table. It was a relaxed group of three humans, although two of them had mild reservations about the third.

"There usually are," Kara said. "In fact, it's better than having a single, rigid plan. One other thing: our safety is paramount, okay? Do not be ashamed to run away. If we're attacked, do not be worried about killing aliens."

A serious-faced Tatia nodded in compliance. "Got that. I guess I also mean, well, it's not very much, is it? I mean, all this way to discover who makes widgets? Just the three of us? Or rather, the two of you, because I'm only here by accident, right?"

It was the question that Marc had been asking; instead of why me, why us? Two against the galaxy. Two against a something that no one knows. The butterfly in Brazil that flaps its wings and causes a star to go nova. And all because a dead pre-cog had once dreamed a future that included an artist, a mercenary and a good-time girl?

Kara was never so sure of her answer as now. "You don't need armies to make a difference. The right person in the right place at the right time can do that. The lone assassin takes down a ruler and starts a war. A scientist is killed by a mugger, so a cure for cancer takes another fifty years. Don't ever think you can't make a difference, Tatia. You can and probably will. Just leave the assassinations to me, okay?"

They left the SUT a few minutes after dawn. Tatia had refused a weapon. She'd never been trained, would probably shoot Kara or Marc by mistake. Instead she carried the medical pack.

They took three scooters, two slaved to Kara's. Where she went so did they, unless she released control. First they checked the craft parked on the apron. One was made from an asteroid, as before on the Cancri planet, so much cheaper than building in space. Another was all silvery beams and girders surrounding a central hub. And there were a collection of globes linked by passageways lying collapsed on the dusty ground. There was no sign of life, so either the Cancri were late risers or somewhere in the city.

The buildings were made of a concrete-like substance that was beginning to glow scarlet as the two suns rose, one a few minutes before the other. The doors were all closed.

"Lazy bastards," grumbled Marc, the self-righteous comment of a man up far earlier than usual. "Do we knock at a door?"

"No," Kara said. "We wait. Let's check out the parks."

There was vegetation of various shapes, sizes and colours with one type predominating, a tree-like organism about four metres tall and with a single thick reddish trunk. Its dark green branches swept down to the ground like a weeping willow. At the end of several was a large round black pod hanging only a metre or so above the ground. Tatia touched one before Kara could stop her.

"It's warm," Tatia whispered. "It feels alive."

"It is," Marc said. "Some sort of plant."

The pod she'd touched fell to the ground, landing with a soft plop.

"You'll have to pay for that," Marc said.

"Shhh. Watch." There was wonder on Tatia's face.

On Kara's face only an intense watchfulness.

The pod moved.

Tatia gave a little scream.

Kara's finger slipped over the trigger of her gun.

Marc checked the immediate area.

The pod heaved and then slowly split down the middle.

Kara pulled a reluctant Tatia away.

Another heaving motion and a thing began to emerge from the pod. It was like a small mound of leather, glistening with mucus. Several bony, jointed arm-like limbs. Short, stubby legs like a caterpillar.

"Fucking hell!" Marc exclaimed. "It's a Gliese!"

It was. Smaller but still a Gliese. A master of technology

that stood for a moment next to its abandoned pod, then scurried towards the nearest dense patch of vegetation and vanished beneath a small bush.

> *It is, right?* Kara asked her AI.

< *Seems to be. Interesting. Tell you one thing. Evolution never produced that on its own. It had help.*

More pods began to fall as the suns rose higher.

"We've got company," Marc warned. "Adult Gliese."

"Out of the park," Kara ordered. "Don't get in their way but observe. There is no record of a Gliese ever being violent, and I doubt they'll start now. But be careful."

A small procession of Gliese came into view accompanied by self-driving low loaders mounted on squishy balloon tyres. The Gliese ignored the humans, moved into the park to collect the newly hatched and place them onto the loaders. A full loader moved off, oblivious of a young Gliese in its way. With a muffled wet-fart sound the loader moved on, revealing the Gliese still alive and quickly collected by an adult.

"That explains the tyres," Marc said. "Still, the little ones have got to be tough."

Kara ordered them back to the SUT. From her own observation, from the AI's comment, it was obvious that the Gliese did not have a society based on science. Plants just didn't. And that's what they were: highly modified, genetically engineered plants.

They saw the Originators' craft as they neared the landing field.

It had to be. It was identical to the one they'd seen after Tse had blown up the Gliese SUT, come to see what had happened to its messengers before vanishing in a cloud of contempt for humans.

A vast skeleton of curved metal surrounded by a flickering force field through which pods of various sizes could be dimly observed. Similar to one of the parked craft, but so much bigger, so much more complete.

"It'll know we're here," Kara said. "Do nothing until I say."

The craft drifted slowly down and landed without raising dust. The force field flickered off, revealing a cobweb of spars and walkways, one large pod and a dozen or so smaller ones. There was no airlock, but perhaps an entrance hall at ground level. As they watched, a large, box-like object floated from the hall and onto the ground outside.

< *Good use of anti-grav*, Ishmael told Kara.

> *Get anything else?*

< *Super advanced tech. You'd expect it. Do they still despise you?*

< *All I get is a sense of peace.*

> *People that advanced can afford to be.*

Kara looked at Marc. "Want to check that box?"

"I'll go," Tatia said eagerly and was off her scooter and running towards the Originators' craft.

Kara didn't bother to call her back. She sensed that Tatia was about to have her own "Why me?" question answered.

The box was made of a metal that Tatia recognised from

the Cancri planet, the containers that had miraculously filled with water and food overnight. Standing on tiptoe she could just see inside it. A collection of objects of various sizes and shapes were piled in the centre. That and nothing more. She knew what they were.

"It's full of tech," she called. "For us!" *But how do I know? Because I just do! Just as I know that they've come for me. My new life is now.*

Marc shook his head. "I get the same. A sense that this is a… a gift?"

"Do you trust it?" Kara asked urgently.

"Not one little bit. Beware the Greeks. Remember the first time we met? After the Gliese ship blew up? We were lower than scum. And now? I think we're being conned."

Kara nodded. "It's too good to be true." She raised her voice. "Tatia. Leave it and come back."

Now was her time. "No," Tatia called back. "I'm staying. With them," she said, pointing at the Originators' craft. "I'll be okay. I will come back, but not now. Maybe in a month, maybe a year. But I will come back. Tell my father. Take care."

"No!" Marc shouted, about to go after her, held back by Kara gripping his arm.

"Don't," Kara said. "It's why she's here. We can't stop it. Don't try."

They watched as Tatia walked into the craft, turned to wave just as the force field flickered into life. The craft floated gently into the sky.

"That's it," Kara said briskly. "Let's get this box loaded and we're off."

"But… Tatia…"

"The box is a gift horse, but so is all the other stuff. No point in wasting it. Tatia will be okay. This is why she was sent with us. Poor kid never had a chance."

Marc stared at her. "Come on! That means—"

"That Greenaway's an even bigger bastard than you thought? Yup. Will an AI please confirm?"

< *She's right, boss*, Marc's AI said. *All the evidence points in this direction, if you accept pre-cognition and psi abilities. Tatia was chosen from the start. It's possible she was deliberately exposed to the Ent to sensitise her mind for these Originators.*

> *That is so shit.*

< *And there's nothing you can do about it.*

They left the Gliese home world in a subdued state of mind.

Kara had lost one of her team. Tatia had gone willingly but she'd never had a choice. It was Kara's job to see that her people did have choices. She'd failed.

The knowledge of being played so comprehensively, of dancing to a dead man's tune, weighed heavily on Marc. As the SUT drifted Up he began to think of netherspace, and then of Scotland, thinking that Tatia wasn't the only person with an out-of-this-world mission. The idea that there was more to come both disturbed and – to be honest – excited him.

They'd been in netherspace for a little over an hour when the alarm sounded. Marc had been in the shower, arrived in the control room wearing only a towel. Kara, fully dressed, was waiting for him.

"We've come to a stop," she said.

"So? We pop back into real space and…?"

Kara shook her head. "Listen."

He could hear it now, a faint scratching as a boojum picked at the protective foam.

"I tried leaving n-space," Kara said calmly. "But it wouldn't work. The SUT's AI doesn't know what to do."

"Yes," Marc said, surprising himself, "it does."

"Marc…"

"It's *my* turn."

"You don't know what the fuck you're *saying*! Just because an old engineer went walkabout into n-space." Tears glistened on her cheeks. "*I forbid it!*"

"They've been calling to me ever since we went into space," Marc said. "You know that. And they are now, I can feel them. You have to get back, Kara. Tell that bastard Greenaway what's happened. Make Tse's plan work for everyone. You get back, park up next to my house and wait. I will come home, love. Promise."

The same promise that Tatia had made. Kara wanted to believe but… but they couldn't remain where they were. "Okay. What the fuck are those things out there?"

"They're connected with the entity I met in Scotland," Marc said slowly, wonderingly, as information poured into his mind. "The best I can explain is that they're like pure emotion, obviously self-aware. I was sensitised the same way that Tatia was. Jeff, my stepdad, was involved and I trust him." He smiled at her. "You have to trust people some time, love. Trust me."

Kara bit her lip. "But we never—"

Marc laughed. "Something to look forward to. Next

time we meet, I promise. Come on, before that curious thing scratches a hole. Let's do it."

One last try. "People have been driven mad in netherspace. SUTs vanish forever."

"Didn't know the rules. Or simply couldn't cope. I will be okay. I'm not being noble. If I thought I'd die, I wouldn't go. I'd spend my time back here with you until the air ran out." He began walking out of the control room. "Watch on a monitor."

"You've only got a towel!"

"According to a book I once read, that's all you need."

"Wait!" She rummaged in her pocket then pressed something into Marc's hand. "Keep it with you, promise!"

Marc cupped her face with his spare hand and kissed her mouth. "Promise." He walked away clutching the strip of wood Kara had taken from her childhood home.

"Find out about the call-out fees," Kara called after him, as if asking him to remember the milk.

He nodded and left the room.

Tears streaming down her face, Kara watched as Marc entered the airlock. Saw him close the inner door, smile at the camera and then open the outer door. She saw again the colours and shapes that weren't, that were always changing, somehow alive. And then, as once before, a tendril that became a tentacle reached up, wrapped gently around Marc and took him from her.

She closed the airlock doors, her mind numb.

And she felt him inside her mind. He was okay, he was marvelling, he loved her. Linked to her by the wood that had once measured her height.

I would think that, wouldn't I?

But no more strange than so much else that had happened over the past few weeks.

He was alive, she knew, just as she would know when he died. Kara didn't know how she knew, only that it wasn't hysteria or shock.

An alarm sounded, the signal they were leaving netherspace. Kara wondered if the engine was broken.

< *No, it's not. In fact, we seem to be orbiting Earth.*

> *What!*

< *Where do you want to set down? Berlin?*

She sat in the big GalDiv office facing an unrepentant Anson Greenaway. There was no need for a personal briefing, he'd data dumped from her and the SUT's AIs.

"You *knew*," she said, wanting to kill him.

"I knew certain people had to be at a certain place at a certain time in order for a certain thing to happen. Yes. Tse's plan."

"Your own *daughter*!"

"Who is alive. And yes, was bred for this. Her mother, by the way, accepted rape rather than disrupt the plan. What she didn't see was that she would also be murdered. Don't talk about sacrifices and betrayal, Kara. You don't know the first fucking thing. I've no idea why Tatia had to go with the Originators, only that she must. Same with Marc and netherspace. And if I thought I was sending them to their deaths, I'd do the same. And then kill myself, as Tse did. You understand what this is about?"

"Kara nodded. Originators, pre-cog civilisation. It's all the same."

"Exactly. The pre-cogs use the Originators to distribute tech and *they* use the Gliese. Result: creativity, curiosity bred out of various races. Death by generosity and kindness. I can't promise you that Tatia and Marc will return…"

"I *always* bring my people home!"

"And maybe you will. No one wants it more than me. Meanwhile, go home. Take some days off. Then back here in two weeks. We still have work to do."

She looked at him in amazement. "If you think I'd ever, *ever* work for you…"

"I do and you will. I'm the contact with the Wild. With the people who understand what Marc met up there and how it's connected to netherspace. You'll be here, Kara, because you have to know. And because I need you. You're the best we've got."

Kara rose to her feet and walked out, no words said. She knew Greenaway was right, but was damned if she'd say so. And it would be good to see Marc's home. Feel closer to him there. He was still alive.

Left on his own, Greenaway told his new assistant no calls or interruptions for fifteen minutes. He reached, not for paper and pen to write to his dead wife, but for the box that Tse had bequeathed him. Time to see what his best friend had said.

Inside was an envelope containing a three-page letter.

Greenaway read the first few lines and smiled. It wasn't so much for him as the world.

> You're reading this because it's still a screwed-up universe.
>
> Humans seek patterns and order everywhere. Not only as a survival mechanism (is that a tiger in the trees, or randomly dappled patterns of sunlight?), but as a reaction to your messy development as a race. Fits and starts with the occasional aberration which might or might not allow its sufferer to survive long enough to mate and pass on its genes, such as single-eyed giants, stomachs with enzymes that can digest milk, or an offshoot of humanity so long-lived and fertile it starved to death. No obvious end in sight, only the blind random drive to adapt no matter the consequences. The need to impose order on chaos. Except that same chaos also gives a sense of mystery, curiosity, always seeking new horizons. It's the great contradiction of existence. Chaos and freedom versus order and tranquillity.

Tatia hung suspended within a large pod inside the curving metal skeleton of the Originators' craft. In front of her floated three metallic globes, each a metre across, connected by a thick, flexible cord of the same metal. She did not know whether there were three beings inside each globe. If it was a three-part hive mind, or an AI.

She had been rendered unconscious the moment the craft left the planet's surface. Had only just woken to find herself floating, enclosed in some sort of transparent membrane presumably to keep her alive.

There was no sense of being loved. No peace, and precious little hope. She reached out with her mind and found only the same implacable coldness she had once known on the Cancri planet.

I have to be needed. She clung to that thought. *Why else would I be here?* She was not a hostage, not an experimental lab rat. But there was something important that only she could do.

Tatia looked more closely at the globes and saw there were differences. One had a thin line around its equator. Another had a small protuberance at what was, for now, its north pole. And the third was shinier than the others. Different creatures inside them? Different functions of a controlling AI? Or even decoration? No. Not decoration. This being was totally utilitarian. She could sense it.

The globes changed position, forming a line with only one directly facing her. She felt a nibbling at her mind, knew it was curiosity, not surprised when it went away defeated. And she understood how misleading emotion could be, that an alien could feel ecstatic joy over an event that would make any sane human yawn with boredom. She thought of Marc and Kara, hoped they were okay. Of her father... but best not think about him. Her situation was stressful enough. It was best not to think about the past at all, only the present. She was needed, valuable.

She would survive.

GLOSSARY

ALIEN

one of a number of non-human species, some of which are in contact with humanity and some of which are not. It has proved impossible to communicate with aliens on anything but the most basic level, that level being trade. Mostly they're named after a constellation; not all city states agree on what a particular species should be called. The most common aliens and the ones responsible for most trades are:

CANCRI

an alien race resembling a small striped greyhound with two arms and carrying a pale white grub on its back in a symbiotic relationship. Neither have yet been dissected.

ERIDANI

an alien race resembling a segmented snake-like creature with multiple arms and a face like a disturbed nest of white worms. It smells of spaghetti bolognese.

GLIESE

an alien race – the first to contact humanity – resembling a pile of wet leather with three spindly arms, dozens of small, stub-like legs, a mouth part hidden by ragged flaps and what might be sensory organs on their outer skin. Dissection of one killed by accident revealed an interior full of a dark, viscous substance in which "floated" various connected objects that could be organs. The Gliese supply the **sideslip-field generators (netherspace drives)** and **updown-field generators** that make space travel possible.

It is estimated by **GalDiv** that up to fifteen other types of alien have visited Earth. However, these invariably land and remain in **the Wild**. What they might be doing there causes GalDiv many a sleepless night.

ARTIFICIAL INTELLIGENCES (AIs)

Most objects – houses, **jitneys**, restaurants – have their own AIs. People have them too, occupying computer chips implanted in their heads that can insert images and data directly into the optic nerve and auditory nerves. AIs evolve the ideal software persona (or "**avatars**") to interface with their "owner", but they are not in and of themselves conscious, although their owners may treat them as if they are. Larger AIs regulate trade between **city states** and between worlds. They also set the exchange rates for the common currency, **virtscrip**. Many people believe that some AIs have achieved a "life" of their own, although the programming is so good it's impossible to tell. Most people prefer to forget that the technical breakthrough that allowed AI development came from alien technology.

AVATAR

the "front end" of an **AI** system; the means by which an AI interacts with humans. Avatars have no legal status as conscious beings: they are just a highly developed version of an operating system's "theme". That said, many people treat them like a valued friend.

BOTS

small, unintelligent robots used for cleaning, construction and observation. They have no individual controlling **AI**, although an AI may control multiple bots.

CYBERDRONES

small insects controlled by electronics. Theoretically it would be possible to electronically control small mammals or birds as well, but this is a moral grey area. Controlling fish is allowed, but not dolphins or whales, although some **city states** will control anything alive.

CALL-OUT FEE

a human who has volunteered to be exchanged for rescue by **aliens** if an **SUT**'s sealed **sideslip-field generator** breaks down, leaving the SUT stranded in normal space. They might volunteer because they are dying of some incurable disease, because they want to pass their salary on to their family, or for some psychological reason known only to themselves. Fees are normally kept in an **induced coma** so that the crews of the SUTs do not become too attached to them. This trade is exclusive to the **Gliese**.

CANCRI see **Alien**.

CITY STATES

were formed in the years after **first contact**, when the concept of nations began to fall apart and people realised they preferred living in self-governing communities. City states often form larger coalitions, especially for defence (hence: The Army of the Anglo-Saxon City States, The Army of the Gallic City States, etc.), but laws are still made and enforced at the local level. Trade agreements between city states are negotiated by each city state's **AI**, and then reviewed by humans before becoming law.

CLOTHES

these can be mood-sensitive and colour-changing. **City staters** tend to dress conservatively, except during public festivals when anything goes. Wilders dress however they damn well please.

COMING OUT see **Out There**.

DOWN THERE

landing on a planet. Also known as **going down**.

EARTHCENT

Earth Central, the administrative organisation that sits above the city states and tries to ensure coherence and stability. Derived from the old United Nations, it is more pragmatic and less idealistic. In reality it is subordinate to its Galactic Division, or GalDiv, which oversees contact between aliens and humans.

EARTH PRIMUS

a political movement that believes humanity's interests should come well before those of **aliens**, and that the unequal system of trade with alien races is a form of charity at best, and callous exploitation at worst. Many in Earth Primus want all alien/human contact to cease; aliens to be recognised as dangerous; and for Earth to develop its own technology, no matter how long and how arduous that process might be. Earth Primus has been accused of wanting to reinstate government by an hereditary, over-privileged elite and of a xenophobia with its roots in a pathological insecurity. Both are correct.

ERIDANI see **Alien.**

FIRST CONTACT

the occasion when the human race and aliens met for the first time. It occurred on the moon, after the **Gliese** changed the colour of several craters so that they could be seen easily from the Earth.

FOAM

an alien technology and a self-hardening substance used to protect **SUTs** in space/**netherspace**. Its strength and effectiveness allows **SUTs** to be made of pretty much anything, including metal cargo containers or, in one bizarre episode, a small thatched cottage complete with garden, which subsequently vanished in **netherspace**. The supply of foam is controlled by the **Gliese** for no apparent trade. Humans consider it an after-sales service.

FREE SPACERS

freelance space travellers based in **the Wild** who use cobbled-together technology and scavenged alien systems to travel to colony worlds and explore outside the jurisdiction of **GalDiv**. They typically launch their **SUT**-equivalents from desert areas or converted oil rigs to avoid accidents. That was the GalDiv version. In fact free spacers provide links between colony worlds that no longer accept GalDiv/Earth hegemony.

GALDIV

Galactic Division of **EarthCent** that looks after the exploitation of space and the trade with **alien** races, and attempts to oversee the colony worlds, although many colony worlds don't want to be overseen and no one knows exactly how many there are. Like many organisations, GalDiv's true main purpose is to ensure its own survival since there is no real way it can regulate alien/human contact – especially in the Wild. It has also been penetrated by agents of the Earth Primus organisation.

GLIESE see **Alien**.

GOING DOWN see **Down There**.

GOING UP

leaving a planet and moving through normal space. Also **Up There**.

INDUCED COMA

derived from an existing medical procedure, a process by which a human – usually a **call-out fee** – is rendered unconscious for long periods of time. Electromagnetic fields are used to "switch off" their consciousness, while their bodies are fed with nutrients through tubes. It is the only real contribution that humanity has made to galactic travel, which is a little sad.

INPUT TATTOOS

sepia keyboard/input devices stencilled on people's forearms used for interfacing with **AI**s. Alternatively, some people prefer interacting using their hands with virtual keyboards/displays which are projected onto their visual field. This is generally frowned on in public.

IN THERE

retreating into a **simulity** and ignoring real life. Also **Going in**.

JITNEY

a robot car, helicopter or boat controlled by an **AI**. Jitneys do not "belong" to anyone, but can be hired or flagged down. When not in use by humans the AI makes decisions about when it refuels the jitney and books itself in for a service.

JOSS

the logical progression of cigarettes and vapes, often containing soft or hard drugs, all of which are legal. Thanks to an **alien** trade, physical and mental addiction can be cured in less than an hour. The commercial search for an addictive, non-curable and highly pleasurable drug continues.

MISSION MANAGER

the person in charge of an **SUT**, usually a technically unqualified administrator. An exception is made for explorer SUTs, where the mission manager is also a back-up engineer, navigator or medic.

NETHERSPACE

the extra dimensions above or below "normal" space where interstellar space travel can be accomplished. **SUTs** that enter netherspace sometimes do not leave it. Human brains cannot find any frame of reference to latch onto when they see netherspace, and they quickly go insane. The relationship between normal space and netherspace has been described as being like the Florida Everglades: if you look at a map of them and want to get from one piece of solid ground to another via canoe, then you might have to follow miles of little waterways. Far easier to row to the nearest bank, pick your canoe up, cross a spit of land, get into your canoe again and row across another channel, go across another spit of land and keep going in a straight line. Netherspace is the dry land and normal space is the water.

NETHERSPACE DRIVE see **Sideslip-Field Generator**.

OFFICIAL ASSASSIN

licensed by what is ostensibly an independent bureau, Official Assassins can be hired to right wrongs when the law may not apply – such as between competing corporations headquartered in different city states – or when the legal process is too expensive. In fact they're covert arms of **EarthCent** used to keep the business and financial worlds reasonably honest, and so secret that not even Official Assassins know who really pays their considerable wages. Most Official Assassins are ex-military. Unofficial assassins also exist, used because they're cheaper or more private than the official variety. Their professional lives are short.

OUT THERE

leaving a **simulity** for reality. Also known as **coming out**.

PRE-COGS

those humans who can, in some way that has never properly

been explained, see the vague shape of the future. Pre-cogs have described their ability along the following lines: they can "see" future events like landmarks on the horizon ahead of them, and they can also "see" roads, footpaths and overgrown tracks that might lead to those landmarks, but the landscape is hilly, with much hidden from sight. Paths that they think lead to a particular landmark suddenly end in a hidden spot, double back on themselves, or turn out to have a wall built across them. Pre-cogs can make educated guesses about which actions or choices now will lead to landmark events in the future, but they cannot be absolutely sure.

SIDESLIP-FIELD GENERATOR

a system for entering and leaving **netherspace** provided by the **Gliese** in three strengths that will power **SUT**s from the size of a caravan to a ferry. Also known as a **netherspace drive**. Any attempt to open the unit results in an immediate shutdown. Moreover, if the unit is opened it is shown to be empty. Humans have the – traded – power to reach the stars, but they don't have the faintest idea how it works.

SPACE UTILITY TRANSPORT (SUT)

a utilitarian vehicle designed for space travel and equipped with an **updown-field generator** (for getting out of a planet's gravitational field) and a **sideslip-field generator** (for entering and leaving **netherspace**). Space Utility Transports do not have names, but randomly generated nine-letter codes: *LUX-WEM-YIB*, *NOL-DAP-KIM*, etc. These are known as trifecta codes. Thanks to **foam** and **updown-field (gravity negating) generators**, SUTs come in many and varied shapes, few of them aerodynamic.

SIMULITIES

all-immersive simulated realities, usually accessed by multiple people at the same time and moderated by **AIs** using **alien** technology and in theory controlled by **GalDiv** and the larger **city states** military. People using a simulity can be made to experience another's thoughts, perceptions and feelings. This leads to a gestalt useful in training **SUT** crews and the military. In practice the simulity technology has leaked into the public domain – probably via **the Wild** – where it is used for gaming, psychoanalysis and virtual sex.

SNARK

a descriptive term used for whatever it is in **netherspace** that sometimes makes **SUTs** disappear. They may or may not have a physical form but can inflict physical damage.

SPACE ACCESS POINTS (SAPs)

what for a while were called "space ports". Areas where **SUTs** take off and land.

UPDOWN-FIELD GENERATOR

an anti-gravity unit provided by the **Gliese** in a form that cannot be opened or tampered with. The generator only "elevates" an **SUT** in a perpendicular direction. Horizontal travel is gained by use of jet propulsion, or by sailing with the wind.

VIRTSCRIP (OR "SCRIP")

the virtual currency originally developed by intergalactic corporations for purposes of trade. At a time when many colony worlds and **city states** have their own currency, virtscrip has become the default one. Rates of exchange are fixed quarterly (Earth years) by three heavily defended **AI**s located in the Asteroid Belt. These AIs represent **EarthCent**; major corporations; and the colony worlds. They also oversee the settlement of intergalactic banking and trade deals. There have been numerous outside attempts to fix the exchange rates, either with false data or a computer virus. None have succeeded. Many of the people who tried are dead.

WILD, THE

politically amorphous and ambiguous areas between the **city states**. The Wild is usually populated by those people who do not follow orders well, don't like **AI**s and/or prefer a libertarian existence. City staters may visit out of curiosity. Many never return. It is known that the Wild trades independently with **aliens** and, via the **free spacers**, with the colony worlds. **GalDiv** is powerless to prevent this, but likes to pretend it can.

WORLDMESH

the loose affiliation of **city state AI**s that allows the free flow of data around the world as well as negotiating trade agreements and facilitating currency transfers.

ACKNOWLEDGEMENTS

Thanks to Gabriella G, world's best beta-reader. Vicki and Dan T for encouragement and ideas. All at Winstone's Book Store for coffee and advice.

ABOUT THE AUTHORS

ANDREW LANE is the author of twenty-nine books and multiple short stories, television scripts and audio dramas. He is perhaps best known for his Young Sherlock series, which have sold to forty-two countries. He has also written three well-reviewed adult crime novels under a pseudonym, the first of which has been optioned as a US TV series. He is currently writing another series featuring Doyle's Professor Challenger. He lives in Dorset.

NIGEL FOSTER began as an advertising copywriter, first in the UK and then North America. He moved on to television and radio factual programming before co-founding a successful movie magazine. Back in the UK highlights include developing and launching *OK! Magazine*; an international non-fiction bestseller about the Royal Marines Commandos; and six of the most popular Bluffer's Guides, worldwide.

THE RIFT
NINA ALLAN

Selena and Julie are sisters. As children they were
closest companions, but as they grow towards maturity,
a rift develops between them.

There are greater rifts, however. Julie goes missing at
the age of seventeen. It will be twenty years before
Selena sees her again. When Julie reappears, she tells
Selena an incredible story about how she has spent time
on another planet. Selena has an impossible choice to
make: does she dismiss her sister as a damaged person,
the victim of delusions, or believe her, and risk her own
sanity in the process?

The Rift is a novel about the illusion we call reality, the
memories shared between people and the places where
those memories diverge, a story about what might
happen when the assumptions we make about the
world and our place in it are called into question.

THE RIG
ROGER LEVY

Humanity has spread across the depths of space but
is connected by AfterLife – a vote made by every
member of humanity on the worth of a life. Bale,
a disillusioned policeman on the planet Bleak, is
brutally attacked, leading writer Raisa on to a story
spanning centuries of corruption. On Gehenna, the
last religious planet, a hyperintelligent boy, Alef,
meets psychopath Pellon Hoq, and so begins a rivalry
and friendship to last an epoch.

The Rig is an SF thriller with two alternating
narrative strands that ultimately draw perfectly
together. One strand traces the story of two boys
bound terribly together, who in time control a vast
criminal organisation, while the other explores an
apparently insignificant murder that opens into
something far greater.

EMBERS OF WAR
GARETH L. POWELL

The sentient warship *Trouble Dog* was built for violence, yet following a brutal war, she is disgusted by her role in a genocide. Stripped of her weaponry and seeking to atone, she joins the House of Reclamation, an organisation dedicated to rescuing ships in distress. When a civilian ship goes missing in a disputed system, *Trouble Dog* and her new crew of loners, captained by Sal Konstanz, are sent on a rescue mission.

Meanwhile, light years away, intelligence officer Ashton Childe is tasked with locating the poet Ona Sudak, who was aboard the missing spaceship. What Childe doesn't know is that Sudak is not the person she appears to be. A straightforward rescue turns into something far more dangerous, as *Trouble Dog*, Konstanz and Childe find themselves at the centre of a conflict that could engulf the entire galaxy. If she is to save her crew, *Trouble Dog* is going to have to remember how to fight…

For more fantastic fiction, author events,
competitions, limited editions and more

VISIT OUR WEBSITE
titanbooks.com

LIKE US ON FACEBOOK
facebook.com/titanbooks

FOLLOW US ON TWITTER
@TitanBooks

FOLLOW US ON INSTAGRAM
@TitanBooks

EMAIL US
readerfeedback@titanemail.com